Also by
JOAN BARFOOT

Abra
Dancing in the Dark
Duet for Three
Family News
Plain Jane
Charlotte and Claudia Keeping in Touch
Some Things about Flying
Getting Over Edgar
Critical Injuries
Luck

Exit Lines

JOAN
BARFOOT

ALFRED A. KNOPF CANADA

PUBLISHED BY ALFRED A. KNOPF CANADA

Copyright © 2008 Joan Barfoot

www.randomhouse.ca

LIBRARY AND ARCHIVES CANADA CATALOGUING IN PUBLICATION

Barfoot, Joan
Exit lines / Joan Barfoot.

ISBN 978-0-307-39705-8

I. Title.

PS8553.A7624E95 2008   c813'.54   C2008-901228-3

Text design: Kelly Hill

First Edition

Printed and bound in the United States of America
2 4 6 8 9 7 5 3 1

Contents

1	AT THREE IN THE MORNING	1
2	GOOD BUSINESS, WELL DONE	3
3	MUSTN'T START ON A SOUR NOTE	9
4	NOT ALL THE OLD MEN	18
5	THE SAME ROOF AT LAST	34
6	THE BABY OF THE PLACE	42
7	AT THREE IN THE MORNING	57
8	A COSY FEET-UP VISIT	59
9	CARPE DIEM	70
10	AT THREE IN THE MORNING	87
11	BASIC ARITHMETIC	89
12	OH HA HA HA, MORE OR LESS	101
13	MEN WITH KNIVES AND TELEPHONES	120
14	AT THREE IN THE MORNING	135
15	EXIT LINES	137
16	GOOD AND BAD WITH LAWYERS	145
17	SMARTER THAN, SAY, YOUR AVERAGE NEANDERTHAL	161
18	NOT AN IMPOSSIBLE ACT	173
19	AT THREE IN THE MORNING	187
20	WHAT FRIENDS DO	189
21	WALKING DOWNSTAIRS IN THE DARK	193
22	GOD CROPS UP	206
23	LITTLE COOKIES	221
24	AT THREE IN THE MORNING	229
25	THANKSGIVING GOOSE	231
26	ALL THE MORAL BUSYBODIES	247
27	THE MAGICIAN AT THE FAIR	265
28	SO THIS IS HOW IT HAPPENS	275
29	AND THEN	304

1

AT THREE IN THE MORNING . . .

*A*T THREE O'CLOCK IN THE MORNING, that defenceless hour when anything feels possible and nothing human or inhuman out of the question, the Idyll Inn's only sounds are the low hum and thrum a complicated building makes to keep itself going. Like any living body, even a sleeping or unconscious one, a building has to sustain its versions of blood and breath, so there's a perpetual buzz to it, white noise in the night.

With only those faint sounds for companionship, three o'clock in the morning is an uneasy hour for the wakeful. It is also the most discreet hour for dodgy, unsavoury acts. Still, while those abroad tonight in the Idyll Inn may find their moods swinging between severely apprehensive and hopeful, there remains potential for a kind of slapstick comedy. If they are discovered, whether too soon, too late, or quite irrelevantly, their lookout will bumble about causing as much tripping and confusion as possible, while the others are to divert authority with exclamations and flailings and jostlings.

If all goes well, there'll be no repercussions. If all does not, they'll be in big trouble. They have chosen nevertheless, not lightly, to draw on whatever reservoirs they possess of determination. Stubbornness. Will. Solidarity in the cause of friendship and, they suppose, of its surprisingly expansive boundaries.

On their side is the unassailable fact that whatever transpires, barring on-the-spot discovery, the odds are decent that no one will ever find out. Resistance is high, they understand, to seeing them clearly at all. Or as one of them has previously remarked, "Most people would rather paddle the Amazon than be tourists around here."

People are cowards, she meant.

So were they, once.

Well, they can't be cowards tonight. In the morning, though, the real morning, they intend to have a bit of a lie-in. Either life will go on as unaltered and perilously as life at the Idyll Inn ordinarily does, or they'll be indulged with extra treats and particularly kind words. Either way, it's nice to have cosiness and comfort to look forward to, if only because the prospect of even a small reward at the end helps keep a person going, really.

2

GOOD BUSINESS, WELL DONE . . .

*N*EARLY FOUR SEASONS BACK, during a blessedly balmy spring run of late-April days, move-in time has finally come to the Idyll Inn. From start to near-finish, from plans and permits to all the necessities and some of the graces, construction on this plot of riverside land in this small city has taken just eight months, including the periodic disruptions of winter. During this time and even before, when it existed only in theory, the place has been an object of interest and curiosity; in some cases, suspense; in a few others, desperation.

This Idyll Inn is the latest addition to a small chain that is not locally based. The corporation is not called something obvious like Idyll Inn Inc. or Ltd., but is a numbered company run by a management group on behalf of a collective of professionals, mostly dentists and doctors, interested in untroublesome, steady investment in what's bound to be a growth industry. The expectation is that as the chain thrives, it will become a bigger firm's takeover target, so from every perspective, present and future, its investors must prosper—how can they lose?

The paved parking lot, which will be adequate for the ordinary run of events, is insufficient for so much simultaneous activity, so each day during moving-in week there's a muddle of small vans and trucks arriving with their loads of possessions, leaving not much later empty. There is, too, considerable risk of dented fenders, bumped bumpers, in all the forwarding and reversing and squeezing by large and small cars, many of them occupied by tense multi-generational groups up to their necks and nerve endings in emotions of one sort and another.

How purposefully strangers hustle through the parking lot, how swiftly and surprisingly movers wielding sofas and chairs in the corridors overtake those slowly taking up residence—how alarming and rude.

Never mind, their day will come.

At this stage in the numbered company's expanding history, there's a vast, detailed, operational template governing services, menus, staffing levels, recreational offerings, cultural and religious observances, decor and other fundamental amenities, right down to the number and location of phone connections in individual suites. Overall design, however, varies from one Idyll Inn to another, depending on lot size and shape. This Idyll Inn, if viewed from the unlikely vantage point of the air, more or less resembles a sperm: a rounded head with a long two-storey tail.

The tail section contains forty suites, twenty up, twenty down, all brightly painted, with shiny fixtures in their bathrooms and large windows in their main rooms. The main room in each suite provides lots of space, adaptable to

individual taste, for chairs and sofa as well as TV set and
sound system, coffee table, an end table or two, and various
meaningful knick-knackeries. Each suite also contains an
array of built-in cupboards, closets, drawers and shelves for
storage and display purposes, which means that bedrooms
don't have to contain closets and drawers, and so can be on
the small side, really only big enough for a human or two plus
bed and side table.

Ten main-floor suites along one side of the sperm-tail's
long central corridor even have decks attached, which will
be useful for outdoor leisure activities such as sitting in lawn
chairs in the upcoming good weather. Those rooms and
decks, which overlook the river flowing by, or in deep
summer, drying up, are more expensive than the rest, and
not everyone can afford the extra cost on top of what is
already a substantial basic rent.

That rent includes the friendly, communal, well-
intentioned features located in the single-storey part of the
building which would, from the air, form the plump head of
the sperm. Circling about from the main double-doored
entrance are several rooms: a large lounge with plants and
paintings, low tables, soft chairs and hard ones, where sociable people are expected to gather to chat and play cards or
word games, or to rattle away at the computer on a desk in
one corner; a crafts and activities room with long schoolroom tables and chairs, and tall cupboards behind whose
doors are the papers, glues, paints, yarns and mosaic tiles
that are to become drawings and placemats and small candy
dishes; a laundry room, another benefit of the place, one
more dull burden lifted; a kitchen outfitted with restaurant-
quality cooking and refrigerating equipment; the open space

of the dining room, where almost everyone upstairs and down will gather for breakfast, lunch and supper at round tables, getting to know each other quite swiftly, if they don't already, for better or worse. Since this Idyll Inn is located in such a small city, a mere forty thousand citizens give or take, it's safe to assume that many residents will already know, or at least know of, each other. Again, for better or worse.

The dining room's grandest feature is a great wall of windows facing, like the most costly suites, the river that winds by bearing ducks, canoeists, anglers, assorted debris. Better than television, is the idea; and also light, as has been proven, affects people's spirits. Research in design indicates that a happy crew, or at worst a tolerably amenable one, should be the result. Not that, once residents are installed, their moods will necessarily count for much—certainly not to the distant investors, as long as the money rolls in. The Idyll Inn is rather like a Brazilian mine or a sweatshop in China that way.

Some afternoons and evenings the dining room will be cleared for various entertainments. Every day there's to be a minimum of one organized activity somewhere in or outside the building, and holidays will be marked as they arise and as they represent the customs and beliefs of the residents. Here in this city, there'll be no need for any very exotic or even multicultural celebration, but whatever does come up is well covered.

Completing the circle, back near the main entrance, is the staff office, which this week, possibly every week, is busy with harried people, women, on a steep learning curve. Across from it is the ill-named library, a dark-panelled room with no books except a set of encyclopedias and a severely out-of-date atlas, but with a wide-screen TV and a fireplace, two large sofas and several easy chairs—rather lush, in an English unlettered-country-gentleman sort of way.

And that's it. The landscaping remains to be done, but otherwise the contractors have met most of their deadlines. Incomplete landscaping doesn't prevent the place from opening for business, although, aside from the parking lot, the property is bogged down in spring mud. Soon, however, it will be covered in sod and dotted with decorative rocks and perennial flowers and shrubs, and no doubt residents will enjoy observing this happen as spring and summer unfold. Many are probably interested in gardening, and the rest should be pleased enough to watch workers working.

It's in the interests of its distant investors that the Idyll Inn be comfortable and attractive in order to appeal to prosperous clients. At the same time, there must be responsible limits, which in practice means that the walls are painted appealing shades of pastels, and the chairs and tables are both efficient and homey, and the floors look like real tile, and the flowers and plants placed here and there out of the way are either full-grown and thriving or fake, and the art on the walls is unobjectionable, mostly prints of gardens, seashores and animals grazing in fields; but which also means that under the paint the drywall is not always smooth, the chair at the computer desk in the lounge is by no means ergonomically top of the line, the floor tiles are stick-downs, and the flowers and plants camouflage a certain draftiness around some of the windows.

Those doctors and dentists with their numbered company and expanding empire have no intention of being directly involved with—of even visiting—this Idyll Inn or any other, so it's fortunate that Annabel Walker exists. She grew up in this city, left at twenty, returned at fifty, and in the interim trained and worked restlessly in nursing, briefly and radically in auto repair, and finally and practically in accounting. She has already worked at a larger Idyll Inn elsewhere, although not as manager. She is unencumbered and plain, and looks fairly worn down by the world, and at this stage is likely to remain unencumbered and plain, if not necessarily worn down, and so can presumably be counted on to concentrate on running this Idyll Inn.

During the months of construction, she has spoken extensively and intensively with a great many people. She has cracked the whip with contractors to keep schedules nearly on track. She has interviewed and hired staff, supervised the distribution of instruction manuals and the showing of corporate videos on required procedures, and is already keeping an eye on one or two staff with a view to possible firings. She has been responsible for furnishing and stocking the place, within the limits specified by the Idyll Inn rules. All that is good business, well done.

She has also, when possible, personally interviewed prospective residents. She has reviewed their histories, medical and otherwise, checked their credit, conducted tours, allocated suites, heard a great many stories. Unlike a newcomer to town, she knows there will be people at the Idyll Inn over whom she'll particularly have to exert her authority, and here, quite possibly, comes one now.

3

MUSTN'T START ON A SOUR NOTE . . .

NOT FOR SYLVIA LODGE an ignominious arrival in the hands of others, that sure, helpless sign of having waited too long. She comes to the Idyll Inn under her own steam, not counting the taxi driver, who gets no tip—imagine honking from her driveway instead of ringing the doorbell, imagine not helping, and never mind that she doesn't particularly need help with only a purse and a small fabric suitcase containing toiletries, mainly.

He can mutter, "Cheap old bitch," if he chooses, but he'd do better to turn his mind to the benefits of courteous service. Another time she might set out to instruct him about who may lie behind the rangy flesh of an eighty-one-year-old female, which in this instance happens to be a good tipper, but today she has other concerns.

She is not one of those superstitious people who hesitate before pride in the nervous belief that it precedes a fall. Pride, in fact, helps hold her upright, and therefore upright she proceeds along the short walkway and through

the two sets of automatically opening glass doors of the
Idyll Inn entrance. There's not much time before her moving
van will arrive, her possessions in the hands of two scruffy
young men she found through the classifieds. She has
culled fairly ruthlessly, but there's still a lot of life travelling
behind her, and she wants to be organized for it and prepared to direct.

Her new *home sweet home*. But mustn't start on a sour
note, or a dubious one.

It is mid-afternoon. She woke early this morning, melan-
choly as any normal human would be. Besides closely super-
vising the young men as they loaded her selected remaining
possessions into their van, she took a last stroll around her
garden, admiring particularly the hardy spring tulips and
tough, graceful forsythia. Indoors she observed the light
slanting through leaded windows, patterning bare hardwood
floors, and ran her fingers over the naked fireplace mantel
and shivered at the echoey sound of her solitary voice when
she made the sentimental mistake of saying aloud, "Goodbye
then, old house." She cooked herself an asparagus omelette
for lunch, on the theory that future omelettes would likely
be of the cooling, rubbery variety, possibly not even involving real eggs. It's been hard not to think of one thing and
another as "last": her last bath in her own tub; her last turn
of the key in the big oak front door with the diamond-
shaped, eye-level glass insert; the last time she can consider
much of anything hers.

Choice, responsibility, blame: all hers. Straighten up.
Buckle down. "I am Sylvia Lodge," she announces at what,
in a hotel, would be the front desk; in a prison, the guard
post. "I have arrived."

She is not unaware that as she approached, Annabel Walker, who somewhat remarkably is supposed to be running this place, was scooting back into her private office, leaving a sprightly young thing to jump up in greeting. "Mrs. Lodge, oh good, we've been wondering when you'd get here, let me find someone to show you to your suite." Such enthusiasm and energy. This is a very expensive place, thousands a month. Evidently one pays for enthusiasm and energy, although one might rather not.

"No need, thank you. Two young men will arrive shortly, however, in a small truck with my things, if you would direct them to me."

"Your sons? Grandsons?"

Sylvia raises her eyebrows. "No, they are not."

Relationships are bound to develop, but obviously it will be necessary to hold out against forced jollity. Presumptuousness. The sort of thing that leads to singalongs, and clumsy exercises from a seated position to the tunes of old ballads.

En route from the front desk to her new *home sweet home*, she pauses nevertheless to admire the wall of windows pouring sunshine into the dining room. Each table holds a bud vase with a single white or pink carnation. Carnations are a cheap flower, but still, a civil gesture. And such light! Nightfall will hit hard. It often does, and how much harder here, on her first night?

She will not think about that; marches on, past a kitchen where two hairnetted staff manhandle vast metallic pans and pots—she was right to make her last meal at home a fragile, irreplaceable one—and continues around the curve to the corridor that leads to her suite. The main attraction of this place is that it is utterly new. Under no circumstances would she be concerned about ghosts or other emanations of former inhabitants, but she does respect the virtues of never-before-used tiled showers and floors, fresh carpets and unmarked painted walls, however unfortunately peach-pink and robin's-egg blue and pewtery grey and faint yellow in tone, along the same aesthetic lines as the tepid landscape prints stuck up here and there. More important, she has a powerful and practical respect for the downspirallings of capitalism's endeavours. In ten years the Idyll Inn will be shabby, but in ten years, if she does not happen to be dead, she'll likely be too broke to live here—the resources of a lawyer's widow are not necessarily as lavish as some might suppose.

Her suite is the seventh door on the left down this wide hallway. Her sanctuary; her vacant sanctuary at the moment, pending the arrival of her possessions. The remains of her life.

Don't think of them that way.

The bathroom is to the right, just inside the door. Its fixtures are purely white for the time being, the flooring blue tile, the step-in shower protected by a pebbly, translucent door. There are three pot lights in the ceiling, and a frame of twelve little bulbs, three to a side, around the mirror over the sink. The toilet and shower feature bars to hold on to and lift off from as need be.

It's the little things, isn't it?

While other little things can turn at the flip of an ankle into quite large things.

To the left, opposite the bathroom, is a cupboard unit with drawers for sweaters, underwear, nightgowns and scarves, and an open space below into which her tiny new fridge will fit nicely. Then comes the closet, with its two doors that do not open outwards but run side to side. It's nothing like her walk-in at home, but it will contain, she supposes, what she has reduced herself to.

She must learn not to think *home* of the place she has left, even if she lived there for half a century and has been here for maybe ten minutes. So much will need swift redefining; for instance, what's referred to here as the *living room*, with its sturdy bluey-grey spillproof carpeting and pale yellow blank walls, where she will shortly distribute the loveseat, easy chairs, recliner, little tables and TV and book-shelves and pictures that are on their way—it will be her *sitting room*. That being, she expects, her main activity in it.

It's the picture window and what lies beyond that clinched the deal. The window is separated from the river by a slow slope and a few metres of cattails and other marsh grasses. Anglers will float by in their boats. In winter—she's not sure about this—there will perhaps be skaters and cross-country skiers. In any event, for the most part the effect should be pastoral.

Beside the window with the clinically white vertical blinds she intends to replace is a second door, this one to the outdoors and her own private deck, where in good-weather seasons she will arrange her own private lawn furniture: a chaise, two cushioned upright folding chairs, a white metal table with legs weighted against winds springing up, and an adjustable yellow umbrella. She sees herself out there in loose trousers and shirt, a book and binoculars, the world of the sitting room left well behind.

It was irritating having to put up an argument for a main-floor, riverside suite with a deck. Annabel Walker—

she must remember Sylvia, although they carefully did not touch on histories and old times—Annabel tried hard on their tour to persuade Sylvia to live on the second floor, where the most lucid and able are supposed to gather in merry segregation. "We'd prefer," Annabel said, "to keep our main-floor spots as much as possible for residents who need a little more help—maybe some supervision with the shower and toilet—or those who can't move so independently." Those would be the residents who, Annabel clearly meant, would be tottering about behind walkers, or bit by bit losing their marbles, little coloured glass balls rolling out of their brains, tripping them up.

Who would therefore keep staff on the hop, and so were best kept handy, saving distance and trouble. "I think not," Sylvia said. "Having a deck suits me best. Have you considered that your plan is entirely backwards? Of course that's up to you. And your other residents. But as for me, this is my choice."

Annabel sighed, an aggrieved, unpromising sound. "Well, as long as you realize that all your neighbours may not be as congenial to you as the people upstairs." It's a shame that Annabel looks like her mother: pudgy and pudding-skinned and, given that she's managing a fair-sized establishment, distinctly unauthoritative. She'd have a better shot at being more, oh, *electric*, if she resembled her father. It was once a mystery to Sylvia how Peter came to be married to a woman like Annabel's mother. Men marry down, that must be it. They may occasionally mistress up, but they do tend, poor short-sighted things, to wife down.

Not that that matters. Sylvia will now be in a world consisting mostly of long-lived women, men who would be her contemporaries being for the most part, like her own husband, Jackson, not to mention Annabel's father, Peter, already dead.

This is also a place where, if she's not careful, people will take to diminishments like *sweetheart* and *dear,* which will not do.

And meals will not sufficiently cater to whims, which is why she bought the little snack-and-wine-sized refrigerator. Whatever happens to major ones, she has no intention of being deprived of minor desires.

Staff will generally be underskilled and ill paid. Some will be kind, some cruel, which she can hope will cause them to be fired, but they're unlikely on the whole to be very bright. Annabel sounded proud of a staff-to-resident ratio that is in fact not awfully remarkable once broken down by simple arithmetic into round-the-clock shifts every day of the week. "A nutritionist plans the meals," Annabel said, "and as well there will always be fresh homemade snacks in the lounge, and free tea and coffee. We're hoping people will gather in the lounge, get to know each other, enjoy the entertainments. And we'd like to build up the library with people's own books." Presumably the mobile and lucid will be able to figure out how to use the elevator to get from their second-floor perches to these assets of the main floor. Sylvia forbore making this remark to Annabel.

"Of course we have an activities coordinator." Of course they do. This will be the person urging Sylvia to make fiddle-fingered crafts, or play word games, or sing along to heartfelt old songs. "And naturally we want everyone to keep up with their own interests." That will rather depend on their interests, won't it? Sylvia didn't say that, either.

The larger point is that staff, however ill paid or unskilled, will arrive when she presses the unattractive button she will wear like a necklace on a cord around her neck. They will help her get dressed and do other personal tasks that require deft fingers. She used to have very deft fingers. "Your father could tell you," she might advise Annabel. Now her clumsy, painful, swollen-knuckled hands look to her like someone else's entirely, which is eerie and jarring.

If she falls in another of those terrifying, bone-defying topplings, no doubt she will still experience the startling sensation of genuine fear as she watches the floor and her body merge in slow motion, but now there won't be the panic about what happens next: someone will come pick her up. These are the trade-offs of moving to a place like this. The trick is never to trade too much, or too swiftly. Not for her the quick, naive, goggle-eyed *Look! Beads! Here, take all of Manhattan!*

Where the hell are her things?

Here they come now, with shufflings and bumpings and young men's voices out in the corridor. This will be fine. Fine enough. It only takes getting used to, and a little time to get settled. It'll remain a shock for a while, being incarcerated even in this genteel, open-doored prison. Not that she intends to be excessively jailed, and sorting out who and what still interest her from who and what no longer do is going to be interesting. As will be the fresh challenge of acquainting herself with people she might not otherwise know; a potentially stimulating project, a means of taking advantage of opportunity, taking charge of a new environment, making the most of necessity.

The most positive possible spin.

Besides, as Jackson used to say about handling the more peculiar legal affairs of so many town residents, "Some shit always happens." It wasn't always funny then, but it is now, and she is laughing when the young men arrive bearing her loveseat between them. Perhaps she sounds mad, laughing all by herself and at nothing; or maybe she just looks typically addled and old. Which makes her laugh again, at the useful camouflagings of age and its occasionally happy invisibilities, which is how it can keep secrets, and even some kinds of freedom.

4

NOT ALL THE OLD MEN . . .

*A*H, BUT NOT ALL THE OLD MEN ARE DEAD. Canting slightly sideways, with a middle-aged man in a dark grey suit at his left, a middle-aged woman in a daffodil track suit pushing his wheelchair, George Hammond is about to take up residence in a room across and down the hall from Sylvia Lodge. He doesn't see Sylvia in her doorway because his leftward vision is blocked not only by the man in the suit, but by the infuriating residues of a stroke.

How well George Hammond has done to be up and about in this surely glorious universe; how gritty and determined a man he must be to have come so far: from his kitchen floor to this spiffy, optimistic new building. He should be pleased with himself, he ought to feel proud and happy and safe.

He does not.

If he can't see Sylvia, she can see him, there's nothing wrong with either her eyes or her memory. Of course she recognizes George Hammond, who ran a shoe store for years.

His surprisingly delicate hands have clasped Sylvia's ankles and cupped the soles of her feet, they have pinched at her toes to demonstrate the roominess of loafers and high heels and golf shoes, although they haven't done so for quite a while now, since he went out of business. The woman with him is likely his daughter. She's of an age to have gone to school, more or less, with Sylvia's Nancy. Perhaps the man is her husband. If so, they live someplace fairly distant—out west, maybe? Sylvia has heard something but doesn't remember exactly, why would she?

He had the beguiling smile of the natural salesman. "Good fit, I'd say," beaming upwards from the stool at her feet. "And they show off your legs." Sylvia had sleek, shapely legs, it was true that a nice pair of high heels set them off. Compliments were pleasing, even from a merchant who, one might assume, only really paid attention to people from the knees down.

He is not smiling now. His face looks dragged down, by stroke or gravity, who can tell? It is enlivened, however, by temper.

Good for him. Young people should not get off lightly when they do these things to the old. Sylvia has avoided the problem by keeping herself out of anyone's hands, even benign ones, or Nancy's. Today's move is in the nature of a *coup* in that sense. A triumphant *fait accompli*. And isn't the French language useful.

Also, *sauve qui peut*. "No, no," she tells the two hired young strangers carelessly distributing her possessions, "that chair goes by the window. Put the loveseat across from the TV, between the end tables." George must be what Annabel meant by the decrepit coming to roost on the main floor.

Depressing, really, and this isn't even a nursing home, the next step downwards en route to incapacity's basement. Unlike nursing homes, with their particular standards for the amount of actual medical care required in the course of a day, not to mention a considerably less elegant ambience, this is a *retirement lodge*, the Idyll Inn—hard to imagine who dreamed that name up. "Sounds like one of those twee cottage names," Sylvia told her friend Mabel when she was deciding to move here. "Dun Roamin'. Bide-a-Wee. You know? The Idyll Inn, my rear end. The Belly-Up is more like it."

And Mabel said, as intended, "Oh, Sylvia, you are bad," and giggled. The trick is not to let people know how much certain things matter. Sympathy is bad enough, pity utterly deplorable.

In which case, Sylvia must deplore her brief pity for George Hammond. For all she knows, he's like her: weighing choices and odds, making his decisions himself. She would certainly resent being used as an example against him, but that's what is happening inside his room as Colette MacPherson, voice pitched high with strain, says, "You have a good-looking neighbour, Dad, did you notice? And she sure doesn't look unhappy, she looks like somebody who figures this place'll suit her just fine."

"Blah blah blah," says George Hammond as clearly as he can manage. "Blah blah blah."

She sighs. "Look, Dad, all your own things are here, isn't that nice? Not just your clothes but furniture and even the photographs—it's the same as your living room at home, and just as big. The only difference is that you won't be alone, and you'll have help if you need it. We're lucky you don't need real nursing care, so we could get you in here. Lots of people want to live in a bright new place—did you notice there's even flowers on the tables out in the dining room?—and for sure I'll feel better, knowing you're safe."

"Blah blah blah," says her father.

"Window," he adds. Because against his better judgment that big span of glass, even though it overlooks mud at the moment, does have its appeals. And according to Colette there's a nice-looking woman right down the hall—who would that be, someone he knows? He used to know practically everybody in town, although he no longer remembers them all and can put names to even fewer. Still, words return one by one, sometimes creeping the entire way to whole and mainly ungarbled sentences. It's like magic when that happens. Like a starburst in his head, something as ordinary as knowing words, making a sentence.

He could just as well say, however awkwardly, "Push me to the window, please," instead of "Window," but it feels useful to emphasize disabilities. Maybe it's pitiful when weakness is a man's best weapon—his only one—but at least it's only an exaggeration, not a lie.

Why is she doing this to him? "Why?" he asks jaggedly. "To me?" It's irritating that Bill, the insurance fellow who years ago took Colette half across the country and still keeps her there, puts a tailored arm around her when she cries. It makes George look like the one in the wrong.

It's also annoying that it's Bill who says, "We've been over this, George. We're not doing something to you, we're doing our very best for you. Look at this place—I'd live here myself if I needed a little help getting along, and let's face it, you do. We're too far away to give you that, and anyway we wouldn't always know how, and besides, we both work all the time. Here, they know what to do so you're safe and well cared for. And like Colette says, you've got your own things, and you'll have friends here, you know. Now," his tone firming, "we had to guess how you'd want things arranged, but if you tell me what you'd like changed, I'll move it around now, no problem."

"Blah blah blah." No problem, says the smartass, but where's the insurance against a perfectly good life turning upside down in a kitchen? What would the premiums on a policy like that amount to, Mr. Insurance Executive? "Why" and "to me" isn't even what George means, really. What he means is, "How does this happen?"

This is how:

An eighty-year-old man gets up in the night because he has a bad headache that requires an Aspirin. He makes his way to the bathroom cupboard in darkness, because after years and years in a house, who needs lights? Then he's off to the kitchen for a glass of water, and next thing he's waking up on the floor in the dawn light with the strangest dead-fish quality to at least half his limbs and an inability to picture just what a fish would be, much less say the word. He lies waiting for answers, and learns that getting up, or unscrambling the sense of things, is not going to come naturally.

He's no quitter, George Hammond. He's a man who, if he can't get what he wants one way, will—except for the store, he finally couldn't save it; or Alice, he couldn't fix her, either—invent another route to his goal and desire. He has a creative nature that way. So he lies on the kitchen floor waiting for capacities to return. He tests this and that and finally gets his right leg to obey him, however reluctantly, but not his left leg. He can only move his left arm by gripping and hauling it with his right hand. He tries saying *help*, experimentally, and hears *fmphf*. There is no one to help. What's-her-name is in a place. Something. Never mind. He's alone.

He wets himself, because he doesn't have a choice in the matter. The prospect of shitting himself is more dire. It would be nice if what's-her-name, Alice, was here so he could close his eyes and be taken care of, but as it is, he has to take care of himself, so he bends his right leg and pushes and slides back slightly on the wet linoleum, and repeats the motion until overhead he can see the grey cord of the telephone reaching down to its plug, and rolling slightly he grasps the cord with his right hand and pulls, pulls again, until the phone teeters on the edge of the kitchen table and he closes his eyes because when it comes down it will hit him, which it does, glancingly, on the forehead.

The light in the kitchen is no longer dawn but full, bright day. Somewhere along the inch-by-inch length of his journey, he has lost time. He has also left his pyjama bottoms behind.

His fingers pursue the phone fallen beside him, but what next? There are numbers for help, but they're gone from his mind. There's a single programmed one on the top row, though, if he can find it. He tries once, shifts his blind fingers, tries again and when he hears the voice of rescue, oh, what triumph!

"Please state your emergency," he hears, and his heart sinks. "Mmph," he says, which is still not close to "help." "Mphlmph," he tries, and then, reshaping his lips around an unwieldy tongue, whispers, "Aylay."

The woman's voice is calm and, to his ears, tender in a new and strange way. "I understand," she says. How could she? But how grateful he is that she understands and is kind. "You just stay on the line. Don't hang up"—as if he could— "I'm tracing your address, and we'll have help on your doorstep as quick as we can. When you hear the siren you'll know we're just about there," and when she rattles off his street name and number he sighs a *yes* down the line, "so you stay with me here and I'll stay with you, and even if I have to put you on hold for a minute or two, you hang on," and she talks him to sleep, content as a baby, slumbering in her arms, sucking her tit. Which wakes him up with a start. Either that or his name. "Are you George Hammond?" she's asking. "That's the name that comes up on my screen—is that you?"

"Ahh," he says. He hears sirens down the block. Now crunching wheels in his driveway. Now fists on his door—as if he could rise up and open it.

"Don't you worry," the tender voice says, "they'll find their way in. Just relax. I'll stay on till they get to you."

"Stay with me forever," he would like to say. "Don't ever leave."

What a crowd in his kitchen! A police officer, two ambulance people—the street must be whirling with lights, what will the neighbours be thinking? He doesn't want to let go of the phone, but is no match for the fingers peeling his from the receiver. He hears a man's voice say, "Stroke," and "Yeah, thanks, we're okay here now," and there's a rumbling of voices before he's rolled one way, and when he rolls back he's on something being raised and clicked into place like an ironing board only on wheels. He tries lifting his right hand in some kind of gesture, but it turns out he's strapped down, all limbs confined. There's a bump and a jolt, and doors slam and they're off, the siren making its rising and descending *whoo-whoo* and a woman in blue fussing above him with one thing and another.

And that's how life changes. He doesn't even get to look around, say goodbye, make a choice about coming or going.

In the ambulance he does shit himself. "It's all right, don't worry," says the woman attendant, but of course he worries, how could he not? Everything, everything gone to shit in a moment.

It's a while, though, before he gets close to comprehending how far everything has gone to shit. Immediately through the hospital doors he becomes meat: juggled and poked and intruded upon, lit here and there, faces, some friendly, some interested and concerned, others not, appearing and disappearing, voices talking too low or too fast or with too many words, gone before he can catch them. At some point Colette's frantic face arrives over him, Bill's beside her, so time must have passed, they have a long way to travel to bedsides back here, his own or her mother's. Then Colette's face and Bill's are gone and he is hauled through more corridors and up an elevator, into another bed, and then wheeled out again and down an elevator and through a tunnel and he's someplace else altogether, although still in the hospital. People ask questions, they have him do this and do that, raising his right arm, for instance, and failing to raise his left one. And all these days, weeks, maybe months, time is nothing. It is day or night, but it no longer extends the way it used to into time passing or getting somewhere.

That, it appears, ends today. Time means something now. It means, according to the traitor Colette, that this room in this barely glimpsed place is his future and he'd better get used to it and even be glad for it, that's what she's saying.

Every Sunday, his only day off from shoes, Colette sat on his lap while he read the Saturday comics to her, even the soap-opera ones that weren't really for children. She was obedient, and not because she had to be scared of her parents either, like some kids. There may have been a few tough teenage years, but they were harder on Alice than him, due to his long hours at work, and other things. Later on, the day Colette graduated, she said, "I love you, Dad," as he took her picture in her windblown black gown, her hand holding the stupid tasselled flat cap from flying away. Also "I love you, Dad" just before they set off down the aisle so he could give her away—give her away!—to Bill, who then had the nerve to take him at his word and actually take her away.

"Blah blah blah," he says now, glaring hard at the two of them, or intending to.

"Please, Dad," she says. "I know it's difficult, but we're doing our best." No. If they were doing their best, they would fix him. They would find somebody to fix him. They would fold time and put him back as he was the night he went to bed with a little headache and woke up with a big one. "Be brave," she says. So even Colette admits this isn't all easy-peasy, nice as pie. Four-and-twenty blackbirds baked in a pie, they used to sing about those, the two of them, when they were, maybe, out in the garden, those precious Sundays again, him weeding the vegetables and feeding her fresh peas in the pod—how did the song go? He's got the first words but then it all falls away, does she remember?

It didn't used to make her look sad. It used to be a

cheery tune, if you didn't pay attention to the baked-alive birds themselves.

Somewhere inside this person with her mother's pink cheeks and narrow nose and wide, thin mouth, this person who makes a living doling out loans for a big bank, must be the happy, obedient blackbirds-in-a-pie girl; just as somewhere inside his own tilted body is the man who made sure she was clothed, fed and loved, who ran with her two-wheeler when she was first learning to ride, who held her up in the water when she was beginning to swim, who had encouraging words for whatever she wanted to try. Well, he foresaw trouble when Bill turned up, but Colette was not asking for encouragement then. George had given her so much of that, she mistook her desire to move far away for the best, right, only thing to do. Even now, even still exiled half the country away, she gives no sign of regretting choices of decades ago. Look at her, with Bill's hand on her shoulder.

So much love, it seems, has made her hard. Now it turns out her mind and heart are much larger than her father's. It turns out she can very well decide not to clothe, feed, love, encourage or care for him in return. Are there debts, then? He shakes his head. At some point things always get muddled. He can't get his brain to go very far.

"Please, Dad," Colette repeats. How old is she now? Fifty sounds about right—imagine that!—although he can't be certain just how big a number it is. "Don't cry." He's crying, is he? That happens unpredictably these days. Sometimes he doesn't even notice till a tear falls into his lap. She probably thinks he's unhappy. *Depressed,* as the social worker at the hospital said people often are after strokes, speaking airily, as if grief amounted to much the same thing as a sniffle or a cut finger. Anyway, he's not depressed, he's damned mad. It's goddamned unfair, events that come out of the blue in the middle of the night, striking a man down on his own kitchen floor, leaving him in other people's pitiless hands.

Colette's included, it seems.

He cannot see a way out. Even when it came to closing the store, he made the decision himself, although pressured by malls and their big crushing chain stores—there were days when almost nobody came through his doors. But he thought the situation through, mentioning possibilities to Alice but not actually consulting her, and chose the closing date, and put the prices with his own hands on his remaining stock for his end-of-business sale, and even managed to be polite to old customers who showed up for the first time in ages to say how sorry they were to be losing a landmark downtown business, not to mention how they appreciated his suddenly cherished attentions to the demands of their growing or bunioned or flattened or high-arched or long-toed or otherwise hard-to-fit feet in years past.

A little late for compliments and regret. As it's late for Colette to be saying, "You're always good at making the best of things. I know you'll manage this too, once you've settled in. And I'll be here to help"—how his heart leaps! "Bill has to fly home tonight, but I can stay on for a few days."

A few days. What about years?

He cannot imagine even a week in this room, with outings to corridor and dining room and damned crafts room and coffee lounge. "And this is our library," said the bloody woman showing them through, who runs the place and whose face rings some kind of faint bell, "with the fireplace and the big-screen TV. We picture it as a cosy alternative to the lounge for residents, especially in the evenings."

Here, people are *residents*, at least to their faces. At Alice's nursing home, they're called *patients*. Is this payback for Alice? But he had no choice, did he? When she did things like turn on the stove and forget, and often didn't know where she was, and took to pummelling him with her weak little fists, and could barely begin much less finish a sentence—what could he do?

Alice no longer knows her own name, never mind his. His situation could not be more distant from hers.

Well, okay, it could be. But still.

And okay, maybe it's not fair to be mad at Colette, but who else is there?

Funny how he sees snippets of life. He can't tell if that's different from before, but what comes to his head is not the smooth, lifelong unfolding of a movie, but snapshots, like the bike-riding lessons and swimming and pea pods. "Sweet," he says, and Colette must understand something of the gentleness but not forgiveness that he intends, because although she does not look happy, exactly, she looks as if he's partly restored in her eyes.

But he's still very angry. Why wouldn't he be?

"So," Bill says, "do you like the couch where it is? We had to guess which cable outlet you'd want the TV hooked up to, so like I said, if you want things moved around, now's the time. There's three phones, one on the end table by the chair, another at your bedside and the other's in the bathroom on the shelf by the sink. You can tell me where you'd like the pictures hung. If you do, of course. Maybe you don't." There's that to be said for Bill: he offers this small choice, he shows that much respect. It's not that he and George haven't gotten along, it's that affections get shifted and loyalties change. George closes his eyes. He is so very tired of change.

"Do you want to lie down for a while, Dad?" She'd like that, wouldn't she? Then later she could say, "But I only left because you were sleeping, and I didn't want to disturb you."

"No. Push." He waves his right arm. "Out."

"Into the hall and around again? Another tour?" Of course not, he means *out* altogether, what does she think? But Alice too pleaded for release in the early nursing home days, and it got her exactly nowhere and isn't likely to get him anywhere either, not with Colette set firm against him, and his furniture already here.

It was hard not to blame Alice for losing her mind. It seemed one of those things where, if a person put some effort into using it, she'd get to keep it; but maybe it wasn't. Dr. Miller kept saying it was to do with tangles forming up in her brain like tree roots in a drain, but to George's mind that's what plumbers' eels are for: to keep that sort of disastrous twining and knotting from getting too big and hard. "*Do* something," he ordered in the early days of Alice losing her grip. "Get some interests."

"What?"

"For Christ's sake, I don't know. You think of something."

He was impatient, sometimes probably cruel. He didn't understand. Now he does, a little. Because it does seem that things can just happen and boom, there you are, struggling for words and other things, for a bit of freedom, some choice independently made. If Colette can't feel the depths of that, well, he couldn't either. Tit for tat. But then too, Colette, like Alice, is supposed to be a better, more, oh, *outward-looking* person than he. "Shit," he shouts, just as loud and clear as he can, slamming his right fist on the arm of the wheelchair. "Shit. Goddamn."

"Shh, relax, Dad, we're on our way." The room whirls and he's turned back to face the doorway so that he can see the side of the room he couldn't see on the way in: the closet, the cupboards, nothing personal on display yet although Colette says, "Look, here's the drawers where your sweaters and pyjamas and underwear are. I've hung up your trousers and shirts in the closet, and there's space for bulk supplies of soaps and deodorants and so forth in these cupboards here. We'll figure out what you'll need, we'll make lists." *Bulk supplies*—so she can fly off with a clear conscience in a few days.

"See the number on your door, the big *14* here? That's how you'll know this is your room when you're coming back." From meals. Games. TV movies. All the promised *fun*. "And isn't this a nice touch?" There's a plastic display box screwed to the wall beside his door. Beside everyone's door. "It's for any little personal item you'd like to put there, or a photo. So people get to know a little about you." Let's see, what would identify him to a passing-by stranger? Maybe a picture of himself as just another old shoe.

He snorts. "Blah blah blah," he says.

"I wish you'd stop that, Dad. It's really rude. And mean, too."

"Can't," he says, very slowly and carefully, "be good all the time."

"Well, you might try, even just for a few minutes."

There, that's his Colette: crisp and sticking up for herself. He expects he taught her that. Alice sure wouldn't have, unless by opposing example. The right side of his mouth curls up in a half-grin. "My girl." And, mischievously, "Blah."

She laughs and slaps his good shoulder; so that's all right.

"Want to go back around? If we do a few circuits from different directions, you'll get oriented for when you're wheeling yourself." When she is gone. Around and around he will go, all by himself, and where he lands, nobody will know.

Besides the fact that he has to get used to a useless left side, which is a very complicated loss in itself, George's vision makes him crazy. One eye cuts out at a fuzzy-edged limit, and is blurred and impossible anyway, while the other works as it always has, except harder. It gets tired, having to see pretty much everything all by itself, and a tired eye causes headaches, and headaches now lead to sizzles of panic.

Or maybe the panic of the moment is due to the woman turning the corner at the end of the hall. She halts, she stands there at the intersection like some goddamn Amazon. George's right eye blinks like mad but it's still Greta, even camouflaged by a lot more saggings and baggings than she had long ago.

How long?

Whether Greta recognizes him at this distance or not, she's quick on her feet, and within a blink or two she is gone. What if she lives here? What if she's one of his many new neighbours, what if the room she dodged into is her own, which he'll have to pass in order to get anywhere in this place?

Then he is even more trapped than he dreamed. It's enough to give a man a stroke, an anxious flare-up like this, and for a moment he has to close both his eyes, although not praying, exactly.

5

THE SAME ROOF AT LAST . . .

*I*T'S ANOTHER BAFFLING VAGARY of George Hammond's condition that old information—Greta's name—can leap spontaneously to the tip of his mind, while he could bang his head flat trying to make some more necessary fact come to light. Timing is also an aggravation, since it's not exactly helpful to remember a word at five o'clock that would have been useful at two.

But possibly his alarm is misplaced; Greta's memory may be even worse, although just to be here she must, like him, be more or less functioning. Not entirely needy. Which doesn't mean she is whole. No one at the Idyll Inn is.

Naturally, as Colette steers him by, he can't see leftward into the room Greta entered. This place is pointless. Truly pointless: in terms of a journey here, there's going around and around, or there's going back and forth or, he guesses, there's a brief elevator journey up and down, still unexplored. "Rat," he says, unable to think of the word he really wants. Then he remembers. "Hamster," he adds ungracefully, picturing futile wheels inside cages.

"Sorry, Dad, I don't understand." Colette has turned right, aiming him through the tables and chairs of the dining room, quite an obstacle course. Many years ago, when George taught her to drive, he was careful to appear trusting and brave, but every muscle was tensed—whose wouldn't be, with a teenager in control of so much metallic power and speed? "Always drive," he told her, "as if everybody else is an idiot. Keep your eyes peeled, and your hands and feet ready." Now she's such a good driver that she can manoeuvre his chair at the same time as she checks out seating arrangements. "This is your table, Dad, think you can find your way to it okay? Never mind, we'll practise, there's plenty of time." Till supper, she probably means. Or till she flies off.

If she's not going to say Greta's name, he sure isn't. He has no idea if it's even familiar to her. If she ever knew of Greta, would Bill as well? Different times, different ways. They probably tell each other just about everything, except their own secrets if they have any. There was more restraint in George and Alice's day. Well, maybe Alice told him everything, he wouldn't know since he wasn't necessarily listening. Now there's no asking her what she might have kept to herself; just as he could tell her anything, everything, and she would never know.

Odd, and funny, and a little bit sad, how things can turn around on themselves. "Don't cry, Dad, we'll keep going." He was doing that again, was he? Pathetic.

It's not just lost words and leftward vision that frustrate, it's a body that won't let him whip around to check what's behind him. There are people and eyes at his back. Anything could be happening. A man shouldn't be so defenceless.

And it's true, Greta Bauer's eyes are indeed at his back. She was able to step quickly (not scuttle, she would not do that—*scuttle: a quick shuffling, a short swift run*) into her room. Now she's out again, peering into the dining room, where a full view of George is blocked by the woman behind him—can that be Colette?

The not-so-alarming way to see this is that over an up-and-down lifetime, a person's heart can become not just weakened but hard, so it may be a good sign that hers is still susceptible enough, and perhaps soft enough, to make that painful leap. Already she is nearly calm again; but it is good that the girls went back to their homes yesterday. It would not do for them to see her even briefly unsteady, or abruptly alert to a person who, with luck and care, is mainly a stranger to them. There was only that instant standing at the end of the hallway, seeing the skewed old man nevertheless perfectly recognizable under the bulk and sway of an old man's body, when she thought, *George. Oh.* Just that, but no shock is good for a woman with a heart that has taken to manifesting its frailties in sharp ways that land her in hospital, and now have landed her here.

Bäuerin, Dolph used to call her, laughing. *Peasant*, of the female variety, as well as a joke on their last name. He meant more than her strong, sturdy build; it was also a compliment to do with earthy pleasures. He was *Bauer* in those ways himself. The word means *farmer* as well as *peasant*, although sadly, Dolph was no farmer.

Bäuerin: also someone who bears any weight of hardship when there is no choice.

All three girls are big-boned like her, but in middle age remain tender-hearted. They tell her she has been a good

mother. They say they are repaying her love and care with
their own. They say they want her to be safe, and insist they
are pleased each to pay some of the Idyll Inn rent. This is
not always what happens to mothers, and Greta is grateful.
They are good girls.

They are also busy. Still, they have come back from
their different long distances, first to hover over her in the
hospital and then to make plans. Emily and Patricia, for
example, found the Idyll Inn during a round of inspections
over a couple of days. "Come see the place, Mum, it's going
to be really lovely," said Patricia, and so it is. It is not the
second-storey apartment with the creaking wooden floors
and warm yellow kitchen and big drafty windows and
tucked-away spaces useful for storing important papers such
as years of photographs and report cards—the Idyll Inn is
not any of that—but it is, yes, *really lovely*.

"And you know," Emily added, "you shouldn't go on living
alone. It's not safe. It's a worry." Greta saw she meant it was a
worry for them, which is an unfair burden for a mother to put
on her children. Also, it would be unfair to suggest moving to
live with one of them, when they have their own complicated
responsibilities, their own households. And so they pay for her
to be here. They are generous girls.

They have come to town as they could to help choose
what she could keep, what they wanted to keep, what must
be thrown out, sold, given to charity: memory after memory
assessed, packed or discarded. She has kept, besides necessary clothing and furniture, her small collection of jewellery,
those gifts from a reckless time, and some photos: decades-
old, yellowy, curled ones of the faded faces of the family left
behind; snapshots of Dolph in his youth; and representative

pictures of the girls through the years, and of their children too, now themselves all grown up.

Yesterday they chose a photograph of her and the three of them, from when she was in her prime and they were still young, for the display case outside her door—"just so everybody knows you've got an army backing you up," Patricia said, laughing but serious too. Other photographs, propped on wide window ledge, TV cabinet, the new space-saving wooden shelves the girls have installed on her walls, form a haphazard kaleidoscope of a great many years. Greta more resembles her father, but last night, spirits at last free to fall, she was swamped for the first time in years by an unexpected longing, like a child's, for refuge in the arms of her mother. Her mother is a plump middle-aged woman staring formally and uncomfortably out of the small portrait Greta brought with her to this country; a woman who has been dead now for two decades; whom Greta has not seen in the flesh for much longer than that, not since she and Dolph waved their frantically hopeful goodbyes to their lined-up families on the left-behind train platform; but who last night poked her way into Greta's newest new world to say, although in her own language, *Do you see again how brave a mother must be?*

A simple tearless wave, such as Greta's yesterday, takes such courage.

She remembers well George's devotion to his daughter. Now Colette is whatever she is—at the moment, a woman in yellow pushing her father around a retirement home in his wheelchair. While Greta's Sally is a librarian at a university, her Emily markets things like laundry soap for a large corporation and her Patricia is a pharmacist. All of them far away, here and there. Busy, yes.

Of course Greta expected to encounter familiar faces at the Idyll Inn, but oh, her heart.

A young foreigner does what she can with whatever she has. Short of the largest sins, she does what she must.

A good mother hoards her affections, and for the most part invests them in her children, where they belong.

A young, widowed, foreign good mother of three must be brave as stone. But she is not stone.

It is all life, all experience. She should be glad, is glad, to be breathing; has come close enough to never breathing again under the assault of heart attack. She was able to call her own ambulance, but what, as the girls pointed out, if she had not been? At the Idyll Inn, by pressing the button that hangs at her throat, the least pretty and most unjewelled of necklaces, she will swiftly have help. Otherwise—as did not need explaining, although the heart doctor explained anyway—she risked dying alone, going undiscovered until one of the girls grew alarmed by an unanswered phone, or a neighbour noticed mail piling up. The word *deliquesce* comes to mind from her days of learning the language. It sounds close to *delicious*, in a sliding, slippery way, but it is instead a terrible damp, rotting word.

There was once a time when living under the same roof as George could have thrilled. It is not very funny when desires come true too late to be any longer desired.

She will return to her room before he wheels past again, and telephone her daughters, as she has promised. That obligation, to care for children even when they are no longer children—that is not love like in a foolish movie or romantic book. It is what remains.

Sally and Emily have similar questions: "Are you sure

you like the place?" and "Do you need anything we didn't
think of?" and "What have you been doing?" and "What are
the meals like?" and "Do the staff seem all right?" and "Have
you run into any interesting people yet, anybody you know?"
Yes, no, getting used to everything new, better than she
expected, as far as she knows to this point, and yes, she has
nearly run into someone interesting she knows. "You sound
great, Mother," says Emily; and "I'm so pleased this is working out for you," says Sally. Patricia's phone rings until her
voicemail picks up. Greta worries about her, the risk of rob-
beries and violence seeming quite high at a pharmacy in a
large city where addicts and other desperate people are likely
to gather, but "Don't fuss, Mum," Patricia always says, "I
don't work alone, and my foot's never far from the panic button, and even if I wanted to be a hero, which I don't, we're
never supposed to resist, just hand over whatever. Anyway,
it's never happened, at least not to me, so don't worry." In
Greta's view, the fact that something has not happened only
increases the chances it will. "That makes no sense, Mum.
Statistically, it's not how things work."

Maybe not. But in life? Maybe so.

Unlike her sisters, Patricia lives in a high-rise, a condo-
minium where, Greta imagines, mysteriously glamorous
events can occur in the life of a woman who, also unlike her
sisters, is not married and does not have children. "I am just
calling to let you know all is fine," she tells the voicemail. "I
am very pleased and grateful to be here, thank you. I am
leaving my room now, so there is no need to call back. There
is always something to do here, you know."

There are more people than George moving in, with
much bustling and clatter, and calm voices, and shouting or

patient ones, beyond Greta's door. This is frightening, so
many strangers among whom she will not belong. This fear
is not unfamiliar. Like other fears, it must be faced promptly
because it will not go away by avoiding it. "It'll be an
adventure, Mum," Sally said yesterday as they were leaving,
which is a good, but impossible, way to think. They mean
well, her girls.

Greta does not have an understanding yet of the staff,
but the administrator, named Annabel, like a cow, was in
Emily's high school class, which led to some friendly conversation as Greta moved in, and may or may not create special
benevolences. Like a good clerk, which she was, Greta
intends to be patient even with the clumsy or careless. Like
a good customer, she will be judicious in her demands and
generous with her gratitude. That is what people respond
kindly to, as she learned in her jobs and raising her girls. She
must begin in this fancy place as she means to go on: with
the courage to be not a foreigner, to be no longer a clerk; to
move as if she belongs, head high and stride sure—she can
do this, she will, but oh, it is a hard, hard thing to do.

6

THE BABY OF THE PLACE . . .

*B*UT HERE IS SOMETHING ELSE TO GET USED TO: rounding the corner too swiftly in her anxiety— what if others are already gathered at tables, with no space for her and no interest either, and she finds no one else ever to talk to or be with and must retreat to her room and be lonely and alone here for the rest of her life, what if all that?— Greta nearly runs down, almost trips over a little woman walking with the aid of one of those contraptions with wheels. "Pardon me, I am so sorry." She knows this small person, although vaguely and in more upright posture, but without at the moment a name—a customer of shampoos and lipsticks when Greta worked as a clerk at Alf Stryker's drugstore? "I am going too fast on my way to the coffee, would you join me? I am by the way Greta Bauer."

Here in this small rush of words is her newest brave start.

The woman is very small, with skin of tissuey softness, and pale brown eyes—faded eyes? Her hair waves in white-sugary fashion, and would once have been brown, like her eyes. Even so, Greta can see that when they were small, her girls might have called an old person of such stooped appearance a witch, although Greta would correct that sort of meanness. "Witches can be good, do not believe all you read," she might say. Or "Appearance means nothing," which of course is untrue.

Freeing a hand for Greta to shake, very gently because how fragile these bones feel, this witch, good or bad, says, "How do you do. I'm Ruth Friedman, and I'd be delighted to join you. I've been in my room long enough. I'm in 3, close to the dining room. It takes me so long to get where I'm going these days, I need the head start."

See how easy?

"You look familiar," this Ruth Friedman says. "Have we met?"

"I worked for many years at the Stryker drugstore. I think I served you then?"

"Oh, of course. We kept our agency's pharmacy account at Stryker's, so I shopped there for myself too." It speaks well of Greta as a mother that they never encountered each other the other way around, in the course of Ruth's duties. "I don't know if you remember, I was with Children's Aid."

That would be interesting, and no doubt sad also, but what should a good mother and store clerk, concerned mainly, like most people, with keeping her own family's head above water, know about the dark, hidden places of this pleasant, treed, rivered, hilled city? Greta knows some things, but not those particular ones. "If you would like to sit, I can get what we want. Would you prefer coffee or tea, and shall I get us cookies also?"

Neither coffee nor tea is recommended for osteo, or for people who've had heart attacks, but this is a matter of first impressions and getting acquainted, and anyway, how much harm can they do? "Coffee, please, with plenty of milk and no sugar. Cookies would be lovely as well." It's slightly alarming to Ruth that in the process of helping her get seated, Greta pulls the walker just out of reach. Ruth can get by without it, but it's a comfort and convenience. Also, she is vulnerable to minor panics if she starts feeling trapped; like in the old days, finding herself in a small, one-exit apartment, for unhappy reasons, with a large, angry man, some unstrung father. This has happened. Still, Greta does not strike her right off the bat as a person inclined to do harm.

First, do no harm, is the pledge doctors make, but that is a much harder, more ambiguous goal for anyone, not only for doctors, than people might think; even quite unrealistically ambitious.

Ruth assumes that this week, with all the commotion and racket of people moving in, will not be typical. At the moment, the lounge is an oasis, and it's thoughtful of Greta Bauer to bring coffee and cookies right to Ruth's side—in these very practical and fundamental ways, the place is not terrible.

As for the rest, well, that will be up to her.

Her reason for moving here must be different from other people's. Otherwise (and how can she not smile at this, so that the nice Greta person across the room at the coffee machine thinks she's smiling at her, and smiles back)—otherwise, such mass catastrophe would lie ahead for the poor Idyll Inn staff! She is proposing a far greater tumble and vault than her lithe former body could have imagined, decades ago, when she was a gymnast performing high, airy leaps.

Here, she already feels almost light again. In the absence of Bernard, the weight and burden of history has been haunting their little white-vinyl-clad home, no escape. Even for only one person—especially for only one—that house is too small to contain so much time, but here, in this newest, most cheerfully inoffensive place there is no history at all, good or bad, hers or anyone else's, steeped yet into the walls. Here too, staff, although no match for Bernard's tender fingers, are efficient and useful, in her experience to this early point. "And so," she asks, as Greta settles into the chair opposite, "do you like the place so far?"

"Yes, it is very fine. My generous daughters help me to pay, or I could never afford it."

Ruth has noted the tinge of accent, the slight labouring over words. There are certain old drumbeats that can cause small hairs to rise on the back of her neck, even though they have nothing directly to do with her or, most likely, with this woman sitting opposite, dipping a chocolate chip cookie into her coffee. Still, there's no getting around the fact that some history is not yet ancient; that the afterlife of war and holocaust is long and may manifest itself unexpectedly. Like now. "That's wonderful. You must be proud."

"I am, yes." Greta beams. Most mothers do. "And you worked with children in trouble?"

"Whole families in trouble, one way and another. Honestly, the people who should not have children but do, without even thinking about whether they have any talent at all for the job—it's shocking sometimes."

Like many parents Ruth has encountered, Greta looks puzzled by notions of *talent* or *job*. "I confess, I gave it no thought myself. But I am fortunate, I know, with my girls."

"Obviously they've been fortunate as well."

Greta nods. Obviously she agrees. "You have children?"

"No. It was more than enough to worry about other people's." No need to mention that, fierce as she may be on the subject of children's general well-being and safety, Ruth isn't all that individually fond of them; whereas in her experience people are normally vastly sentimental about their own children, but have no broader affections when it comes to weighing personal comforts against keeping the offspring of strangers here or anywhere else in the world fed, safe or even alive. But a familiar, infuriating pity has flickered across Greta's face—no children, too bad, what a shame! "I saw far too many examples of ghastly families," Ruth adds. "That alone was far from encouraging."

Again Greta nods. What a large head she has, made larger by a mass of thick silvery hair, and blunt features, blue eyes—a striking woman, Ruth expects, in her youth, back in a time, unlike now, when voluptuousness could be much the same thing as beauty. "That is so, families can be terrible, I know. In the apartment downstairs from mine lived for a while people who shouted and struck each other. I would go to their door to say I would call your very agency, or the police, and they would be quiet then for a time. They moved away finally. You would see much worse than that?"

"Yes. Although you never know. It seems to be hard to decide when to call in the authorities." Ruth hopes she hasn't implied that Greta's downstairs neighbours moved away and kept right on yelling and landing blows on each other when they might have been stopped by a phone call. They would not have been stopped. Only crises and catastrophes ever were. Sometimes.

Ruth is exhausted by tales and images that take up space she needs now for quite other purposes.

So many people these days seem too young for their duties—firefighters, police officers, lawyers, they all look like apple-cheeked innocents. Bernard's oncologist, too: Dr. Lucy Holmes, a mere infant, arriving in town to take up her practice just in time to stick Ruth's husband into a long, claustrophobic scanning machine, and later to lean forward and take his and Ruth's hands in her own and say, "I'm sorry. It isn't good news."

Indeed it was not. What Ruth and Bernard had taken to be swellings and tweaks of pain associated with aging were instead cancers busily consuming, one by one, his most necessary organs. "I see," Ruth and Bernard said, "I see," but of course they did not, right away.

Whoever does?

"We can try treating aggressively," Lucy said. "There's always a chance." But her tone suggested otherwise. "And you know, there are wonderfully effective pain control methods these days, as well as all sorts of other resources. Survivor groups, counsellors, therapists."

"Thank you." But Bernard's life was not a democracy. Ruth, even Lucy, could offer opinions, but only Bernard and the cancer had votes.

Ruth has heard both lovemaking and sleep referred to as *the little death*. They are delicious in their quite different ways, but what is either compared with the real one? Back home, she and Bernard wept and shouted and cried out, "Why me, why you?" and held tight to each other.

And then they got on with things. "I'm a widow," she tells Greta. "My husband died just over a year ago. You too?"

"A widow, yes. Not so recent, however."

"I expect most of us here are."

"Yes."

Ruth told Annabel Walker that, living alone, she was finding the osteo made it too difficult to properly look after herself, as well as occasionally dangerous. Helping Ruth choose a suite, Annabel took care to point out that the Idyll Inn was not a place for the seriously medically needy, but for people able to cope, with some help. "Well," Ruth told her, "I may be slow, but I get there. There's no question about coping." In its way this is true enough. Reminders of purpose do sizzle-bubble, though, causing her to close her eyes briefly in anticipation and alarm when they erupt, which reasonably enough is fairly often, including right now.

The nice Greta person is asking, "Will you know many people who live here?"

"It wouldn't surprise me. There could be an exceptionally successful child from the past who's managed to get a job in the kitchen, or as one of the aides." This is possible, but the odds were always against those castaways and brutalized youth, that infant debris, growing into thriving adulthood, even minimum-wage adulthood. "Or an old board member taking up residence. A different category, that would be. I mean, different from both the children and me."

"As I will see customers, but not other clerks?"

"Exactly." A matter of class; a bond of sorts even though, strictly speaking, Ruth herself was once among Greta's customers. "The way it's maybe not as easy for us to afford the place. I only have my little pensions and the money from selling our house. My house." That's been one of the problems, hasn't it, that so much has refused to become singular after devoted decades of plural?

But Ruth is surely singular here.

"I did not have a house," Greta tells her. "Our home was the apartment in the upstairs of a house. Only because of my girls can I be here." Yes, yes, as she keeps mentioning. "So I have wondered about fitting in."

"Me too, I suppose, although I bet we can both hold our own."

That is kind of Ruth to say. "There is also being used to living alone, and now being with so many people, do you think about that?"

Of course Ruth has considered that; for her own, still very personal reasons, not just because everyone here must have had to contemplate in advance these new, quite different circumstances. "But there's nothing wrong with spending whatever time we need in our own suites. In a way it'll be interesting, figuring out our preferences from scratch, as we go along."

What is *from scratch?* "I have thought also I shall miss watching the children going to school past my apartment—all the sounds of the young."

Good heavens, what *isn't* Greta fretting about? But "I expect there'll be lots of young visitors," is all Ruth says.

"And don't forget," comes a dry voice from behind, causing Ruth to jolt her head automatically leftward, causing in turn a great cascading of pain across her shoulders and right down her spine, "don't forget the schoolchildren who I gather will be turning up to amuse us. Keep us soft-hearted. Or soft-headed. Have you seen this thing?" The voice belongs to a narrow woman in pale linen trousers, white blouse, and two slim coppery bracelets, waving the same sheet of paper that was waiting in everyone's suites when they moved in. "How do you do, I'm Sylvia Lodge. May I join you?"

"Yes, of course, please. I am Greta Bauer."

"Ruth Friedman." Ruth notes arthritis that looks rheumatoid, the cumbersome, misshapen joints in a different category from her own osteo. She knows Sylvia Lodge, as a matter of fact, or used to when Sylvia, as Ruth moments ago predicted, was on her agency's board and Ruth was occasionally called on to flesh out, as it were, the blood and guts behind the agency's numbers: this many homes investigated, these charges laid, those families under close supervision and counselling, these children seized, injured, once or twice dead.

So: this Sylvia Lodge a board-joining Lady Bountiful. Who looks puzzled, as if realizing she should recognize Ruth; maybe Greta too, for all Ruth knows. Sylvia waves her piece of paper again. "Have you taken a look at this so-called activities schedule?"

"Yes," Greta says, "I thought to learn knitting, or to crochet. I have not ever made anything except for my girls' clothes when they were small, and I might like to."

Each day of the month is blocked out in a large square, and each square tells what's organized for that day. "Knitting group"—Greta's choice, evidently—"10, crafts room!" Or "Word games, 2, lounge!" or "Music by The Golden Cowboys, 2, dining room!" Wednesday afternoons there's to be "Bingo, 1:30, dining room!" and on Friday and Saturday nights "Movies, 7:30, library!" Plus there are "Mall outing, 10!" or "Spring countryside tour, 2!" Next Tuesday, "Sylvester School Grade 6 Choir, 10, lounge!" "All those exclamation marks!" Sylvia says. "As if punctuation will make any damn thing interesting. Sorry, Mrs. Bauer, I didn't mean to insult knitting. But really, if a person were depending on that girl for entertainment, the days would be long and uninspiring, don't you think?" *That girl* is the recreation director, Linda Swain, a muscular, peppy blonde who could be somebody's granddaughter. Great-granddaughter. An optimist, it appears. "Honest to God, we're just old, we're not morons."

"Call me Greta, please."

"I expect," Ruth says, "it's hard to program for so many different kinds of people. I mean, of just the three of us, only Greta's fingers look as if they can manage knitting. Maybe the activities are for people in the middle."

"Or the lowest common denominator. Although I do understand the desire for productive new skills—perhaps you'll have knitted up new sweaters for us all by Christmas, Greta?"

Sylvia Lodge seems to have a strange sense of humour. "Or if I am not so clever, perhaps a plain scarf?"

"Anyway, nothing's mandatory," Ruth says. "Maybe the schedule's just a fallback, and they figure most people will have in mind using their time in their own ways."

"Such as?" Sylvia asks.

"I don't know. Keeping up with what they're already interested in. And thinking, I suppose. Preparing. Focusing forward." A curious remark. Sylvia frowns. "How did you decide to move here?" Ruth asks, leaving unsaid but perhaps not unheard, *if you're going to be critical right off the bat?*

"A pre-emptive strike. I thought I should take matters into my own hands before anybody had a chance to do it for me. Or to me. I've taken a couple of spills, and as you can see I have awful arthritis, so I foresaw more and more trouble getting around without breaking bones." Sylvia leaves unsaid, but not unheard, *although not as much difficulty as you, you poor crippled thing.*

Nevertheless Ruth notes Sylvia Lodge's inclination toward pre-emptive strikes.

"Me also," says Greta, "I am here to be safe. I have had two heart attacks, and to think of another and not being found, it frightened me, and my girls, too. Do you have children?"

"A daughter. I guess I should call, let her know where I am."

"She does not know?" Greta is startled; Ruth, too. This sounds like yet another way to abuse a child, even though any daughter of Sylvia Lodge's will be a long way from childhood.

"Not yet. I didn't feel it was a matter for debate. Now it's done, I'm hoping she'll be grateful to be spared all the trouble."

"Goodness, my daughters would not have liked that. They have been a great help."

Ruth moved unaided. It's not an impossible thing to do. Her sympathies slide back toward Sylvia; Greta may be one of those women who lean on their children for every damned thing. Then again, obligation is different from love. Maybe Greta's daughters, as she suggests, just love her to death. Maybe Sylvia is simply cold. Ruth shivers. "Are you chilly?" Greta asks. "I could get you a sweater."

"Thanks, but I'm fine." It's hard not to be warm in a track suit, and track suits are pretty much Ruth's uniform these days, if only because most of the time she can get in and out of them on her own. Today's is a bright and misleadingly athletic red. She also owns a purple one, and another in a rather unpleasant green shade verging on lime. Her theory is, now that she's gotten so stooped, people could easily trip over her like a crack in a sidewalk. As Greta nearly did anyway.

"*Scheisse*," Greta whispers.

"What?"

"Pardon me. Someone coming into the lounge."

"You know him?"

"I did once."

The man slouched in the wheelchair looks as sullen as one of Ruth's unhappy adolescents. A younger fellow, middle-aged and dressed in a dark suit, is pushing him, pausing, eyes landing on Sylvia, Greta and Ruth. Perhaps they look welcoming.

The man in the suit—a son?—leans over and points. "How be I wheel you over there where there's people to talk to? You can start getting acquainted with the place while Colette drives me to the airport shuttle, okay?" His voice carries. To Greta he sounds cajoling—*cajole: to deceive with soothing words or false promises*; to Ruth he sounds patronizing; to Sylvia, inconsequential. The old man's right hand waves vaguely, as if his sentiments are more or less Sylvia's.

"Look, George," the man continues; not a son, then, unless it's one of those progressive families in which everyone uses first names. "Look, when Colette gets back, go easy, okay? I know you don't want to make her feel bad. If you try to make the best of being here, that'll be a kindness to her, and it'll help you as well. Go into this with a positive outlook and good things will happen. Shall we start by joining the ladies?"

The old man flings his right arm out, brings it down hard on the arm of his wheelchair. The man in the suit says, "Good. Here we go, then."

"I know you," Sylvia says as the wheelchair reaches them. "You're George Hammond. You ran a shoe store on the main street."

As if he doesn't bloody know who he is. "Mmmph." George's head bobs up and down, back and forth.

"Yes, he did," says the suited man. "See, George, we told you you'd know people here."

Greta takes a deep breath everyone can hear and leans forward. "George," she says. One more time to take a first step. She looks at his hair, which is still lavish; at the off-kilter shape of his lips, into his alarmed eyes. Her gaze travels across his arms and down his body, fixes briefly on his slippered feet propped on the wheelchair's footrests. Abruptly she leans back, raising her coffee cup as in a toast. "George," she repeats. "We meet again." From a spy movie she saw long ago.

"Right, then," says the middle-aged man, "looks like you're all set with old friends for a while, so I'll be off. Colette expects to drop back in after your dinner to make sure you're doing okay. You can get back to your room when you need to, right?"

"Rummph."

"That's great. You guys have fun now," and he's off, his step light and eager, his relief so evident that all three women at the table feel the insult. The young who don't want to be bothered. The young who fail to see life in the old fellow yet. Any old fellows. Including the women.

Did that suited man not feel, coming through the automatic doors earlier, the breeze of his own future entrance?

The tangles and complications of families—here's another one, as Annabel Walker comes into the lounge, clapping her hands like a cheerleader. "Isn't this lovely, you're already getting together, just what I hoped for, what good examples you are! Don't forget to ask for whatever you need—cards, cribbage boards, anything."

Good God. Cribbage. Good examples. When Annabel turns away, Sylvia's narrowed eyes remain on her back. Peter's genes, all in all, were pitifully weak. Never mind. "We were discussing this activities schedule before you arrived, Mr. Hammond. What do you think of it?"

George took one blurred look at the damned thing this morning and threw it into the trash. What does he care for stupid things to do? "Be pleasant, Dad," Colette keeps telling him, "and people will be pleasant to you," but who gives a bugger about *pleasant?* He's a man who could rely not only on knowledge of footwear but on charm for his living, and now he's just supposed to be *pleasant?* Hell, he can consider himself brave when he musters a smile, half a smile; stoic when he isn't in tears. "Useless," he blurts finally, and the women look startled.

"Exactly," Sylvia says after a moment. "We'll have to come up with our own entertainments if we want any stimulation at all."

Ruth thinks: a natural board chair, setting agendas, organizing, moving events right along. A thin line between that and bullying. But a leader of sorts, not to be sniffed at.

Frankly, Ruth is a little shocked by the age of the people she's seen here so far. At seventy-four, she looks to be the baby of the place—this bunch must be hovering around the eighty mark. And all these people have simply kept going, no matter what. Does that make her a coward?

No.

But it is true that she has come here to die.

She does not mean this in the shadowy fashion that applies to every Idyll Inn resident—every human on earth—but as a resolution packed along with her cosmetics and painkillers and photographs and nightgowns and best bits of furniture.

She has taken a large, hard lesson to heart: if in Bernard's democratic dying there were two votes, his and cancer's, in the dictatorship of Ruth there's to be only one.

Like any prudent dictator, she has made certain plans, devised certain strategies. What she needs now is a dictator's military support. The Idyll Inn may not look like a barracks where good soldiers reside, but if she can find one ally, one friend, that's all she should need. Two would be better; more most unlikely.

Still, she has some faith that while they are often enough properly nervous—about tripping, about falling and breaking, about being abruptly struck down whether by heart or by stray, running youth—the old are not easily bone-deep frightened. Having, like her, survived decades of large and small ups and downs, and being well aware of what is capable of being endured and performed, they surely can't find much truly terrifying still; really, just one or two things.

7

AT THREE IN THE MORNING . . .

*P*INKISH, TRANSLUCENT, RIDGED AND UPTILTED wall sconces light the after-dark corridors of every Idyll Inn, including this one. From a distance they resemble valuable old glass, but in fact they are made from recycled plastics and are pleasantly inexpensive when bought in Idyll Inn quantities. And who can tell the difference? They're set high enough that even the most skeptical residents won't be leaping up to examine them closely.

There is a density to the dim radiance, too, that creates its own silence. The first person to set out on the night's journey at the appointed hour feels wary and out of place, even though this is the same smooth, handrailed, plain-sailing corridor regularly travelled in daylight.

The sole overnight-shift staff member gloomily or sleepily or irritably responsible for covering the main floor made her last rounds an hour ago, and now, barring some kind of alarm, she will be settled in the office down the hall, around a corner, past the dining room, well out of sight and sound of a shady first-floor corridor, till the kitchen staff start arriving to set up for breakfast. This is a well-scouted, predictable pattern—who expects aged residents to be skulking around at this hour, when they're supposed to be tucked up in their beds?

Still, care is required.

The tall, narrow figure taps on a door, steps inside. In foxholes, the bullying old saying goes, there are no atheists; which is a lie, she believes. Hoping for mercy and grace under fire isn't at all the same thing as belief.

Because what sort of god would put people in foxholes to start with?

"You're ready?" she whispers to the waiting figure, a bulky silhouette against moonlight. Then, "Courage." Which is not to be mistaken for a prayer; more a battlefield exhortation.

8

A COSY FEET-UP VISIT . . .

On the Saturday afternoon in late May that ends the Idyll Inn's first full month in operation, the taxi bringing Sylvia's daughter Nancy for her first visit arrives just in time to take George's daughter Colette away after her second. From this flying trip Colette will again catch an airport shuttle to the city, and then her long flight home to Bill and her much-interrupted career. "Jesus Christ, what were you thinking?" are among Nancy's first words to her mother when she reaches Sylvia's suite. "There's a guy at the front door in a wheelchair making weird noises and crying. You don't belong with people like that."

How flattering. Really. "I'm sure that's meant as a compliment, thank you. But I *am* living here, so why don't you sit down, relax, and when you're ready, I'll show you around. If you'd like to stay for dinner, we'll let the kitchen know—they're happy to serve guests, but they need some notice and the dinners are early."

Here the meal is called supper, and it's appallingly early.

By five-fifteen, which is about the time Sylvia in her previous life, last month, would have been choosing among predinner wines, everyone is gathered at their place settings. By six-thirty, a good half-hour before Sylvia would have even been starting her meal, everyone is gone from the dining room as if, like messy plates and used cutlery, residents are to be cleaned away as smartly as possible. It's early days for a campaign of civil disobedience, but Sylvia has been considering an obdurate, chair-gripping refusal to move. A group sit-in would be wonderfully literal, and bound to be more effective than George's periodic tantrums; the ones that caused Annabel Walker or one of her minions to call Colette to fly here again to get him calmed down because otherwise, despite previous promises, "we might not be able to keep him here after all."

He's been pushing the envelope, that's for sure: gritting his teeth against taking his meds, specifically the prescribed antidepressants, which personally Sylvia thinks he should be taking as many of as he can get; refusing to propel himself in his wheelchair, demanding the services of an aide instead, if good-hearted or too amenable Greta isn't around; plus the last straw, when he deliberately tossed, as opposed to dropped, his lemon cake and custard dessert on the dining-room floor, loudly pronouncing one of the words he can actually say clearly, which is "crap."

His methods may be unfortunate, but Sylvia is basically sympathetic to his aims. It's a matter of power, and trying to exert some control—aside from going about it foolishly, he's putting up a pretty ordinary and admirable struggle. Nancy's right if she's implying that most Idyll Inn residents are not what one would call sprightly, but mistaken if she thinks nothing is happening. Which would hardly make Nancy unique when it comes to assumptions the not-old make about the old, but it's annoying. It shouldn't be so hard to realize that there are some strenuous wrestling matches going invisibly on. Or visibly—look at George.

"Before you sit, Nancy, why don't you fetch us some wine from my little fridge—it's beneath the counter by the door, and there's a corkscrew and glasses on the shelf overhead, if you'd do the honours." Sylvia's hands can barely perform that trick any more. One virtue of the Idyll Inn is that there's always somebody to corral into opening a bottle, even if she has to wait awhile sometimes.

"Should you be drinking, Mother?"

"Should I not be?"

So swiftly they leap to belligerent tones. The trouble with families: there you are, locked to people you'd never even meet otherwise. If Nancy were not her daughter, how would Sylvia ever encounter a personal trainer for the reasonably wealthy and terrifically self-indulgent in a city a couple of hundred kilometres away? Personal trainer! And an aging one, at that. Perhaps Nancy's concern here is for her inheritance, despite doing well enough for herself with the inheritance she has already received: Sylvia's bones, Sylvia's long, lean, previously flexible body.

Plus Sylvia's sharp tongue, not necessarily an advantage, although perhaps reserved for her mother. "I'm glad you came," Sylvia tells her now, and having said it, finds that in its way, it could almost be true. Or at least that making the small effort to say so makes her feel warmish and semi-benevolent. "A cosy feet-up visit with a couple of glasses of wine, what could be nicer?" But she goes too far, that doesn't sound like her at all. "I do enjoy an afternoon sip," she adds.

"I know."

What the hell does that mean? Sylvia is hardly a lush, so what's Nancy's problem?

Nancy's problem goes back years. For four decades she has cherished her great grievance, which by the way was really Sylvia's, and moreover could have been, could still be, much, much worse—Nancy has no idea. As it is, Sylvia would wish to have raised a daughter who didn't *dwell*, but it seems Nancy is addicted to dwelling. Permanently attached. Over time this must become deliberate and at this stage, Sylvia suspects, is even a kind of delight. Still, one of them has to try. "Now you're here, I hope you can see the place is perfectly fine." *Perfectly* is pushing it; relatively fine, better than lying helplessly alone in a big old house with broken arm, broken leg, broken hip—that kind of fine is what the Idyll Inn is.

Or, all right, it's also fairly fascinating, although how long this fascination can last is a question. But for the time being there are new voices and sounds and new people, a two-storey Petri dish of adjustments among the lame, the halt, the partly deaf, the half-blind, the liver-damaged, ovary-missing, joint-stiffened, determined veterans of decades of breathing: quite a crew. Every sag and wrinkle in the place a medal for some kind of valour.

"The point is, you moved without even mentioning you were going to. You didn't even ask what I thought. Or about the house, and everything in it."

"Well, it's not as if you were ever going to come back here to live. And if you waited before you jumped to conclusions, I'd remind you the sale hasn't closed yet, so you can still wander through the house to your heart's content." To do that, to be there again, with light glancing from window to sideboard to candlestick to bookcase to shining hardwood, to be home to the heart's content—it's no wonder George cries out and flails. "As to all our things, everything I need is here, and a lot of the rest is in storage, more than you could possibly want, from some really good furniture to boxes of books, and the bookcases, and your grandmothers' china and silverware and most of the paintings and prints, and a carton or two of old photographs—all sorts of things. After you make your choices we can arrange to get rid of what's left, but there's time, I've paid storage for another couple of months. And look at it this way, I've put myself into storage as well, at no cost or trouble to you. I'm not a nitwit, I did think it through."

"All by yourself."

See? There she goes, *dwelling*. "Consider yourself lucky, then. Often enough it's families that get stuck making decisions, so there are some very unhappy faces around the place—you met one at the front door—but mine's not among them and yours shouldn't be either. Really, think what I've saved us from." She should leave it there, she should bite her tongue, but no. "Can't you just say *Thank you, Mother*, and be pleased?"

"Thank you?" Nancy has her own lines at her eyes and her mouth—medals for which acts of courage?—and the beginnings of puckerings down her throat. Sylvia remembers when that started happening to her own throat: a touch of despair and, yes, even horror to start with, then a brief, futile battle with creams and upward strokings of skin grown unfirm. Eventually acquiescence, because—what the hell. It happens. Does Nancy know that, that it happens and you might as well ride it? Nancy is leaning forward, hands tight on her crystal glass—Sylvia hopes she doesn't break it, it's one of the five remaining of the dozen that were a wedding gift to her and Jackson. "You didn't think I should have something to say about you and my home?"

Nancy hasn't lived in this town since she was eighteen. In her subsequent thirty-five years, shouldn't she have found another place to call home by now? "I knew you'd be interested, but think about it, what was there to say? I didn't feel easy living alone after those falls, and I know you'd agree that moving in with you, or vice versa, would be considerably less than ideal. I thought of trying to find an unusually helpful tenant, but how likely would that be? And this place is new and clean and not unattractive, and there's company, and help if I need it, and so—what more do you want of me? To talk? Go ahead then, say your piece if you must." Sylvia crosses her arms. It crosses her mind, too, that that cry of *What more do you want of me?* is an old one. She relaxes her arms. "Nancy," she says. "My dear."

A distinctly unlavish effort. Oh, to be like George Hammond, capable of weeping at the drop of a hat for love of his kind, unwilling daughter.

What will Nancy see, going through the photos in storage? They gave Sylvia herself pause, contemplating the many gaps between then and now. There were she and Jackson, she in flaring-out skirt and twin-set, he loose-limbed in charcoal trousers, sky blue sweater over paler blue shirt, only its cuffs and collar visible. Both of them young and angular then. Both sizzling, too, never mind twin-sets and peeping-out collars. They were obviously not the only ones in town climbing zestfully into back seats, but they must have felt like the only ones.

There is an album of wedding photographs. In the end, some things go better than, at certain points, could have been dreamed. Or deserved.

There are golf tournaments and celebrations at the country club, a table for four very often when everyone was still young, all glasses raised and much tossed, buoyant hair and white teeth. Cigarettes between fingers—everyone smoked in those days. Bright lipstick stains on filters stubbed out in glass ashtrays.

Barbecues and birthday parties at various homes, including their own, and Peter and Susan Walker's. Children in the frames: first Annabel; two years later Nancy, in bare feet and playsuits, a jolly child showing off for the camera; a couple of years later Annabel's brother, young Peter. How contained the dramas of those days, behind several sets of eyes giving nothing away. So many cameras over the years taking hundreds of photographs, and the striking thing about looking rapidly through so many is how lightly and easily important themes of the time flow through the fingers, while themes undiscerned then are obvious now. "You'll never guess," Sylvia blurts, because this has popped into her head in terms of Nancy the energetic, adorable child, not Nancy the cross grown-up in the easy chair facing her, "who's managing this place." A blunder as soon as it's out of her mouth, so she hurries on. "Annabel Walker. You should say hello if we run into her while you're here."

"Really?" The word is drawn-out and forbidding. "Are her parents here too?"

"No. They both died. He had a heart attack, she had cancer. Breast, I think." Ridiculous to go through this sort of alarmed conversational dance years after everyone's emotions, except Nancy's, apparently, were thoroughly settled.

"I see. You never said."

"No, well, why would I?"

Nancy looks down into her wine, looks back up. "Weird for Annabel to end up back here if her parents are gone. And running a—what's it called?—retirement lodge."

"Yes, and I can tell you people are touchy if it's confused with a nursing home. I don't know why she's come back. Her brother is off being an engineer someplace in Asia, I think. But some people do seem to want to return to where they began."

"I can't imagine anything worse."

No doubt.

Nancy sighs. "You'll need to give me whatever authorization gets me into the storage place so I can get started on sorting. I don't suppose there's any furniture left in the house?"

"Well, no. Because I wouldn't be going back. And it needs to be empty on closing day."

"Then I'll have to look around for a place to stay. Can you suggest a motel? Is the ABC still in business?"

Oh, that Nancy. She's got far more of Sylvia in her than bones.

"I have no idea," Sylvia says curtly. "But I could scarcely recommend it anyway to someone as virtuous as yourself. I can, however, recommend you grow up and get over it. You can be very tiresome, Nancy." What a shame. It's all gone wrong. Again. Sylvia pushes herself to her feet. "We're both too old for this. Let's take a tour, so you can see that if nothing else, this place will do fine." Both their wineglasses make discernible clicks on Sylvia's coffee table. How much blood does Nancy want?

Perhaps she wants something more tender, more, oh,

maternal than a mere uncrossing of arms and that single dragged-out, dredged-up *My dear*.

In the lounge, Greta and Ruth look up with interest from what appears to be another effort to cheer George. Greta's effort, anyway, since it's her hand on his knee. Ruth is in the soft nearby chair that's become hers as long as there's someone to help her out of it. By and large she strikes Sylvia as a person who observes closely and carefully, although not maliciously. It would be interesting to know what she watches for. "You must be Sylvia's daughter," Greta says. "You are the very image."

Indeed. "Yes, this is Nancy. I'm showing her around, trying to reassure her I was smart to move myself here."

"Oh yes," says Ruth, "it's quite pleasant so far. We're just talking with George about how we should enjoy ourselves while the staff take all the cares and chores off our shoulders. And then too, your mother," she advises Nancy, "encourages us to keep lively."

"I bet she does."

There's a silence as they absorb the mystifying chill of that before Greta says, "It is nice you visit your mother. I have three daughters who were here to help me move in, and George's daughter has been here twice from far away. She has left again today to go home, and we are reminding George that our children have their lives and we must get on with ours. Would you not say so, Sylvia?"

She certainly would, and given Nancy's mood, the sooner the better.

Except that's not the entire state of affairs. It's also true that now and then, although usually not until nightfall, when there's no seeing the river or skyline and even the best suite grows barren and cramped, good reason to pour a little more wine—at any rate, it's true that now and then, including right now in full daylight, Sylvia's spirits plunge downwards like stones from the sky. It's hard to stay armoured. Love and history—even without looking too closely, those can be hard to bear. "George's daughter," she tells Nancy, "was pleased about her father moving here, especially since it's new and in demand. She and her husband live out west, right, George?"

"Umph," he says sadly.

"And," Ruth pipes up, "since she's a busy banker, it's unusual she's been able to get away as much as she has. How long will you be staying, Nancy?"

"Only a couple of days, and I gather I have a lot of sorting to do. In fact, now I've seen around the place, Mother, I'll be off. I'll find a hotel and drop in here tomorrow, but if there's as much to deal with as you say, I won't have much time." And off she marches. As stiff-necked as her mother ever has been.

If imitation's what it's cracked up to be, there should be a way to feel honoured by that.

Sylvia sighs. She rests a hand on George's shoulder, which means he has her hand there, Greta's hand on his knee, which is a great deal of attention and comfort for the one man among them, so she takes hers away so that he doesn't grow spoiled. Perhaps he is already spoiled by women, perhaps that's his problem. "Really, George, you must know we can't rely on our children. Certainly not to make us happy. And it's years since they've been around all the time anyway."

"Umph," he says again. How determined he is to be downcast.

Still, even when they're gloomy, Sylvia doesn't consider these unuseful companions. George keeps the fierce little ember of rebellion alight, however misguided his tactics. For her part, Ruth knows from her work a staggering and reassuring amount about truly bad mothers; although that's balanced by the sterling Greta, whose daughters evidently care to such an extent that most evenings right after dinner, one or another calls to check how she's doing, or she calls one or another of them. Presumably that is love, and presumably among mothers and daughters—among anyone—it must be a very nice thing to feel.

9

CARPE DIEM . . .

*S*YLVIA HAS GIVEN uncountable dinner parties in
her day, organized charity auctions, canvassed for
political purposes, danced charmingly at the country club
with total strangers, served at various times on the boards of
the local art gallery, the theatre, the child welfare agency for
which, as it happens, Ruth Friedman worked—an irony, perhaps, given the abuse Sylvia's own daughter feels she has suffered. She has lived with a husband and daughter, then just a
husband, and for the past three years as a widow in a large
house alone. She has travelled with that husband to quite a
few countries, visiting museums and cathedrals and hotels,
and restaurants with unusual foods, although never, and this
is too bad, to the many places on earth where the sights
would have been radically foreign to her.

Whatever else all that means, she has plenty of experience in adaptability and shifting gears. So Ruth, Greta and
George are a breeze, all things considered—not particularly
deferential, but with their own virtues; including a mutual

determination, not by any means shared by all Idyll Inn residents, not to maunder on endlessly confiding their ailments. Also, they don't really gossip much. Discretion is often underrated when it comes to companions, but not by Sylvia. Rummaging about in the nature of humans is a worthwhile endeavour, no doubt about that, and she's acquainted with a fair number of residents and enjoys a good natter herself, but it's . . . unnerving how much time some people can spend performing autopsies on the lives, real or fictional, of their fellow citizens.

"He drank, you know," someone in the lounge or dining room will remark. Or "She'd come into the hospital bruised up and down and swear she'd tripped and fallen downstairs." To which someone else will point out, "She had all those children, though, one after the other. What was she to do?" "I don't know, but if Bob had ever raised a hand to me, he'd have been a goner. And it's no favour to the children—look at hers, two of them hellions who landed in jail."

It's not so much the tales themselves, but the undertone of satisfaction at other people's misfortunes—*schadenfreude*, one of the few foreign words Sylvia's used that Greta has grasped. "A drug addict, you know," a beamish Pauline Parker will announce with regard to someone else's grandson. "Joined one of those cults, and no one sees him any more," Jocelyn Reynolds will offer about another. In the telling their own offspring are, by contrast, professionally successful and personally triumphant. Rather like Greta's librarian and soap-seller and druggist—never a mention of disappointments or failures.

Well, people don't become *better* humans for being old, and here, where idle hands may well be the devil's workshop, it seems to Sylvia that a lot of decorative embellishment goes on well beyond the walls of the arts and crafts room.

She herself knows all sorts of private stories, and Ruth must have some grim ones indeed. Greta, working in a drugstore, would have learned much about local lives—who used what sort of birth control, for instance, or dyed their hair, and who was prescribed antibiotics, and for what—and who'd have a clue what George knows but has doubtless forgotten? Imagine the stories that've been woven around Sylvia, and Jackson too, over the years; or what gets said about Nancy. Speaking of whom, "Nancy opened a bottle of wine but we didn't make much of a dent in it, so why don't I bring it down here? We could drink to our daughters, how about that, George?"

"I shall help," Greta offers, and off they go, and when they return Sylvia is clasping a corkscrew and two bottles— half a Riesling and a full Chardonnay—and Greta is holding four glasses. Greta pours—the good helper, as well as the one with good hands.

Sylvia raises her glass. "Right then, here's to our offspring present and absent, and to that excellent advice to for heaven's sake get on with our lives." Immediately she feels she has misspoken, as she sometimes does, sounding as bitter and unpleasant as, oh, Nancy. She used to be, if not exactly merry, more amusing, wasn't she? In old laughing country club photographs, did she not look genuinely lighthearted? Now there's rust in her voice, and it seems to have spread, as rust will, to more significant parts, and when did that happen?

"Yes, we don't want to waste the time we still have." Easy for Ruth to say, never mind the grim tone. She has no children to wound, or be wounded by.

"Your daughter cares to come a long way for you, George," Greta adds. "I think you must be content about that." She means *with that*, but now and then these days her grasp of language takes minor slides. This could be worrisome. George has told her haltingly about his wife and her Alzheimer's. "Alz," he said. "Head," tapping his own head with his right hand. "Not her fault." Greta would not wish to be cruel, but she herself does not surrender willingly to her heart, and if George's wife had similar fortitude, she would not have to give in to her brain. It is necessary to be determined. George used to know this. "So we have a toast to our children, but to ourselves also."

They don't need to keep saying it over and over, bloody women. George's eyes are as furious as his heart as he lashes out with his right arm and *splash*, there goes his wine flying over the table. Greta dodges back. Sylvia leans forward. Ruth watches. "Room," he says. "Shut up," he adds.

Women and their preaching, lecturing, demanding. As if he could be content at the snap of their witchy fingers, as if he couldn't burst with Colette flying off again today with an easy "Try to be happy here, Dad. Do your best. I know you can." She kissed his forehead the way she does, and danced away before he could hold her. Maybe she forgot that he can't move the way he once did, that he's not the same father who could give her a swift hug before leaving to, he'd say, meet a salesman passing through town, or refresh his inventory—anything that explained getting out and heading to the interesting and sometimes even thrilling parts of his life.

She said, too, "If you keep behaving badly, Dad, they'll throw you out. And another place . . . well, it might not be so nice. You really do need to think about that." She meant a nursing home. She spent time visiting Alice, who doesn't even know if Colette's coming or going, and was shocked he wouldn't go with her. Shocked too when he said, "Waste."

Any day he wants, he could call a cab or be hoisted into the Idyll Inn van to go and see Alice. Does she ever wonder where her husband has disappeared to? Does his face ever rise up in what remains of her mind? She has no way of remembering that he's been ill, has been in hospital, is now here. Maybe in Alice's world it's easy come, easy go; now you see him, now you don't. Time can have no meaning for her. She used to say, "I hate when you're out in the evenings, the time drags so." Not for him.

If he could, he would throw himself to the floor and howl and batter his fists like a two-year-old.

If he *could* do those things, he would not *want* to do them.

If he could be gathered up into somebody's arms; if he could be consoled, and other unspeakable words; if he could be restored to his feet—then wouldn't he run and run! Home, if he knew what house number, which street, how the rooms fit together. If he could be himself there again, whole and free, not like this. "Room," he commands more loudly. Why is Greta looking at him like that, why is her big warm hand not at his knee any more? Sometimes she wheels him around, it's not as if what he asks is impossible or surprising.

"No, George, if you want to, you can work the wheelchair yourself, or you could call for an aide. Or you could change your mind and stay here with us. We shall have wine and not be sad in our rooms." Perhaps it's a collapse of will, or of temper, perhaps it's a loss of some kind but—all right. "Good," says Greta, "good for you."

He hears Sylvia say to her, "Good for *you*."

Their voices resume rising and falling around him. Who the hell knows what they talk about all the time? Sylvia said one day, "At least at our ages there won't likely be time to get fed up with each other," and Ruth drew a sharp breath and then laughed and said, "Too true, there's no time to get bored." He guesses they talk about women's stuff, little things, but it can be kind of like music, their voices, and maybe he's been too meek but Greta's right, this beats being alone. Her living here is funny, in a strange way, not ha-ha, even if she's not as agreeable as she once was, except when she is. Here's time making a man dizzy with words and the round-and-round voices of women, and with wine, too.

"We can't go on drinking your wine, Sylvia," Ruth is saying, "just because you were clever enough to bring your own fridge. Did anyone mind?"

"I didn't ask. They'd object to a microwave, but a little fridge won't burn the place down. I don't find the meals quite as advertised, so I like having my own treats on hand."

"I guess the food's bland so it doesn't upset anybody."

"Well, but what about people who find bland upsetting? There seems barely any point to having taste buds and teeth, does there, for the meals they've been serving so far?"

Ruth giggles. "You're right, and if we don't get what we want now, when will we?" Another remark that creates a pause. "We could ask, I suppose."

"You could," Sylvia says. "Or Greta. I have such an awful time dealing with authority, I'm usually just inclined to demand, and you're more diplomatic."

What an odd point of view. From Ruth's and Greta's perspectives, Sylvia carries authority around in her slacks,
blouses and bracelets, in her voice, in her very bearing.

Greta's needles go *click, click, click* through their conversations now, with the first knitting classes under her
belt. It is hard to talk and knit at the same time, however,
even plain practice squares. "That Annabel Walker, she
said she wishes to please"—a moment to frown over a
loose stitch—"so would it be fair to let her know ways she
can do that?"

Fair—something to know about Greta. "All right. Then
carpe diem, don't you think?"

Greta hopes the talk will not reduce to carping, if that is
what Sylvia means. Complaints risk retribution—*retribution:
the dispensing of punishment.* But she will not say so to Sylvia
in case it would sound like criticism. She would not care to
criticize Sylvia.

"Maybe we could get somebody to shop for treats for us
all, to keep in my fridge," Sylvia suggests. "So we wouldn't
have to bother with Annabel, but nobody'd have to rely
entirely on the kitchen, either." There. How gracious and
redemptive is that? Not that she's keen to turn her suite
into an open house of people wandering in and out, root-
ing around.

"As long as we were careful not to intrude on your privacy," says Ruth, "it would be nice to have some things of
our own. It's very pleasant having an afternoon sip like this."

"It is, isn't it? And not to be sniffed at in the middle of
the night, either. Those times, you know, when you wake
up and can't get back to sleep, and you sit in the dark and
look out the window and have a little drink." Did that

sound peculiar? It's been Sylvia's cosy custom for decades, the waking up into darkness, the slippering off to a soft chair with a glass of wine in the silence of night.

Then back, more calmly, to bed and to sleep.

"Drunks," George bursts out—so he's been listening after all, and now half his mouth is upturned, and his eyes, even the left one, look unexpectedly merry.

After a startled moment Sylvia says, "We could ask an aide, in return for a little spare cash. The poor things probably don't make much more than minimum wage." *The poor things.* Ruth frowns. "But it should be one of you. My name is already mud with some staff, there's a certain *froideur* in some quarters."

On Sylvia's very first night here, the evening-shift aide assigned to the main floor barged into her suite without knocking. "Hi hon, I'm Diane, I'm here to help you get ready for bed and give out your medications and night-time snack. Okay with you, sweetie?"

Did no one train these people? If they lacked the wits themselves, did someone not suggest that residents might be lonesome or homesick or just plain sad, or be lost in their own thoughts and adjustments, and shouldn't be startled by some perky thing bouncing into their private space all unannounced, as if that were normal at the door of a stranger? There was so much wrong, Sylvia hardly knew where to begin. She raised herself from her loveseat, then paused to make sure her voice wouldn't for one reason or another carry a tremor. Ditto her legs, and her hands. "How do you do. I am Mrs. Lodge, and I am by no means your *hon,* or your *sweetie.* In future, too, I would like you to knock, as you would at any home. Also"—she peered at her watch—"it's only seven-thirty. If you come back at ten, we'll discuss what you might do for me then."

Hard to tell young people's ages. This Diane looked more than twenty, maybe even thirty—old enough, anyway, to be less intimidated than Sylvia intended. "Fine," and she slapped a plastic glass of orange juice and a tiny paper container of Sylvia's two powerful nighttime anti-inflammatories on the end table. She was cool later when she returned to help Sylvia into her nightgown. By the end of the day, as at its start, Sylvia's joints are exceptionally painful and stiff, although in a pinch she can usually manage to change her own clothes. One purpose of the Idyll Inn is to eliminate such pinches.

George is frowning. "Nice girl. Strong." What was wrong, anyway, with being called *hon* or, as he was, *sweetheart*?

When the girl came to his room his first night here, Colette was still visiting, but she jumped right up. "Did you need my dad, am I in the way?" It could not have been clearer that she'd spotted a means of escape. A stroke is scarcely more hurtful.

"It's okay, I can come back. I'm just making the rounds, helping people get toileted and ready for bed, and there's cookies and juice and Mr. Hammond's pills, but I can go do somebody else first."

"No, I should leave anyway. I'm going back to the house now, Dad," Colette said more loudly—did she think he'd gone deaf? "I'll see you in the morning after I pick up the things on our list"—the massive supplies of toothpaste, soaps, aftershaves and tissues she stacked in the cupboards, intended to last him for months. It costs a shocking amount to live here, but even so, these modest items, like racing stripes on a car, count as extras. "I'll pick you up a couple more pairs of pyjamas, too. There's no such thing as too many pyjamas, is there?"

Not if he was supposed to go to bed at eight o'clock. That used to be right about when he was leaving the house, excusing himself to Alice and Colette, creating shoe-related reasons for absence.

When Colette was gone, the girl said, "My name's Diane, I work evenings so you'll see a lot of me at bedtimes. Want to start with a trip to the bathroom?" She looked friendly and strong, and he didn't too much mind having her arms locked around him as they located his place on the toilet, although he did mind that first she had to tug down his pants, and then he had to sit with his shanks showing, and under some pressure. But there too she was kind, because she said, "Are you okay here for a few minutes on your own? I can deke out and check on one or two of your neighbours while you have your privacy, okay, sweetheart?"

"Good."

Except immediately she left, he began worrying about how soon she'd be back. Because what if she forgot? He remembered the button hanging from the cord at his neck: the way to remind her. He shifted more comfortably, nicely protected by the frame surrounding the toilet. All in all, safe as a chair. She was gone quite a while though, and was a bit rougher when she came back. By then he'd risked twisting his right arm back to the flushing lever, which required him to lean forward, so that he might, if the manoeuvre had gone badly, have toppled headfirst off the toilet. "Oh," she said, "you shouldn't have done that." Maybe that's what made her rougher: alarm.

She'd be a good one to get to pick up food and booze for them, right?

"It's still early days," Ruth is saying. "I don't think most of the staff have much experience, so we're learning together, them and us both. It's not their fault we don't always enjoy being their jobs."

"Ruth Friedman, what an annoyingly good person you are. You put us to shame."

"Oh no," Ruth starts to say, before she realizes that Sylvia's teasing; and also that a real remark is buried inside the joke. Ruth doesn't mean to put people to shame. It's only a side effect, sometimes, of wishing people were kinder. And what does any of them know of Diane?

"You just tell me what you need, hon, and how we should do it," she said on Ruth's own first night here. "I don't want to cause you any discomfort." Someone, Ruth imagined, had taught staff to say *discomfort* rather than *pain*. She took no great offence to the *hon*.

"Well, dear, I'll hurt whatever we do, so it's just a matter of managing in ways that hurt least. I'm sorry if I slow you down, you must be very busy trying to take care of so many people."

"Yeah, and in a new place it's hard on everybody. It'll get easier as we go along, I guess."

"Is this your first job in a retirement home?"

"It's sort of my first job altogether since I graduated."

"From?"

"I did a nursing aide program. I didn't like school so I quit and worked in, like, a variety store, but then my grandmother died and left me some money, but only if I went back to school. My grandma was kind of bossy sometimes."

"Good for you. And good for your grandmother. Did you mind?"

"Not really. Working in the store got boring real fast, and the pay was bad."

"Not great here, either, I imagine."

Diane shrugged. "I don't mind helping people, and that's all it is. Everybody's different so far, but I guess I'll manage."

"I'm sure you will. You're doing just fine." So she was. Her arm was strong to lean against, her fingers quick and gentle getting Ruth's arms into her bright zip-up nightgown and its matching red robe. It was nice seeing her eyes light up at just a morsel of praise. "I used to be a social worker, so I tried to help people too. Although," and Ruth smiled at Diane, "you'll have more certain results. We'll be grateful, and then we'll die, so you won't have to worry about whether you've set someone on a good road to the future or not." Diane looked shocked. "Oh my dear, you'd better get used to it, don't you think? Death, I mean. It's bound to come up." She patted Diane's hand. "Never mind, I shouldn't have mentioned it. You'll do fine with whatever happens."

"Thanks, yeah, probably," but now she looked anxious.

Okay, if the girl didn't entirely realize that Idyll Inn residents weren't children or pets, well, she wasn't alone in that, was she? The old, as they might remember from their own youth, are like a separate species: more or less useless, even repellent, and certainly irrelevant. It may even be, Ruth supposes, that they *are* all those things, and that's just one way the world propels itself onward, and the best trick the old can perform involves acquiescing to the harsh rule of becoming unseen.

While continuing to go, as she must, about their own urgent business.

"The plump girl with short brown hair?" she asks. "I don't mind asking if she'd run errands for us now and again. I find her an agreeable girl." Sylvia needn't think Ruth's a pushover. While Sylvia swanned around serving on boards and playing golf and bridge and throwing parties, Ruth was being honed by genuine danger: from raging men, rapier-fingernailed mothers, sullen and dangerously unpredictable adolescents, and youngsters in awful distress. As a small person, she made herself large with straight back and head always held high—possibly amusing, given the present shape and state of her bones.

But she has never been defenceless. And she is surprised to find that at this late date she can still be angry at women like Sylvia Lodge, with their easy, casual lives.

Even though it's better to be on Sylvia's good side than her bad; and it's somewhat flattering to be on her good side.

They've finished the Riesling, and gone to work on the Chardonnay. "Then that's settled," Sylvia says. "Now, I don't mean to harp but what else could we be doing, do you think? Besides drinking the days away."

"Well, nothing very *active* in the way of activities works for me, I'm afraid," Ruth says.

"No aerobics, then."

"Or dancing."

"Or yoga or jogging or shotput or three-hundred-metre dashes."

"Or three-metre dashes." Ruth again.

They are giggling now, Greta too, like six-year-olds at a birthday party. "Oh, I hurt," Ruth gasps.

"So laughing's out, too?" Causing more laughter; how
unseemly. Or perhaps they look senile. A passing aide smiles
but then frowns. That's funny too.

Annabel Walker drifts into the lounge. "Hello, ladies.
And gentleman. Nice to see you all enjoying yourselves, is
there a joke you could share?"

Why, does she have a sense of humour? One hasn't been
discernible in this first month. And if she does, from whom
might she have inherited it? "Probably not. You had to be
there," Sylvia tells Annabel. Who holds her tight smile as
she sighs. Naturally.

"All right. Only, this looks like a good time to mention
that I've been a little concerned you may have been drinking a bit on occasion."

"There's no *may* about it. We have."

"Well, it's not a good habit to get into, especially since
we serve a glass of wine at supper, which is already more
than some residences permit."

Permit? "Would you care for some?" Ruth asks, so innocently that Sylvia thinks, *What the hell is she doing, offering
my wine around?*

"Me? Heavens no. It's the middle of the afternoon, and
I'm working."

"Then I too don't understand your interest."

Good for Ruth.

Annabel now looks, Sylvia thinks, even more like her
mother in middle age: cross and disapproving and plain. That
can happen when people are disappointed again and again—
it starts to show up in expressions and postures, even their
features grow heavy or pinched. One may feel sorry for people
who've been deprived of their hopes, but one does not

especially care for them. "What I mean is, drinking is dangerous just for getting around, never mind for mixing with different medications." They might sympathize with this point of view if Annabel didn't go on to say, "It's for your own good."

What an intimidating little thing Ruth can be; she has Sylvia's and Greta's attention, and even George watches as, best she can, she draws herself up and together—here's a view of how she must have operated out in her tragically dangerous world. "Oh, I don't think we care for *that,* I don't believe we're paying to be deprived of our pleasures because of what someone else thinks might be for *our own good.* I don't think that's what we've signed up for."

"But," Annabel leaps on the word, "you did sign our contract."

"It says nothing on this subject," Sylvia says, "not even in the small print, and believe me, the wife of a lawyer learns to read carefully." She says this deliberately, poking at the past to see if anything stirs. And something does. Annabel's eyes harden.

"So does the daughter of a lawyer, Mrs. Lodge. Which I am, as you know. And I'm sure you remember that the contract says if management decides a resident is not best served by this kind of accommodation, the tenancy may be terminated. Including on medical grounds, and drinking can certainly be medically inappropriate, I don't think there's much doubt about that." Hardball, and more impressive than Sylvia expected. Also unhappily similar to dealing with Nancy. It doesn't do to retreat, but she rather wishes she hadn't taken that poke.

Fortunately Ruth takes over again. "You know, among us we have more than three centuries of experience with our own bodies, so I think it's safe to say none of us is going to get falling-down drunk. If you think this is depravity of some kind, I can only think you've been lucky. In my time I have seen real depravity, and this is not it."

Clever Ruth, pulling rank in that sweetest, sternest of voices, so that Annabel is left tamping down air with her hands. "No, no, I was just talking about taking good care of yourselves. I don't want anyone falling and hurting themselves. I understand about knowing your own bodies, but bodies change."

"Oh, my dear," Ruth says more gently, regarding Annabel almost tenderly, "we know that better than anyone."

Again, Annabel Walker sighs. "All right then, I just wanted a chat. Take care, though, all of you, won't you?" When she leaves, Ruth recedes into her chair as if the air's been let out of her. Sylvia notices that her own hands are unsteady. Greta also is shaken, as she generally is when there is conflict. She looks at George. It is a little cruel to see him in this state, although there was a time she might not so much have minded. Perhaps it is true that he should not be drinking. A glass of wine or two is not so bad for someone who has had heart attacks, but what are the effects on a survivor of strokes, whose attention drifts even at the most sober of times?

George has heard in Annabel's tone how she would have spoken to Colette about him and his behaviour and prospects, and he shivers, and hopes he doesn't start the damn weeping again.

"Honestly," says Ruth, "some days this place is just like starting school. The first day of kindergarten all over again." Although as she recalls, her parents were far more fretful than she was. She had other kids, and games, and everything new to look forward to. They only had losing her to a whole world of menace.

"There's sure no rest from change, anyway, even now, when you'd think there should be," Sylvia says. "But never mind, come on, we're about as far from kindergarten as we're going to get, and we've got this bottle to kill. Better a dead soldier than one that's just seriously wounded, wouldn't you say?"

Yes, at the moment, they would.

"So drink up," she says, and they do.

10

AT THREE IN THE MORNING . . .

*E*VEN IF EVERYONE WERE CAPABLE OF HURRYING—
and in good conscience none would deliberately
dawdle—no one cares to rush toward their middle-of-the-
night appointment. Just because, until something happens,
it hasn't yet happened.

Courage may have been the exhortation, but as the first
two now set out together to fetch their more difficult,
unwieldy third, *nerve* feels a more precise word for what is
required.

They are keenly alert to the brevity of the corridor, no
matter how cautiously they move. Every day and often
enough in the evenings they travel it back and forth, back
and forth. Every step should be utterly safe and familiar, but
tonight feels uncertain, as if they're on foreign, uneven soil.

In the pinkish uptilted light the atmosphere is dim and
mysterious, but it's not only a matter of distance and light.
It's the hour, as well. However often they've made this journey after the sun has gone down, they have never done so at

this dense moment hung on the cusp between one day and the next; nor in this deepened silence in which the only sounds are the building's inhalings and exhalings, and their own fast, shallow breaths.

At the third door they rap lightly and, no need for invitation, go through. Here they have to exert themselves; there's some effort and clumsiness involved in adding this companion to the last leg of their journey.

They are, all three, grateful for each other's presence. They have long since discovered the comforts of companionship, but now the knowledge is sharp and specific and shared: whatever would they do without each other tonight?

Probably they would be sleeping, safe and unanguished and innocent; it will soon be too late to say.

11

BASIC ARITHMETIC . . .

*R*UTH HAS NEVER BEFORE BEEN much of an arithmetician, but recently she's been calculating like crazy. One, two, three, she adds, subtracts, even multiplies and divides, as if bound to arrive at a total that will amount to something; although nothing as unlikely as meaning, her math not as hopeful or pretentious as that.

Smugness and arrogance can be toasty comforts some days and nights, and it's quite smug, of course, to suppose that everyone—barring the everyday abrupt, surprised finales of car crashes, planes falling out of the sky, bombs likewise, heart attacks and so on and so forth—that everyone should be prepared to set their own deadlines. And it would be arrogant to recommend the usefulness of arithmetic toward a particular end point, but Ruth can say it definitely sharpens the attention, and is a considerably more useful occupation than aimlessly putting in time, which looks to be the choice of at least a few Idyll Inn residents; as if their lives freeze-framed when they moved here, and there's nothing to be done now but wait.

Or alternatively grow attached, as Sylvia says, to "embroidering other people's lives and offering up far too much information about bladders and bowels." Of course she overstates, and Ruth misstates. And Ruth's own counting is a means, not an end.

The end is something quite different.

So: Ruth has here these one, two, three new friends. Or friendlike persons. She hoped to spot possible allies, but she did not expect any great affections and is surprised by how much she appreciates Greta's steadfastness, and Sylvia's bold, bitter laughter in the face of what they're all up against. And she likes, not George's occasionally excessive sentimentality, nor his sometimes peremptory words, but the solid banister of angry stubbornness, however unrealistic, that he hangs on to so tightly. These are not minor qualities, generally speaking or specifically, so—lucky Ruth to have landed among them.

There are other options. Ruth knows a number of people from public occasions—fortunately not private ones—attendant on her work and Bernard's who might, she supposes, be cultivated for conscription to her cause. And plenty of people recognize George, and Sylvia can, when she feels like it, float through lounge, library and dining room like an arthritic butterfly, touching down briefly here and there as she pleases. Even Greta is acquainted with a few residents besides former customers, including a couple of retired teachers who once taught her girls. But almost always they wind up together, the four of them, for some part of the day.

From Greta's knitting to exercise, afternoon concerts and crafts, TV programs, card games of, mainly, euchre and hearts, the Trivial Pursuit tournaments the recreation director Linda Swain organizes and even Sylvia periodically agrees to take part in, although not without pointing out that "Really, every day here is a trivial pursuit in its way, so what do we need with the game?"—Linda has already lost some of her perkiness although not, it seems, her determination—all this and much else could add up to waiting, or it can count for something.

Ruth would have been smarter to realize this so acutely years ago. As it is, her counting has to include wasted time: an average of three hours a day minimum spent, say, dawdling unnecessarily in the bath, watching foolish programs on TV, puttering about the yard in a heedless frame of mind, amounts to twenty-one hours a week, which are nearly one thousand, one hundred hours a year. Multiply that by sixty-five, to exclude childhood, when not an instant of time is wastable, and she has lost roughly seventy-one thousand hours that could have been better filled. Eight years, more or less; an eternity, practically. How might she use those years now?

She would donate some of them to Bernard; although only to Bernard without cancer.

No doubt he had wasted time of his own, but if he ever counted it up, she didn't know.

She counts, too, the curves of a life: the sweeps and arcs of event.

So: parents first, those two small, dark, anxious, brave people running their side-by-side clothing stores, one for men and boys, one for women and girls. With their one late-arriving child, Ruth. Whose preciousness was in part because they had no other children, in larger part because they had no other family at all. More prescient or more shrewd or more fearful than far too many others, they came

to this country when some catastrophes, but not the worst
catastrophes, were beginning to happen in the place they
came from. Leaving them, finally, no one. People like, perhaps, Greta's parents, grandparents, saw to that, although it
would be wrong to hold this against Greta, and Ruth mainly
does not. Indeed, they carefully do not discuss history
beyond the bare tales of Ruth's parents, and how years later
young Greta and her Dolph abandoned the same country.
Greta says old lives must, with determination and concen-
tration, be left behind, and so, Ruth supposes, they must.

   History has its terribly personal effects, however, not
only large ones. Until she started school, Ruth spent her
days bouncing back and forth between the two stores, underfoot in a world of long legs. With their customers, her parents' voices were enthusiastic and soothing, their eyes bright
with praise and encouragement. With Ruth alone, their
voices dropped to darker tones, drilling her in their one rule,
one lesson: "Be careful, beware," they said, because there is
no trusting the abrupt and evil, unpredictable turns the dangerously unreliable hearts of men may take. Or God's heart,
either. They had no faith, why would they?

   They must have had such courage, before—look what
they did, creating lives out of wreckage, the same wreckage
Greta and her young husband set out to escape, but from
entirely different perspectives. But how blind the young are:
to not only their elders' private passions, but their fears.
Now Ruth could say, *I'm sorry, I didn't know about being
frightened then; especially for somebody you love.*

   Too late now. Then, callous child, she scared them to
death.

   Too small or too useless for the rigours of team sports,

she was steered instead at school toward the solo, personal feats of gymnastics.

People who play well in groups are said to play better with others later in life. Ruth wouldn't know. She still has singular goals.

It was thrilling, even dazzling, learning to rise up and fantastically over, through and across beams and bars, rings and floormats, her ankles and wrists performing like springs, sending her soaring upwards and rolling downwards like a tumbling, blown feather. As freedom goes, this was a massively disciplined sort. The thrill lay not only in the moments of being weightless and airborne, but in the exacting, focused, excluding attention required—a toe placed here, a fingertip there, a particular twist of the spine and tilt of the weight, all in the interest of perfect balance, graceful performance. Done badly, bones could be broken; but hers were not. "Oh, I wish you wouldn't," said her mother and father. "Please be careful. You're all we have." That's a lot of weight, two grown people, for a small person to carry. A wonder she could get off the ground.

Now, when bones bend and turn on themselves, the flamboyant boldness of the girl, along with comprehension and pity, are visited in old age on the woman, but what child thinks of these things?

What child *should* think of these things?

Give no thought to the morrow—that's fine for youth, but is it a sustainable concept with age? Maybe. Maybe that's just what it is, and there's no point in giving thought to any morrow whatever.

Her parents' house smelled old. All Ruth's life there— her lives there—it smelled dark, wary; filled, too, wall to wall and floor to ceiling, with love. The Idyll Inn doesn't smell remotely of love, its air never thickens or chokes. It is never allowed to smell bad, either, never carries any reek of warehouse or prison, zoo or nursing home. Other countable benefits of life here: having her laundry taken care of, even if in the process stockings and panties and bras sometimes vanish; having meals, even mediocre, bland ones, served up with no effort from her beyond getting herself to the table; being helped by aides in getting dressed and undressed, and if one or two staff are more brusque or indifferent than chatty Diane, well, why shouldn't they be? Their job is to be competent, they don't get paid to be happy. Although happy is nice. Diane has a new boyfriend, so she's especially cheerful these days. He's a mechanic, thirty-two, divorced with a little son he sees on weekends. "He's really cool. Cute, too." By *cool* and *cute* Ruth understands that Diane means there's hot, fresh desire going on. Such a sparkly thing desire is. Even Diane's complexion is better. "I remember," Ruth remarked, immediately realizing that Diane could have no idea what Ruth remembers and anyway would consider it ancient, therefore irrelevant and even pathetic history.

The privilege, and the doom, of the young: to consider everything that comes new to them to be previously unknown and unique.

As is, often enough, the correct shiny outlook.

Armed with this same correct shiny outlook, Ruth left home for university. The young are supposed to abandon, and good parents raise their children to do so, and so Ruth tumbled and vaulted out of town toward lights, noise, darkness with sweet, sweet scents, and one at a time, three so-called lovers. *So-called* because they count only as practice,

devising with her pleasing, adult forms of buoyant limber-
ness that later, with Bernard, had real beauty.

She chose the work she would do to echoes of "Be careful, beware"; took a job, part-time that might lead to full-
time, in one of the very first shelters for women battered and
abused by husbands and lovers. These were people who had
suffered badly for love, been unhappily used by their hopes.
Even so, pitiful, victimized adults could be unenchanting to
deal with. If they'd ever had many charms, for the most part
they no longer did.

The children, though—could they not be saved?

Ruth was wrapped in her robe, exhausted by another day
of rescue and salvage, watching TV—what program?—with
a drink—what kind?—when her mother telephoned, weeping. "Your father's had a heart attack. He's in intensive care.
Please, can you come home?"

One event, one telephone call. Of course she could go
home, for a few days. And then a few more, and later on
more. Her father left the hospital shaken. He was only in his
sixties, although that seemed quite old to Ruth at the time.
He would have to sell his store, his doctor advised, and take
it very easy. Times have changed, care is much more intru-
sive and vigorous now, but that was then. Overnight her
father was an invalid, and her mother told Ruth, "I don't
know what to do, I don't know how to manage him. What if
I do the wrong thing? What if something happens and I'm
here by myself? It was terrible, Ruth, watching him fall.
Calling the ambulance. Sitting in emergency all alone.
Frightened to death." Any remnants of her mother's younger
courage had run down like a clock, and so finally Ruth gave
up and gave in and moved from her apartment and job and

city, back home. That's what responsibility and duty and compassion are for, far beyond love.

"Just for a while," she said. "Till you're both back to normal."

She found work, temporary she thought, at the children's agency, and began learning more about this town than she'd dreamed, growing up. She took care of selling her parents' stores and invested the proceeds, still under the impression that once their lives were organized, she could leave.

In a year, two years, three, a person grows *accustomed*; or loses hope, and any clear view. She could even see herself, like a camera, watching herself slide right into place.

And then Bernard walked into her office.

Move on, keep counting.

She has saved three little lives. Probably there were more, but she'll only count what seems certain, no fudging or guessing. They are:

The two-year-old toddler who, while her mother was at work, was set by her mother's boyfriend on a hot stove element. To make her stop crying, he later said. The child's entire backside and thighs were branded and seared. The boyfriend was sentenced to eight months, got out in three. The child, fetched by Ruth from the hospital where her mother had taken her when she got home from work, was put into foster care. The mother said she loved and believed in the boyfriend and would not abandon him, and no, since she was a good mother she would not attend a parenting course, nor would he, nor would she allow any outsiders into her home. The boyfriend said he'd just lost control for a minute or two—imagine the length of that minute!—and would never harm the baby again, but who cared what he said? Not

Ruth, ferocious with the mother, with the court, and with Bernard's backing, in the cause of keeping the helpless out of the hands of the exceedingly harmful. Because the next time, or the next, the outcome would doubtless be fatal.

A seven-year-old discovered, when Ruth took him to hospital after his teacher raised the alarm, to have multiple bruisings, four cracked ribs and many previous healings and scarrings, not to mention the possibly more permanent hopeless, dulled look in his eyes. Both father and mother had been ganging up on him for a long time, although they got to keep his little sister, who was doted on and untouched. "It's only regular discipline," the furious parents insisted. "He's a bad boy, just bad. What would *you* do with such a bad boy?" Rescue him, obviously, before their small broken-boned bad boy wound up in the morgue.

An eight-week-old featherweight on the very verge of floating away when Ruth carried her off from her stupid— literally stupid, although one wasn't supposed to use the word—young parents, who could understand neither how to feed her properly nor how to ask for advice nor, when it was given, how to follow it, and so let her starve and dehydrate nearly down to the bone. How that pair wailed, how distraught and baffled they were, crying out their confusion and grief. They spoke loudly of love; as if love is enough to keep any creature alive.

Whatever those children went on to endure or be broken or even redeemed by, Ruth can say she saved them from their first and worst fates. It would have been nice if the burned toddler's young mother and her boyfriend, if boyfriend there had to be, had buckled down, taken parenting and anger management courses, settled into demonstrating responsibility and compassion, those hard things harder than love, and had earned the little girl back and lived happily ever after— that could happen, it's somewhat possible. But it didn't happen, of course.

Nor could the scapegoating parents learn to embrace their bad little boy; nor would the stupid ones ever get smart. All that could be done was to try to save children from the most extreme mutations and malformations, like birth defects, of love. What people will do to each other.

It's no minor achievement, even in a universe of griefs, an infinite swamp of things that need fixing, to pick one single small goal to pursue. Not that a child's life is small. But there are so many, many desperate children in the world—to save a few must be a tiny triumph, but surely it's also enormous.

Of course most children did stay in, or return to, their homes. That was the prevailing child-care philosophy: supervise families if need be, but keep them together; a tragically pragmatic philosophy, reliant on dubious parental pledges. There was nowhere near enough money, or people, to shift kids willy-nilly into new, improved lives, but there was also this: children will love just about anyone. Or they'll hold as hard as they can to the most vicious known against any unknown. Ruth can feel frightened arms tight around her neck, but also little hands struggling to free themselves in order to flee home again. She can find these hands and arms, surprisingly, right on the tip of her skin, any time, day or night.

It would be interesting, if not useful, to know the endings to their stories, but for the most part she doesn't. She has come more recently, though, to understand better why those children might have clung to what was familiar.

A person can cling too long, and create terrible hardship. Keep counting.

So far at the Idyll Inn, like consolidating many small debts into a single large one, Ruth has managed to roll many minor terrors into a big single ball of—what? A grand tension, anyway. A discernible, terminal purpose.

Such absurd dreads rose up when Bernard was gone and she was alone in their house. Something of a revelation, really, for a woman who considered herself reasonably fearless, to find that beyond grief, and much else, there was shock that some of what she'd assumed she was must have relied on knowing he was behind her, backing her up, holding her up, simply *there*. Where he no longer was. So that—talk about wasted time—suddenly she was fretting over upwards-sliding property tax and utility bills denting her careful budget, potentially threatening how long she could keep the house (not all that long, but for other reasons entirely); becoming alert to strange sounds, animal or human, outside in the dark (but the strangest sound her own anxious heartbeat in the silence of listening); and picturing, quite vividly, the even more far-fetched possibility that, say, a plane overhead might dip radically to slam into her street, or an electrical appliance—hair dryer? radio?—could splash into her bath (what were the odds, ever? But you never know); or in high, howling winds that a tree might crash through the roof (but the old backyard maple stood the test of time more sturdily than she has, for sure).

Whatever happened to flying high and free through the air? Still, she is starting to feel the days whirling along as fast as when she was young and lithe, with a body so light and flexible it turned and tumbled at her slightest shifting command.

Those were the days.

These are the days, too: for advancing an intimate bal-ance, balance being a trick for which she once had a fine aptitude; for proceeding a step at a time through her many count-ups to her single countdown. Admittedly, persuading at least one of the others will be a subtler and more difficult matter than balance, or even soaring solo through air, but she has some ideas for getting her desire to add up in their minds, just as it moves toward a dark, still secret total in hers.

12

OH HA HA HA, MORE OR LESS . . .

Spry granny climbs Kilimanjaro.

Feisty senior beats off purse-snatcher.

Also, 8o-*year-old charged with child porn.* "Good God," says Sylvia, "you'd think it was a miracle anyone our age could do anything livelier or more complicated than wake up in the morning. *Spry. Feisty.* Can you imagine?"

Of course they can. Qualities of spryness and feistiness do not, in truth, abound at the Idyll Inn. Unexpectedly, after the first relief and delight, days without chores and duties—laundry, vacuuming, cooking—feel a little too free and weightless. They lack heft; which is why for an hour or so every morning Sylvia, Greta and Ruth now converge on George's room, where, although they don't put it this way out loud, he is a project. Greta's idea. "George," she'd asked, "do you have exercises from the hospital, as I have from my doctor, that you are to do here to improve?"

Yeah, there was some crap he stuck in a drawer, and no, he wasn't doing them. "No point," he said.

"For heaven's sake, of course there's a point." Sylvia, in that snappy voice of hers. "Do you want to get better or worse?" As if those were his choices. But that's how come Greta and Sylvia are spending time every weekday (weekends off) manoeuvring his limbs and egging him on while Ruth, who can't really help, perches on his coffee table reading aloud stories from the national newspaper she gets and the local one Sylvia subscribes to. "A physical *and* mental workout rolled into one," as Ruth says.

It's not that every day's stories are necessarily funny— the opposite, in fact, when Ruth does the choosing—but today, *oh ha ha ha,* more or less, laugh the women. What they find funny isn't generally what George thinks of as jokes, they're not little stories with punchlines. Aside from that he has to admit, although he would not to them, that it's kind of pleasing to see Greta's head, even her old, altered head, bent beside Sylvia Lodge's, pushing his left leg, then his right, upward and back, and then to feel them close beside him, one on each side, rotating his arms, flexing his fingers, except when Sylvia stops because she says that while the exertion helps her, not just him, it gets to hurting her too.

Sylvia Lodge being in his room—not so much the others—makes him see through her eyes, or one of them, anyway, that his furniture, years old, is worn and its arrangement a bit hodgepodge. When he looks at it that way, Colette and Bill didn't go to much trouble to make sure he'd fit in, did they? Even more uncomfortable at first, though, was having her fooling around with his feet. "Goodness, George," Sylvia said, "think how many times you've had your hands on my feet. This is just turnabout." But that was a long time ago, and except for admiring a good set of legs, it was business. This is—maybe not pleasure, but it sure isn't business, and there's nothing to admire about his feet now, all blue-veined as they are and half-helpless. Still, he doesn't say no. He could tell them they can shove him around till the cows come home and he won't be fixed, but to be honest he can feel blood moving, at least on his right side, with a vigour that is secretly, privately heartening.

Then there's the flash now and then, looking down, seeing Greta working away; just a flash like a quick bright porch light in a storm.

She and Sylvia make him use Ruth's walker as a brace or a weight or a pullbar for some of his exercising, which is a lot of hard work. It can also be hard work listening to Ruth read out loud from the newspapers. If they've heard fire trucks racing by one day, the next day she'll try to find an item in the local paper that says where they were going and what they found when they got there. Court cases are interesting for the names of people, sometimes children and grandchildren and even great-grandchildren of those familiar to them, caught driving while drunk, breaking into variety stores—and today, the larger, interesting crime of creating counterfeit money with a fancy photocopy machine. Ruth keeps saying that none of them knows half of what goes on in this town, but even she sounds surprised by this one.

What Sylvia says is, "We should get ourselves one of those," meaning the photocopy machine. "Nobody'd suspect a bunch of old crooks in a retirement home, would they? Even *spry, feisty* crooks. We could manufacture enough money to keep ourselves going forever."

Ruth kind of spoils it when she says, "If forever could be bought," in that down-bringing way she has sometimes. Left to her own devices, she'll go on and on about the most grue-some stuff: stonings, beheadings, starvation, disease, dead children, brutalized women—before George protested this morning, she'd already dragged them through a painstaking account of a rebel army of kidnapped teen rapist-killers and kidnapped child slaves far away, with some really nasty infor-mation thrown in about one bunch of people hacking and burning another bunch, leaving rotting bodies in dusty streets, torn into by hungry dogs, victors prancing around wearing necklaces festooned with ears and, of all things, dry-ing fetuses carved and sliced from dead wombs.

Unbelievable except that since there it was in the news, it must be believed.

Even hearing these things felt painful. "Expendability," Ruth said, as if that explained anything. "The value of life. Anyone's. What's it worth, after all? What's so sacred about it?" Which was a plain strange thing to say, especially for somebody whose job involved saving lives. All those things Ruth tells them they don't know the half of.

"No good!" George cried, meaning any number of things: that knowing does him no good, since these stories make his head hurt again, when he's already here because of a stroke; that they're in no position to do any good about distant matters; also that Ruth doesn't read more about the good things that some humans somewhere must be doing, or else the whole world's out of whack. Ruth claims it *is* out of whack, but then she found those old-people stories that

made the women laugh, and then the one about the photocopy machine.

One day last week Colette phoned while they were in
his room, and Ruth answered and told Colette her father
was busy and would call her back. "What on earth, Dad?"
Colette asked when he did.

"Exercise."

"With a woman? In your room?"

"Three." He couldn't help sounding pleased. Colette
should know that if she's not going to be here, he has other
options.

"Staff?"

"No."

"Well"—how doubtful she sounded—"I guess it's good
you're making new friends." Yes, it is, although by the time
they leave he's pretty worn out, and has to lie down for a rest
before lunch. He supposes he's lucky compared with a whole
lot of other people, but he wouldn't say that to Colette. Or
to Greta, or the other two, either. People take advantage;
women always want something.

On the other hand, it wouldn't hurt to press the point
with Colette. "They really wear me out," he told her. "I
always need a good rest when they've gone."

"I see. But try not to overdo it, okay?" Colette didn't say
what she imagined the "it" was that he might overdo, but he
thought she sounded slightly and satisfyingly unhappy.

Just keeping her on her toes.

Today when they leave him to his pre-lunch lie-down,
Sylvia stops Greta and Ruth in the corridor outside his door.
"It's a beautiful day, do you feel like sitting out on my deck
for a while?" Because there are these late-June days now,

when the sun shines and the river glitters and the air smells somehow bright green, when her deck is exactly as she pictured it could be when she moved in: a place to stretch out in the warm light, with a book or without, easing heat into her bones, and luxuriously remote, worlds away, from the day-to-day Idyll Inn rhythm of TV being watched, songs being sung, meals being eaten, tall tales being told, people coming and going: residents, relatives, staff, the rare but inevitable corpse, with attendants. Today, when they've settled and adjusted themselves, Sylvia on the chaise, Greta and Ruth in the upright deck chairs, Sylvia—just because she's in a curious, *Tell me a story* frame of mind, and just because this late in the game where's the harm, and just from a kind of languorous mischief—Sylvia turns to Greta and says, "You used to know George much better than well, didn't you?" Greta frowns. "It seems to me you're a lot more attentive to his well-being than if he was just any old fellow. It looks as if you touch him like an old habit, and you lean toward each other sometimes. You have ways of talking and sitting I bet you're not even aware of."

Sylvia would win such a bet. Greta has not realized that others might notice. She likes touching George. It is a good sensation to rest a hand on his knee, shoulder, arm. It is different skin than it once was, but so is hers, too.

Otherwise what is there to touch? The woolly materials of her knitting, the needles, metal or plastic. She would most happily embrace Emily, Sally and Patricia, but they say she can make no more long journeys to them, as she has before, because travel is too hard, even for someone strong, who has heart attacks. So they say they will continue coming to her; but they cannot very often, having already given up much time to her sickness and health. Once she is more skilled, she has in mind knitting birthday-gift scarves for them, possibly also for chilly underdressed strangers, perhaps even children who are wards of Ruth's former agency. People say the best gifts are made by a person's own hands. The main part, though, is sensation and touch; the understanding, too, of beginning and end. Shape and boundary. Of one stitch, one row after another: how a scarf, a life, a person proceeds.

For the time being she is still practising the arts of casting on, holding a steady tension, attempting to purl and not losing or gaining stitches row by row. She likes the need for paying attention. "Then there is how to end well," she has mentioned. "Cast off, it is called."

"Yes, that's important." This from Sylvia. "Otherwise you'd risk getting stuck on one great long scarf forever, and we'd have Isadora Duncan all over again." Who? Sylvia says these things that are as mysterious as her foreign words.

Occasionally Greta slips into foreign words too, except they are not foreign to her, and she is nervous of them because they are slips.

Now a stitch slips as well. "George was good to give me my first job when I had to find work." As they know, because they weeks ago told their stories of widowhood—cancer for Sylvia, another kind of cancer for Ruth. Greta told her different tale as briefly as possible, because George was present at the time and grew quickly restless. Well, he had heard it before. Perhaps he remembered. It is not always easy to know what George can remember.

He may at least recall that there could have been no question of him if there had not already been Dolph.

With whom she came here blithely—*blithe: joyous*—and with relief like a deep breath, and with gratitude for the small savings and large sacrifices made by their families, and for the offer of work from a distant cousin of Dolph's father who'd come here a generation before, so that the two of them, at least, would escape from the terrible country whose war had been lost, along with much else, and whose name, easy to say these days but which she nevertheless tries not to speak around Ruth, because there were those difficulties, atrocities, even though they should not matter so much here and now; Dolph's name also a problem perhaps, although not his fault either—Greta and Dolph came here hand in hand and thigh to thigh, willing and hopeful and strong, leaving all their people behind with the brutal ease of the young, no good looking back.

This is when she learned what she has since always tried to remember: how the young do what they do.

Dolph was beautiful. He still is beautiful. Greta is much, much older than he. Photographs of him could be of her grandson. This is a nearly indecent thing to consider.

Glad for escape from the hunger, the debris, also the retribution, and thrilled by possibilities, and entranced by desire, although, to be sure, lonely too, they rented a shabby house in this small alien city, intending to save money so that soon they could buy. Then from their busy bedroom came Sally, Emily and Patricia, all in Dolph and Greta's first seven years in this country. They chose the strange-sounding names from a book, to be sure their children, those new citizens, would not be lonely; would be unburdened by foreignness, unlike she and Dolph, toward whom there were moments of unkindness. A passing group of boys, young, on the street: "Fucking Kraut."

Letters came and went over the ocean with news that was more and more remote. Some of it, too, best put out of mind and forgotten. Here, Dolph and Greta were like pioneers. They might now and then miss faraway mothers, fathers, sisters, brothers, but faraway meant what it said: out of reach, grown vague and impossible to imagine.

How happy she was then! Busy, always busy: baking and cooking and washing diapers and sterilizing bottles and sewing on her second-hand treadle machine her girls' little outfits. Dolph had work at his father's distant cousin's garage, where he became skilled in the repairing of cars, tractors and trucks and came home more muscled each day, scarred and blackened and smelling of metals and oils. He earned more money with odd jobs on a farm, and some nights smelled of manure and grains and the hot breath and flesh of cattle and pigs.

He brought home new words and stories, like pearls to be draped around Greta when they were alone in the night. They breathed each other's skin. He said she smelled of laundry: clean and airy like wind. She traced his spine, those bones, long and narrow, holding them all here together. Holding the two of them, too.

They had yet no house of their own, but were still young and hard-working, stubborn and hopeful. They had still, too, the rapture—*rapture: ecstatic delight,* of skin. They saw no end to this; why would they?

But endings come. They come in the middle of a day, girls in school, Greta pounding with a hammer a cheap cut of beef to make it tender for supper—an ending comes with a distressed, awkward young man in uniform blue on Greta's doorstep, clutching his uniform cap. There was an accident, he told her. He said that Dolph, no *Bauer* except in name, no farmer, had lost his footing while loading a silo; that he had fallen in; that he was at that very moment inside the silo, being crushed and smothered by feed corn. Much frantic digging was occurring, the man said, but the prospects were bleak, and she should not have hopes.

She dropped the hammer where she stood and he drove her to the place, where she saw for herself the desperate, pale efforts of men on ropes and chained platforms, wielding shovels and even bare hands, clambering over the silo and into it and back out, faces and clothes coated in corn dust and horror. While behind the blank, grey, curved silo wall was her Dolph, his long bones being crushed, his golden skin gone battered and dark, his story-and-word-bringing voice choked into silence. There were police, there was an ambulance, there was a woman in a brown dress with small pink printed flowers trying to put her arms around Greta; but Greta would not be touched.

There were no words in any language for the white light of *How can this be?* As Greta sat trembling later before the girls, they may have thought her as mysteriously and terribly vanished as their father. As Dolph. Who had been beautiful.

They did not see his body. The undertaker said that would not be possible.

To have this thing that there could be no undoing, no way back, no hope forward—it was as if she was as broken as Dolph. Also more lonely and frightened than she had ever supposed to be possible. Three girls and all up to her—what was she to do?

She thought first of going back to where she and Dolph came from, where there were people who could comfort and support her, and help with the girls; but their families had already given the help of sending her and Dolph here. Their circumstances were improved, but defeat lasts a long time, and they still did not find it easy to care for even themselves.

More important, her girls belonged here, with their names and futures and her own and Dolph's hopes.

And that is how she learned to grieve and manage, mourn and cope, all at the same time. This was possible. She was more *Bäuerin* than Dolph or she had ever dreamed.

She left the rented house for a cheaper apartment on the second floor of one of the town's old brick homes. She considered her skills, which were to cook adequately, clean sufficiently, sew somewhat, love and try to comfort and keep safe her children—what could she do, heartbroken young foreign widow, with any of that?

When she first recounted this, Sylvia said, "How awful for you," and even Ruth added, "Tragic."

While George said, with raw, singsong clarity, "Too bad, so sad."

Now, in the sunshine of this deck, it is the absent George that Sylvia inquires about. So many years. Does one betray long-ago interests in favour of new? Perhaps yes. Greta nods finally. "Ah," Sylvia says in her dry way. "You astonish me."

So.

In the nights, Greta watched Dolph struggling hopelessly against a storm of corn raining down. In the days, she went knocking on doors. Up and down the main street and side streets she went, from hardware to florist to bakery. People leaned close, frowned, shook their heads. Language was a difficulty; or rather, accent. History also, she was curtly

given to understand at certain shops. She knew there would
be no purpose in trying to say that she was herself guilty of
nothing; that yes, certain events must have occurred, but
she had not herself known or done anything; that she had
been young, not quite grown up.

George Hammond frowned too. "Do you have experience selling?" No, she did not. "Do you know anything
about shoes?" No, although she had bought shoes for the
girls from George Hammond himself.

"I will learn fast," she said.

He told her about sizings and the related subject of tact.
He showed her stitchings, lasts, tongues and soles, and spoke
much about service. She could think of customers patiently,
as her children, she told him, and he said, "Then that's who
you can deal with. I'm not always good with the kids. They
get bored and start acting up. Although sometimes the mothers are worse."

"And you—" she risked smiling—"are good with them."
Well, he would be, wouldn't he, a handsome lean man bending over their delicate arches and toes?

A man, too, of a certain courage. "All right, let's try it,
we can see how it goes."

Oh, at last.

He paid her not a large salary, but with care they could
manage. Some entertainment was free: at the kitchen table in
the evenings, homework spread out, the girls grilled her with
words. "Regress," Sally or Emily or Patricia would call out
while Greta did dishes or ironed, "what's *regress*, Mum?" They
would read from the dictionary. "It means *movement back*."
She learned with them, in this hopscotch fashion, *malfeasance. Enlighten. Mortality. Uvula.* They laughed, making non-

sense sentences together. *My uvula is regressing. My mortality is enlightened by malfeasance.*

To be happy would be different from laughter. Even so, there came glittery moments when Greta could see peace in her kitchen, and even gladness to be there. Those were not the moments, which were fewer and fewer, when she could place Dolph among them. Memory is harsh in that way. It is true that some wounds will not close, but it is also true that the first shredded, soft skin around them will finally toughen. During the days she was smiling and helpful, obedient as she reached down to small feet, reached up the racks of shoeboxes to find the right sizes and styles. She knew a need to be careful. People could so easily take a dislike: to her foreignness, her circumstances, her very flesh, bones and voice. Anything.

George called her Greta. She called him Mr. Hammond. It was impossible for her to be very interested in shoes, although he was. "This is working out fine, don't you think?" he said after a year, and gave her a raise. Another after her second year, and again after the third. This by no means meant an end to frugality. The girls grew into and traded each other's clothes and got discounts on shoes. Sometimes when she got home they had made a tuna or macaroni casserole for their supper. They quarrelled and teased and played jokes, but "We must look after each other," she told them. "We have only ourselves." They did jobs ordinarily done by neighbourhood boys: delivered newspapers, mowed lawns, shovelled snow. That money they kept for movies and treats, birthday gifts for their friends. Unlike Greta, they were not without friends. She did not, as she saw it, have time.

Also she remained fearful of the long memories; the grudges of time that might still be turned against her.

Her girls, easy with their fitting-in names, compared their changing bodies, dated boys, went to parties and sleep-overs. Sometimes the apartment was empty but for Greta, even her youngest, Patricia, with a life of her own.

They must have looked after, leaned on each other, more than most had to.

Then. It is a little bit shocking how unanticipated affections can be. Greta would not have dreamed of making first moves, but first moves having been made (unexpectedly, inexplicably—*inexplicable: incapable of being accounted for*—during inventory in her fifth year in his employ, as she rose from counting shoeboxes on a dusty lower shelf while George hovered above with a clipboard which he put suddenly down on a higher shelf, the better to take first her elbow, then her shoulders, her chin, her head, her breasts in his hands), she found in herself a sudden flare-up of hope.

She took this to be desire, as it was; but desire deriving abruptly from hope. She was in that moment not struggling foreigner, widow, mother of three, but a woman standing on her two feet, reaching upwards: to George Hammond, with his deep brown, intensely interested eyes, which had not been so obviously interested before, and his long trousered legs, his shiny, top-of-the-line shoes. He had a half-smile even then. "I was watching the back of your neck, and I couldn't resist. You probably don't know how tempting it is, do you?" No, she did not know; although in her own bathroom, using a hand mirror and the one over the sink, she tried later to see what he saw.

Of course she had met Alice and Colette many times in the store. Husbands may be taken at any time, however, in any way, by any hand, God's included. Then why not by her?

Not that she could *take* George. There was no question of that. There were her girls. There was scandal. What he said was, "My marriage is, well, it's a marriage, I guess, but I love Colette down to the ground." Once he explained *down to the ground*, Greta understood precisely. In the same way, her love for her daughters had a ferocity that was in a separate category from adult interests, and could not be shaken by adult vicissitudes—*vicissitude: a fluctuation of state or condition.*

This, although in shorter, more restrained form, is what she has now described—should she have?—to Ruth and Sylvia in the warm balm of the sunshine on Sylvia's deck.

"Where did you go?" Sylvia asks.

It is bad to say, but "a motel, most often. The ABC."

"The ABC, oh my God!" and Sylvia claps a hand over her mouth. Of course, even someone like Sylvia will have heard stories of the ABC on the outskirts of town, with its incurious management and its parking lot hedged by cedars guarding it from too-easy roadside view; although she cannot know how, over decades of people like Greta and George as well as unwary travellers, it grew shabby; worse than shabby, with mildew around windows, and peeled paint, and sheets that smelled musty although surely they were not.

George said, "It's not very nice, I know, but it's private."

The surprising, secret pleasure was what mattered, not comparings; the luxury of unwrapping each other's long limbs, rediscovering warm skin, which George said applied to him as well as to her. To *belong,* that was a grace in itself. She told him he was beautiful, although in different form from Dolph and his beauty. George said, "Men aren't beautiful. We can be good-looking, or handsome, but *beautiful*'s a woman's word." Perhaps he was correct, but she thought he was not.

They captured their moments between obligations, as when Emily had a school concert or Sally a play or Greta an interview with a teacher regarding Patricia, or when Colette was suddenly sick. Although other demands—on George, not Greta—came, in time, to injure. An anniversary dinner Alice was planning and counting on; that sort of thing. He said, "I wish we could fall asleep and wake up together," because it was hard having to leave the ABC by a respectable hour, and "If I could get away for a weekend, could you?" Yes, twice there was walking hand in hand in a distant city, going to a movie boldly together, dining in a restaurant at a table for two. But how many reasons could a shoe-store owner devise for leaving town on his own? How often could Greta leave her growing-up girls to look out for each other? Twice only. There was a fear, which neither of them could speak, of disastrous event in their absence: burst appendix, accident, fire.

"What about your daughters," Sylvia asks, "did they know?"

A good question. They did not inquire about, among other things, the woman friend, unknown to them, with whom she said she went away on those two weekends. Perhaps that was delicate of them, not incurious, but "No, I do not believe so. Nor George's daughter."

"The precious Colette."

"Yes. Precious Colette."

"But even now," Sylvia adds, with an odd, angry laugh, "there are the children to worry about, don't you find?" Greta is puzzled, more by Sylvia's tone than by her words. And although of course it would not be good if the girls learned now of George, it would be far, far worse if they ever learned of what followed. "Why Greta, you're blushing."

Yes, but not for George.

"How long did it go on?"

"Almost seven years." Which is altogether too much and too little to tell.

"You must have loved him, then, did you?" Ruth asks. So personal a question, is it not?

"We said so. It was long ago. Some feelings, they are hard to remember." So they are. But whatever they were, Greta cannot truthfully say she has often regretted them. Because she and George, their entanglement—*entanglement: the condition of being deeply involved*—helped make her brave again. It also gave shape and touch and plot, when she most needed those things, to her days. Flesh and bones. An adult attachment to life. "I cared as well as I could."

"Then that's good," Sylvia pronounces. "That's what counts." A surprisingly romantic remark from a woman who was herself, after all, someone's wife for a very long time. "What happened?" To bring an end, she must mean.

One by one Greta's clever, hard-working girls left with their scholarships and loans and ambitions for futures that were not to be in this town. "I love you, I am proud, your father would be so proud as well," Greta said, waving good-bye. By the time Patricia left, Greta was forty-six. How young that seems now. All her girls are older than that.

Then Greta and George no longer needed the ABC Motel, but could be in Greta's apartment with food at her table and each other in her bedroom. Her apartment without the girls was a terrible vacancy, but in those hours with George there was the consolation of desire and familiar affection. For him too, he said, because by then Colette also was gone.

Perhaps too easy, those consolations and comforts. Someone noticed George's car, although he took care to park around the corner on a shorter, less-travelled block than hers. Someone remarked—took the trouble to remark—on this to Alice. "I made up something about dropping off a special order of orthotics at a customer's on my way home, but whoever it was has seen the car a few times. I wouldn't mind so much if it was just her, but there's Colette. It doesn't matter she's left home, I can't have her finding out. I'm sorry, but I can't take any more chances of everything going right down the tubes."

From which, although she wasn't sure of *right down the tubes*, Greta understood that here was something she had failed in all their time to perceive: that while George liked, even perhaps cherished, their parallel life—why would he not?—Alice had powers that rooted him in his other world in ways not, after all, to do with Colette. "I'm sorry," he said, and he probably was. He even put his head on her shoulder and for a few moments wept.

"And that was that," she tells Ruth and Sylvia. "But life goes on very well." Which was not true, of course.

Her experience in sales, and perhaps the familiarity of years in this town, got her work in Alf Stryker's drugstore. She was astonished when George said, "But there's no reason you can't keep on working here"—was he so stupid after all, or so cold?

Then what happened? Then, having learned the virtues of home and repentance, George maybe settled down with refreshed attentions to Alice, who would be surprised to find him permanently restored to her kitchen table and bed; or he found someone else, a series of someones, with whom to

journey to the highway and the grimy charms of the ABC
Motel—who knows what George decided to do? They had
used the word *love*, but what is that? People think love is
naturally scattered about in everyone's hearts, as thick on
the ground as shiny bits of sand on a beach. It is not. It is
rare as gold, as emeralds, as compassion.

"It's dicey, for sure," Sylvia says.

In no way has Greta expressed to them those years. Even
now there is no replacement for touch, although she must
try to make herself content with the soft spilling, row by
row, of yellow-and-red scarf into her lap. "Please do not tell
George what I have said."

"Don't worry." This is Ruth. "We have to trust each
other. We must take care of each other." What is in her
tone? Some passion beyond the words. This is the
difficulty—one difficulty—with learning a language: not
always knowing if words contain more than they say.

"Yes, of course we won't say anything," Sylvia says, but
then suddenly she is laughing. "Although—*Old gran spills
lurid secrets*, how's that for a headline?" As if what Greta has
said matters only as an amusement? Or as if Sylvia and Ruth
have already begun keeping a secret, which is a better, nicer,
warmer idea. Because they are friends, another word, it may
be, that can contain more than it says.

13

MEN WITH KNIVES AND TELEPHONES . . .

*E*VERY DAY, ten minutes or so before every meal, people begin lining up at the two dining-room entrances. Are so many Idyll Inn residents persistently gullible, does hope really spring eternal that this time, contrary to all previous experience, mealtime will bring something different or new?

But darned if today there *isn't* something different and new: a man with two knives.

Occasionally there are these disruptions, although others have been less compellingly public. Two staff members have quit, having discovered a serious distaste for the old, and one was fired abruptly amid reports that she was rough in her handling of residents and then made a dangerous mistake in the distribution of meds. Nobody wants that sort of person on staff, not only those on the spot, but distant, lawsuit-leery doctor and dentist investors. As well, there have been three sudden deaths—two heart attacks, one huge stroke—with doctors and ambulances called, stretchers wheeled in and out as discreetly as possible, but death isn't exactly disguisable so everyone knows, and they all feel the chill.

Then there are residents' own eccentricities to contend with. Poor old Amy Perry, for one, who used to be a town librarian, but more recently, like today's man with two knives, suffered a food-related downfall; because at the Idyll Inn, where presentation is reasonably dainty, the butter and margarine come formed into little yellow balls on small flowered plates, and Amy Perry took to furtively picking up the butter plate at her table and dumping its leftovers into her pockets and purse. "It was gross," Ruth heard from Diane, who said that another aide, collecting laundry, "stuck her hand right into a pocketful of nasty old putrid butter. I guess Adele screamed, and then she got kind of mad. When she asked Mrs. Perry what she thought she was doing, Mrs. Perry said she was collecting it for her knees—she's got arthritis, like you. So Adele said, 'You were going to put it on your knees?' and Mrs. Perry said no, when she had enough she was going to slice them open and put the butter—she said margarine was no good—right inside the bones so she wouldn't hurt any more, and now Ms. Walker says Mrs. Perry is too dotty to stay and has to go to a nursing home. And everybody's supposed to make sure the butter plates are off the tables as soon as first course is over."

There's the lesson: don't falter, because action will be brutal and swift against any residents who let down their guard. Evidently Art Fletcher has not taken this lesson to heart. Perhaps he hasn't been here long enough to have absorbed it, as a relative newcomer, a replacement for one of the dead, and not a happy one. Even George has been less morose—indeed George took the trouble to wheel up to greet him, in faint hopes of a little male companionship, but Art just glared mutely and gave him the finger. His manners have clearly slipped since their nattier days, when George was a customer of Fletcher's Menswear and Tailoring, and Art would tell him he was perfectly built, from shoulders to hips to the long thighs Greta also admired, for the suits Art fit around him. Art was—is? Do these inclinations dissipate with age?—homosexual, which, although everyone knew, most people did not much care about, or understand, or discuss. Whatever he did, he didn't very obviously do it around town, but George expected that it gave Art a sharp eye for who looked good in a suit, even though it took getting used to, being assessed by another man in that way.

Now for ease and convenience George wears loose zip-up shirts, and pants with stretchy waistbands, and he wonders if being homosexual has somehow led Art Fletcher to knives.

Probably not. Why would it?

Something has, though; some kind of rage.

What happens is, between courses, while staff are out in the dining room clearing plates to make space for apple cobbler dessert, Art rises from his table and hikes pretty fast into the kitchen. Where he picks up two fair-sized chopping knives and starts to wave them around, surprisingly vigorously. When a couple of staff take ill-considered steps toward him, he shouts, "Fuck you," and "Back off, bitches," and "I'll kill you if you take one more step." It looks as if he would, too. Even if not on purpose, although he does appear to have purpose, just from the flailing knives he could really hurt someone.

Annabel Walker comes out of her office. "Everybody stay where you are," she says, in calm if quivery tone.

"Everything's fine. Now, Mr. Fletcher, I know you don't want to be so upset. Just put down the knives and we'll talk over what's troubling you, all right? We can fix whatever it is, so just put them down and come out of the kitchen and we'll go into my office and have a nice chat. All right? Will you do that for me now?"

No, he won't. His lips curl back. He looks like a wolf. "Bitch," he says. "Back fucking off."

Nobody gets paid enough to deal with a situation like this, certainly nobody at the Idyll Inn, including Annabel Walker. She leans to an aide. "Go to my office and call the police," she whispers. "Don't run, just slip away." She herself continues talking to Art. "Can you tell me what's wrong, Mr. Fletcher? Can I get something for you? Call someone you'd like to talk to? Please tell me so I can help. We all want to help, we just need to know what we can do." And so on and so forth, to no effect except for Art starting to sway on his feet.

There are no sirens, and when two police officers come through the doors it's at a leisurely, ambling pace—who expects urgency at a retirement home? This changes when they see the knives, and behind the knives, even if an old man, also a furious one. "Drop it," one calls out, unbuttoning his holster as if he thinks he's in a shoot-'em-up movie, while the second pulls free his baton. Will there be gunplay? Head-cracking? Pepper spray? Do the cops' pockets or belts hold one of those electrical gadgets that knock grown men to the ground? How exciting. Everybody is watching, some leaning forward or, at the back, standing up as best they can for a better view of the action. What do they hope for? Not harm, surely, just . . . something. Better than TV or any weekend-night movie, but laced with a kind of horrified pity for one of the many ways a life can go sour.

It looks as if it's the uniforms, not the shout or the weaponry, that cause Art Fletcher's eyes to shift as if a channel's been changed, so that he regards the knives as if he has no idea what they're doing there in his hands. He lets them fall clattering to the floor, and his head drops, his shoulders slump—a defeated man. There are sighs here and there in the room.

And that, as he's hustled out the doors, a cop on each side, is the last they will see of Art Fletcher. A rather more vivid departure than Amy Perry's, or any of the dead bodies that have rolled out these doors, but just as final. Poor Art. Or as Sylvia says afterwards, back in the lounge, "Do you suppose he was having hallucinations? Please, promise to put me out of my misery if I ever start doing things like swinging imaginary golf clubs. I swear I can put up with swollen ankles and wrecked knees and these horrible hands as long as I don't lose my marbles. If that happens, shoot me."

"With an imaginary gun, I presume," Ruth suggests.

It's interesting to Ruth, hearing the thumbs-up, thumbs-down weight Sylvia gives to her mind. Even joking, she's serious. But come the crunch, like most people, including the old facing more or less imminent encounters with death, she would probably turn out not to mean it at all. "Just kidding," she'd say, "for God's sake, don't shoot."

Whereas Ruth hopes she herself would command, "Fire away."

Later in the afternoon George, wheeled back to his room by an aide, thinks Colette would be interested in what happened at lunch. She might remember Art Fletcher, and since there's hardly ever much new to tell her, this makes a change. Colette claims she calls George every couple of days before she goes to work, or even sometimes from her office, but he swears that's not true. It's his impression that they would never talk if he didn't phone her, which he doesn't do all that often. Even so, this afternoon she says, "What's up, Dad? Did you know you already rang today? Think of your phone bills!"

Mustn't complain. Complaints roll out anyway. "Did not. Where are you?"

By which he means, "Why aren't you here where you should be?" but she sighs and says, "You know where I am, Dad, I'm at home. It's the weekend, it's Saturday, and I'm at home." Up the street and across town? "No, not your home, my own."

All thought of Art Fletcher has vanished. "When are you coming?"

"Pretty soon. In a few months. I was there not that long ago, remember?" Not really. And *soon* and *months* are totally different. She doesn't have a clue about time, no wonder she can't keep track of telephone calls. Still, her words and his, and their tones, ring a bell. Maybe she's right, maybe they have already spoken today. It's easy to pick up the phone on the little table by his right hand and press the single number programmed to magically dial Colette in her faraway household, or the next one, which rings her direct line at the bank, although there she's apt to sound busy and quick. There's something else about time: that hers is different from his. Once she answered as if he'd wakened her up, even though it was way past breakfast here. Now she says, "Listen, Dad, I'm sorry but we've got company coming later on for Bill's birthday, and I've got a cake ready to come out of the oven, so I can't really talk now, okay? Anyway, you'll be eating soon, won't you? It'll be your suppertime in a few hours. I wonder what you'll be having tonight?"

"Some crap. Never mind. Sorry I bothered you." He tries to slam down the receiver but misses on his first try—damn it, a man should be able to do something that simple the way he means to.

Bill gets a birthday party, that figures. How does she carry on with parties and cakes as if nothing is wrong, or if anything is wrong it has nothing to do with her? What did he do to deserve this?

Oh. These thoughts, like the telephone calls, come new to his mind but then are immediately and completely familiar. Even back in the ambulance, and in the hospital, he surely thought, *What did I do to deserve this?* His sins from decades past catching up finally? But he has never murdered or even stolen, unless a person counts time. He has never caused mayhem. All he ever wanted was *more*, and doesn't everyone, and is that so terrible? His sins, if that's what they're called, amount to mere promise-breaking, and is it so bad to hanker for passion, as well as affection?

That's a word that hasn't come to him for a long time: *hanker*. But there it is, another one gained, although perhaps to be lost again, whoever knows?

Greta once told him, now tells everyone, that after her husband died, her daughters took over teaching her language. Lucky Greta, to have daughters who would patiently, even as she tells it cheerfully, put word after word into her head.

George does not have such a daughter.

He never met Greta's girls—well, he did when she was buying them shoes or they turned up in the store to ask her for permission or money or whatever girls ask for from their mothers—he guesses he means he never *knew* them. Greta was careful—he was too—about keeping family separated from pleasure. What a pleasure she was, he thinks he recalls: big and strong, golden and tall, kind and willing—all of which qualities together meant he didn't need to worry about injury or breakage in any way. How free he could be with her! Although in the end it doesn't make much difference, does it? Now Greta is big but not so strong, tall but more pasty than golden, more or less kind and even sometimes willing, but not always thoughtful; that is, not always thoughtful of him.

And there's Colette, in a whole different time, busy getting ready for somebody's birthday. And there's her mother, in another place, lost completely for memory and words.

How long has he been harping on this way? There's another word—*harping*—popping back unexpectedly for a visit, just like *hanker* did moments, or it might be hours, ago.

Perhaps this is an H day. *Help me*, he thinks, or possibly says.

Colette isn't here to help, and she's not going to be. Maybe nobody really helps anyone else. There was Alice, her defiant little voice saying some helpful person at church had pulled her aside to remark on George's car being regularly parked where it had no good reason to be—and then there were choices to make, no help for it.

What would Alice have been like if she'd had a job besides being married to him and raising Colette? It's strange now to think of a person not going to work, although that didn't occur to him at the time, and if it occurred to Alice, he's pretty sure she never said so. Anyway, what could she have done?

She could have got off her ass, the way Greta had to, and made a life, and a living.

Greta once called him *hard,* and not in the good way she sometimes meant. Come to think of it, Alice too called him hard. Or as she put it, *hard-hearted.* He feels soft now, that's for sure. Malleable and helpless, most often.

The aide who wheeled him back here from the lounge this afternoon helped him from the wheelchair into his easy chair, saying, "There, that's more comfortable for a while, don't you think?" At the time, yes, he did. Now, no. He is trapped, helpless as a turtle turned on its back.

Colette and Bill and Greta and that Lodge woman and the little one, Ruth, still go on about making the best of things, or the most, and it still sounds like the sort of stupid thing rosy-tinted people can say, blah, blah, blah. But look what he can do now that he really is stronger, perhaps due to time passing, perhaps thanks to the women. He can rise up slightly using his right arm, then lock the elbow for bracing. This way he can, elbow locked, hover—another H word!— just off the easy chair's seat while he leans forward and gets a good grip on the floor with his right foot so he can propel himself forward and upward and over and down into the wheelchair—so pleasing, a move-by-move plan that will have liberating results.

Moderately liberating.

So it's an unhappy surprise when he succeeds in locking the elbow and hovering, and leaning forward and planting his right foot firmly, and as he is preparing to rise further upward and forward and over and then safely down, that his arm starts to tremble and the locked elbow collapses and his right leg shifts to recapture his weight, and he finds himself falling leftward, just missing cracking his head on a wheel-chair footrest, and then there he is, landing with a thump, sprawled on the floor.

Staring down into carpet instead of up into light, but otherwise much as before.

Useless old man.

He is winded, and very frightened. The carpet is a mass of bluey-grey fibres that look plastic up close. Is anything broken? Busted hips can be killers. He didn't hear anything snap, but he also can't feel half his body. Give him a second and he'll figure out what to do, though, same as when he was alone in the night and the day of his kitchen floor.

One way is simple. If he presses the button at his throat, someone will come and raise him up, check for bruises and broken bones, rescue him. But he can hear Annabel Walker saying sternly, "I'm sorry, but we can't be responsible for such dangerous, careless behaviour," and off he would have to go. He might, after all, wind up living with Alice again—there'd be another cruel twist. No wonder that for as long as she could, she begged to get out, even though as nursing homes go it's a decent one. Of course he wouldn't have put her in a bad place; but people arriving there seem to observe their dazed new companions, sniff at air that always smells slightly fetid, and start their swift journeys to happier, or at least more useful, pasts. Within weeks he might be a lost, loony man cupping people's feet in his hands, measuring their toes and assessing their arches, probably getting in trouble for touching.

As bad a fate as whatever Art Fletcher's will be.

The point is, pressing his buzzer would lead to nothing good, except for being raised off this damned floor. "Help me," he says aloud, nevertheless. "Help me." It must be good news that he can say those words almost clearly.

"George?" he hears from the doorway. "Is that you? Is something the matter?"

"Umph," and he's facing a pair of fat wheels and some chrome, and two flat brown shoes—mass-made, imported from some cheap-labour country where individual stitchery is not a concern or an art—and thin ankles.

"Oh my goodness," says the voice of what's-her-name, Ruth, "are you hurt, can you get up?" Of course he can't. If he could, he'd be up, wouldn't he? "Would you like me to press your buzzer for help?"

. "No!" That comes out loud and clear, which is good, although it causes the wheels to roll slightly back and the plain brown shoes to do a small shuffle.

"Oh. Yes, I see." Does she? "Do you think anything's broken?"

"No."

"Is it another stroke, or a heart attack?"

"No. Fell."

"Does anything hurt?"

"No." Just what he can feel of his pounded, bruised body, and his pride. "Get me up."

"Well, you know, I can't do that myself, but let me go and see what I can do without bringing staff. You just gather your strength for a few minutes so you can help get yourself back on your feet, or your rear end, or whatever you want to be back on."

Is she making fun of him? "Thank you," he says, however, and the wheels and shoes disappear. She is like Lassie, gone looking for help. He and Colette used to watch *Lassie* reruns. Colette begged for a dog, but Alice opposed it. "The trouble is, honey," he said, "you're at school every day and I'm at work, so your mother would have to look after it most of the time, and that wouldn't be fair, would it?"

"You could take it to work with you, it's your store. I'd feed it and take it for walks after school every day. Mum wouldn't have to do anything, honest." The fact is, customers might not have minded a store-dog at all. Does Colette have a dog now, or a cat, or a bird, or a goldfish? It's the sort of thing you'd think a person would mention, but he doesn't think she has, although he cannot be sure.

Look, here are different shoes at his nose, and thicker ankles: Greta's white sneakers, nasty things. Also a pair of expansive sure-soled yellow slippers belonging to Sylvia Lodge, whose enlarged, knobby foot-bones and ropy ankles he recognizes; and the wheels and little feet again—what a crew. He hopes he doesn't look too revealed and pathetic, but expects he probably does.

"Oh dear," Sylvia's voice says. "This'll be tricky. Should we block the door shut with the doorstop, Greta, while we try to figure this out? We don't want anyone blundering in."

The sneakers go away, then return.

"I can't lift," Ruth says, "but my walker might be useful. Maybe George could pull himself partway up it. Then if we got him standing and braced, we could use it to nudge him back into his chair."

"Like a snowplow?" says Sylvia.

"Something like that."

They sound to his ears interested mainly in solving a puzzle. Also pretty cheerful about having a problem to solve. Beggars can't be choosers—there's an old expression zipping back. He rolls slightly leftward, raises his right hand and digs his right foot into the carpeting to show the contribution he can make to the effort.

"Good," Sylvia says. "All right. We'll only get one chance, so what do you think of this? Greta, if he can reach up the walker and grab onto that bar while you get under his shoulders, so you're raising him up but not holding his whole weight, and I come in from behind and push best I can to help get his knees under him, and he hauls himself upright with you helping him from beneath and then me coming in on his left side—could that work?"

"I guess," Greta says dubiously. "It sounds complicated and we do not want to put strain on you or on my heart, but I do not see a better way. Can you help so much, George?"

He'd better, hadn't he? One chance, as they say.

"Just think," Ruth sings out, "how many men would give their eye teeth to be in the hands of so many women." Does she think that's funny? Apparently so. The helpful women laugh; even Greta.

Women are cold. But still, here they are.

Now he can feel Sylvia behind him, and here's Greta's face—how loose-skinned and large-pored it has become!—coming down close to his. "All right, George, remember, right arm up to the bar, and right leg forward for the push onto your knees."

He does as he's told. Rolls leftward enough to lift his right arm, find the bar, wrap his fingers around it while Greta wriggles under his shoulder, burrowing farther until she has shunted his left shoulder upwards. He hears Sylvia yelp as she shoves at his legs with her twisted hands. There's sacrifice going on, which is not cold. Greta rises beneath

him as he pulls as much of his own weight as he can, raising
him higher, breath by heavy breath. Not like the old sounds
of Greta beneath him; not like the same flesh and bones,
either. Hers or his. How horrified is she by his softness?

Finally, triumph! He is unsteadily up on his knees, gripping the walker, and Greta is sliding away, taking a moment
to climb to her feet, also using the walker, and then she's
alongside Sylvia, pulling on his left side, helping him upright
in a last exhausting burst of effort, and—he is trembling, but
he is standing.

"When you're ready, George," Ruth commands from the
coffee table, "move straight backwards. You'll feel the chair
at your legs, and then you can let yourself down. It's not far.
Just a few steps."

Sylvia guides the walker, Greta guides him, only a couple of steps, as Ruth said. "Thanks," he guesses he must say.

"You are welcome," says Greta. She looks flushed and
high-blood-pressured. Sylvia's jaw is fixed, and she is stroking
her arms with her wrecked hands. "Oh my, that was a job,"
Greta says, then quickly, "I am sorry, George, I did not mean
you were a job, only the struggle." *I am sorry, I didn't mean
this, I didn't mean that*—more familiar words. How many years
did he spend, as often as he was able, with Greta? How long
are years? How long since he crashed to the floor, and how
long have they spent raising him up? He hears Colette saying
something like "It'll be your suppertime soon."

From across the room, where she's opening his door
again, Sylvia says, "Yes, you're entirely welcome, George.
Actually, it's rather useful to know we can look out for each
other. I'm all in favour of not letting our guard down with
authority. Staff."

"That's a good way to look at it," Ruth says. "That we look after each other."

"Oh, and listen, here's the headline, don't you think? *Grannies save fallen senior.*"

Again the women find this funnier than George does, and they're still giggling when Diane bounds in, calling out gaily, "Supper, George, do you need to pee before we head to the dining room?" Then, "Oh. I'm sorry, I didn't realize you had company. But aren't you the lucky one, surrounded by so many ladies."

Ruth could safely say something like that, but from any outsider, including Diane, the joke insults them all. The four of them, even George with his slow-moving eyes, glance at each other. Then:

"We shall get out of your way, George," Greta says.

"See you in the dining room," Sylvia says.

"Thank you for inviting us in," Ruth says.

"Thank *you*," George repeats, meaning it this time. Gratitude and belonging look different from a newly rescued, sitting-up point of view. It's true there are days when a man could easily feel like picking up a couple of knives, but at the moment he is fervently touched, and warmly disposed. "Hungry," he tells Diane, happy for another H word come in timely fashion to mind, and then "Hungry," he repeats, and again "Hungry." Just from the blah-blah joy and relief.

14

AT THREE IN THE MORNING . . .

*T*HE SUSPENSE TONIGHT UNDER THE DIM LIGHTS of this Idyll Inn corridor, in a barely breathing silence of cautious, reluctant, step-by-step progress—oh, the suspense is a killer.

Which in happier circumstances might be a good joke, well worth a laugh.

As it is, it's a wonder skin isn't scorched by electricity arcing from one to another, then skipping its way down the hall before rolling back in an angry, dangerous ball—a wonder the whole place doesn't burst into flames.

If it did, there'd be alarms and sprinklers, shouting and sirens, the whole saving apparatus of panic and, mainly, people. People would witness, and their witnessing would bring a halt to this right here and right now.

The three of them can't count on any such luck. Disaster comes out of the blue, not when it's needed.

If not smoke, something does hang in the air: an unpleasant scent embedded in hair, seeping from pores; the faint, acrid stink of human anxiety. That's all right, though. It would be strange if they were bouncing along as if they hadn't a care in the world, all sweet-smelling and full of zest for their task.

Prepare for the worst and hope for the best, that's a good motto. Views vary on what will be worst and what might be best, but here they are, on their way and about to find out.

15

EXIT LINES . . .

*T*HERE IS NO EASY, GOOD, NATURAL TIME for wrecking a perfectly glorious summer afternoon, and maybe much else, but: for any number of reasons, it's time.

The setting is right. Ruth doesn't want interruptions, or for anyone's alarm to be noticeable to a passing aide or Annabel Walker, so where better than Sylvia's deck, beneath Sylvia's big yellow umbrella, with George in his wheelchair wedged into the opening between deck and living room so that even if they wanted to, nobody could make a speedy getaway?

Thanks to Diane's errand-running they have wine and a big bowl of grapes. The end-of-July sun is shining, the air is neither too humid and hot nor too breezy, and Sylvia must be feeling benign or she wouldn't have invited them to join her out here at all. And Sylvia's mood counts. Everyone's does, of course, but Sylvia has a way of setting reactions and tones, and her benevolence is by no means guaranteed every moment, much less every day.

And speaking of time: if need be, there'll still be almost five months for cultivating other means; other people. To be precise, a hundred and thirty-four days.

And among these three, there is promise. Ruth's best bet is probably Sylvia, rigorous in her regard for good argument, and readily detached from mere sentiment. There may also be hope for Greta, with her kindness, her meek willingness to bend; or alternatively, with a history that may have bequeathed her a yet-untapped talent for death.

George's views don't especially matter. He'd be little help to Ruth, willing or not. But here he is, a voice at least.

How gorgeous and grand the world can be. Out here, overlooking the glinting river, the tall, waving wetland grasses, the far trees under the bluest of pacific, uplifting skies, there's no sign of life beyond themselves. Well, that's not quite true. There's always a hum of traffic, an occasional honked horn or siren. In aid, though, of presenting a bleaker, less serene view for their consideration, Ruth has done a good deal of careful spadework. It is not accidental that while Greta and Sylvia have bent over George's limbs every morning, Ruth has taken charge of what she wants them to know: implanting, reinforcing, the easy-come, easy-go nature of life on the planet.

Two unhappy newspaper stories read aloud every weekday amount to ten tales a week of plunder, destruction, viciousness, greed, just plain carelessness. So that out of such clear blue balmy skies, as Ruth hopes she has inclined them to know, bombs are falling. In tall grasses elsewhere, mines will be waiting for unwary feet, while other feet will be kicking in doors to rooms where other old people and women and children will cower, waiting for slaughter.

Surely this knowledge adds up.

Fingers crossed. People may say they hold profoundly to certain beliefs, or disbeliefs, but they're still apt to balk when the time comes to act. Ruth knows that herself. Also, sheer squeamishness is a hindrance. In the kind of news she chooses for reading aloud, the problem is that far too many people aren't nearly squeamish enough. Hence wars and tortures, children blown to bits, polar bears drowning and barren deserts expanding while floods rain down massively elsewhere and whirlwinds storm through unlikely skies—all that, in one, two, three, a thousand ways, demonstrating mortal injury to the planet, the nature of its human portion eternally unimproved.

Just her luck that her friends aren't, as far as she knows, among the marauders and killers. This would be so much easier if they were. She takes a deep anxious breath. "I have a great favour to ask."

"Of course," Greta says. How hard can a favour be? Greta is working on another of her scarves, this one yellow and blue. Sylvia has been wondering if it would be rude to offer a little subtle colour advice, since Greta's tastes run to the garish, as if she's making school-colour scarves for a high school football team or cheerleading squad, nothing any normal person would reasonably wear out in public. Ruth's addiction to loud sweatsuits could also bear guidance. Sylvia has been thinking a joint clothes-shopping venture might be in order.

Ruth holds up a hand. "Wait, don't be too quick. I'm talking about a large favour. Enormous."

Not, then, a time to discuss sweatsuits and scarves. "All right, you have our attention," Sylvia says instead. "Don't look so worried, you don't need to be nervous with us."

"I do, actually. You'll see. Because what I want is—all right, here goes: I plan to end my life fairly soon. The favour I'm asking is for you to be with me come the time. And much more than that, even, I need you to help me."

What? Ruth wants what?

"I'm intending to die, and I'd like your assistance."

Greta's scarf loses two stitches. Sylvia is gape-mouthed; blindsided, when she'd have sworn she was by and large beyond shock. While George remains unruffled, assuming he's heard wrong, as sometimes he gathers he does.

Ruth cannot be serious. Except if she's not serious, she's making a far worse and more unlikely joke than anybody among them has yet managed to crack. "You're kidding, right?" Sylvia asks, but Ruth shakes her head. Who would kid?

Then who does she think they are?

Perhaps she considers them cruel people, or arrogant, or compassionate or righteous or vulnerable or guilty.

Or she thinks they're her friends. And so they are, in a haven't-known-each-other-very-long way. Only, friendship is supposed to be companionability, compatibility, trust, empathy, challenge, warmth, goodwill, consolation and sustenance. Not this. What she's asking has to be—or is not?—beyond all possible bounds.

And how she's gone about it, sneaking up like a clever little snake in the grass, lulling them in the warmth, under the sunshine—what a slyboots, known to them till this moment as a fairly kind, smart enough woman of, okay, immoderate pessimism, but with a lifetime of good works behind her, and presumably goodness rampant throughout her soul.

"I realize this is a surprise." This makes Sylvia's eyebrows fly upwards. "But I can tell you that helping is not as grim as it sounds. And you know, we've already shown how we can look after each other."

"Well, yes. But that was about getting George up, not putting you down." Honestly, it must be some kind of reflex—bad, frivolous Sylvia. But really!

There's no longer much chance they've misheard, so—how can this be? Isn't living the only thing to be done about life, isn't that why George demands some *good* news when Ruth's going on and on with her doom and gloom? Hope, even if he can't say exactly what for any more? "No," he breathes, but there's no sign Ruth hears.

Greta's knitting has lapsed into her lap in a spill of bright yellow, bright blue. This is terrible. Poor Ruth, who must be so lonely with no one to love. If she had another person in the world to be responsible to, or to care for, this could not cross her mind. A hand reached out to Ruth's will count for nothing, compared, but Greta reaches out anyway and touches Ruth's hand. And withdraws. It is almost like touching someone already dead, so remote.

But poor Ruth.

Who says, "I'm sorry I've upset you. I guess I was bound to, but I needed you to know and start thinking about it. I expect just knowing is a burden, and I'm sorry for that but frankly, the time I have left, it's moving along. There's this, too: we know we can trust each other's discretion"—a glance at Greta—"as well as help each other out when need be"—a glance at George. "So I'm trusting you all not to tell anyone." As if discovery would be the larger catastrophe.

"Please understand, my mind is made up. It's only my heart, for want of a better word, that I'm still working on. And now yours."

There aren't enough words in Ruth's vocabulary, not enough eloquent, pleading exit lines in the lexicon, to make her intentions sound anything other than harsh. To be honest, once put right out into the sunlight, they sound even to her unnervingly—well, frighteningly—real.

And her approach may, after all, have been counterproductive, although she can't think of one that wouldn't have left each of them looking bushwhacked.

And if they had leapt to agree, and cheerfully buckled right down to the specifics, how insulting would that have been?

"I'm not saying it's the right thing for anyone else," although that isn't quite true. "Not at all."

"Oh, well, good." Sylvia again. "That's a relief. I believe I'm too old for death cults." Not very funny, but the best she can do. "Sorry, Ruth. In theory, at least, I do believe people should be able to do any damn thing they want with themselves, but in practice . . . that's rather difficult and different, you know." Yes, Ruth knows that. Of course she does. "So you've taken us badly aback. And think of Greta's heart."

In Ruth's experience, people do not have heart attacks on other people's behalf. Greta looks as solid as ever, except she's not knitting, and her mouth is open.

Then there's George, whose expressions are often hard to decipher. Who knows if he's even listening? But he seems to be. He's frowning, his head making little negative shakes.

Ruth's three Idyll Inn friends. "I know there has to be a lot to consider."

Yes, there is. Monstrous questions unexpectedly and unpleasantly arise in the course of an innocent day, and suddenly they are having to begin urgently asking themselves some of the largest ones. Chief among them:

What do they believe? What are their values, and if any, their faiths? How do these apply to the small but real figure of Ruth sitting here?

What is compassion, how important is trust?

What, specifically as it relates to Ruth, and generally as it relates, well, generally, is the nature of goodness? Of badness?

What exactly is so exceptional about human beings? A single human being? Besides the fact that only human beings can even contemplate such a question.

Who gets to decide? Ruth says she does. How did she decide that?

Is she sure? Because everyone's entitled to a few moods and diversions, and friends make allowances.

Friends don't do this, though, they don't take an ordinary afternoon get-together, and a deep breath, and suggest such a thing. Ruth must be mad, and terribly sad. Sadder than any of them could have dreamed. How could none of them have known that? Yet it's not how she appears, mad or sad. Of course she's looking at them intently, narrow-eyed, naturally she'd be keen to see their reactions. It's her life, after all. Or it's not.

Is it strange that the air among them now contains sizzles of anger?

"Just think about it, okay? It's truly not so outrageous, believe me."

Really? In what way is helping Ruth kill herself likely to become less outrageous, and how long does she think that will take? Who, honest to God, does she suppose them to be?

That's not even to mention, what on earth are they going to talk about from now on? The weather, Greta's knitting, their children, the latest flood, fire, war? Everything, everything lies in a distressing new light, and this is Ruth's fault. There were the months before she said, more or less, "I'm planning to end my life fairly soon, and I'd like you all to be with me, and beyond that to help me," and now there will be after.

All this in such a few moments; a sliver of time.

Not one of them has a single reliable word to add; until Sylvia says, in the chilly tone they've previously heard mainly when she was talking to Annabel Walker, "You know, I think we need time to ourselves now." Meaning she is pretty much kicking them all off her deck.

What a relief. Greta gathers up her knitting and turns to steer George from the doorway. No one meets eyes. No one is sure of meeting eyes ever again. Ruth nods and rises. Now there is not only lost time to count, an infant or three whose lives she has saved, these three companions, a single grave act, but another sort of arithmetic too: a possibility, a doom and a hope. Three more different things, adding up maybe, finally, to one grand subtraction.

16

GOOD AND BAD WITH LAWYERS . . .

One doesn't like to believe that the older people get, the more grindingly slowly they think, but maybe it's true; otherwise, how to explain none of them immediately inquiring into the basics? Ruth's why and when, not to mention the how of the thing? Even taking severe startlement into account, that's got to be embarrassingly slow-witted.

Oh, there are all sorts of reasons to be angry. Having kicked everyone off her deck, Sylvia's now tormented by questions like itches. She'd like to stomp right down to Ruth's room and demand a few answers. Get things straight. Set Ruth straight, as well. How dare she, and exactly what does she have in mind? Does she picture Sylvia, Greta and George feeding her pills one by one, hanging her from a doorway, slitting her narrow arthritic wrists? While Ruth, passive as a peach, gives instruction?

Still, she must have a reason, and it must be terrible. The obvious one is a desperate illness she hasn't been able to put into words, the sort of eventuality anyone—almost anyone—is bound to consider. Even at that, unless Sylvia were too incapacitated to do otherwise, she wouldn't think, herself, of asking for help. Wouldn't, for that matter, know whom to ask. She has not had those sorts of friends.

Perhaps she has them now.

Whatever the reason, Ruth's aim and request are extraordinary. If she weren't utterly serious—but maybe she's crazy as a bedbug; maybe they all are, it must be hard to know for sure when brain cells are slip-sliding away—but mad or not, she must be serious or she wouldn't have raised such a subject. Which by extension would seem to imply that she chose her Idyll Inn companions right from the start with an eye to who might be amenable, useful. Which would mean that— perhaps barring George, who is mainly Greta's project as well as more or less a group pet, veering between spaniel and unruly pit bull—barring him, Ruth must have sized up Sylvia and Greta as potential killer conspirators; at the very least as extremely, indeed almost uniquely, flexible in their ethics.

Hardly a compliment. Not necessarily inaccurate either, although bending to Ruth's proposal would be a stretch beyond all previous flexibilities.

Or not. There are certain faint precedents.

Looked at one way, adultery is only an act, an event, so ordinary and clichéd that no one could possibly care besides the terminally righteous and those directly involved, the husbands and wives and lovers and children with their little individual lives ravelling and unravelling in romantic, troublesome, delicious or shattering but at any rate insignificant-to-the-wider-world ways. So ho-hum, and still ho-hum when all sides, husbands, wives, lovers, children, wind up decades down the road beneath the same roof.

On the other hand: Sylvia could argue that adultery is a grave matter if only because the entire human portion of the planet operates, or fails to operate, on understandings of trust and faithlessness, truth and falsehood, generosity and greed, promises and shifting loyalties, treaties kept and treaties broken; and where are these most intimately formed and demonstrated but in kitchens and bedrooms and sometimes motels and parked cars?

Nor is it necessarily a straightforward judgment. Not only are there such things as multilateral treaties, but it can also be wise to keep some agreements, break others. As blood and history show, these are not minor decisions, and neither is adultery, however common as dirt.

Ruth, with her interest in bleak historic and current affairs, might well agree. Maybe it's exactly what she thinks concerning Greta and George: that for people who carried on in adulterous fashion for such a long time, assisting a death would be a mere bagatelle. Or, more far-fetched and against all personal evidence, that a trickle of leftover cells in Greta's blood might lean her toward destruction, specifically of people like Ruth.

But what has led Ruth to suppose that Sylvia has successfully auditioned for an executioner's role? Perhaps Sylvia's own excursions into infidelity, except how Ruth could know about them is a mystery, even if there's no discounting the power of rumour, accurate and otherwise, in this town.

To be honest, as far as Sylvia can see, Greta and George's fling, even though it lasted so long and in much-mutated fashion lasts even now, is a not-very-dramatic, possibly somewhat steamy but fundamentally banal soap opera involving a

clerk and a shoestore owner. Whereas Sylvia's is an epic
poem, an opera, some great *Guernica* of a canvas.

Or hell, maybe hers is also a cheap hour or two of melo-
dramatic afternoon TV. At least no living soul knows the
whole story, because the only soul who did died almost a
decade ago. Jackson's law partner was the fellow she dallied
with. Dallied with twice, as a matter of fact; no point making one mistake when a person can go on to make two. *Dally*
is a nice tipsy word. Besides being Jackson's law partner, her
lover was Annabel Walker's father. Circles and circles, dizzying dallyings.

Marry in lust, repent at leisure—no, wait, that's quite
wrong. The very word *repentance* is wrong. It's true, though,
that lust casts a blinding, shining mist over the vision, so that
when an admirably attractive, promising young man, son of a
former mayor, comes home from law school and runs into an
admirably attractive young woman feeling her oats, certain
matters grow hazy. But it seems there are risks in being a
young woman flung from the limber gropings and thrills of
illicit affections into a multi-tiered gauzy white dress, licitly
aglow with promise and hope, and then into a big multi-tiered
house—who considers what will be lost rather than gained?

Oh, what a whiner. What did she lose, what great ambitions did she otherwise have for herself that were so impeded
by Jackson, that exemplary man? None, is the answer to
that. She got what she'd wanted and even what she'd
desired, if not, thank God, what she deserved.

Which only means that desire's real outcomes can be
disconcerting. Which are pathetic grounds for self-pity.

"We're a team," said Jackson, eyes turned toward pros-
perity, consolidation, making not only a living but a life in

this town. A two-person job, not only his—"I do the law, and down the road maybe some politics too, and you do the tough stuff," and unlike any other man she might have fallen into back seats with and married, he meant it. Joining boards, playing bridge and golf with women who were sometimes a bore, as Sylvia was often enough boring herself— that was her share of the work. Matching the china and having enough kinds of forks and spoons to manage large dinner parties. Making up menus and invitations and seating plans, scrutinizing the finances of the public art gallery, one of the first boards she joined—everyone gets better with practice if they stick with what they've set out to do; but some things also fall into patterns, then habits, which may well lead to grievance.

Jackson's civil law, however mundane, had to be more entertaining and challenging than her pursuits, even when he ran for council and she found she enjoyed making little speeches concerning his virtues, and shaking hands and air-kissing any number of cheeks, and standing loyally at his shoulder as he made his victory speeches—even then, she came over time to consider that she had several reasons to smoke a little too much, play bridge a little too fiercely, laugh a little too loudly at country club dinners.

She cannot imagine now, in this sunny hour, how she could have felt so hard done by. Surely it was pleasing to chair a meeting, encounter a certain deferential recognition in stores; find real gratification, not just social benefit, in planning a library addition, arranging to buy a new painting for the gallery, adding in these ways some knowledge and beauty to the community. And she was certainly free to pursue her own interests and acquaintances, had the leisure to read and the money to shop and the liberty to drive in her own car with her own friends wherever she wanted, including to out-of-town theatres, galleries, restaurants. She and Jackson went away some weekends themselves, finding that between her trim body and his increasingly bulky one, lust in strange hotel rooms could acquire a festive glamour not always present at home. How ungrateful and spoiled she must have been. Look at Greta, working and raising three daughters all on her own during what must have been more or less those same years. Sylvia didn't even have children to care for; was wondering, actually, if Jackson was shooting blanks.

Jackson and Peter Walker were old friends from law school. When Peter joined Jackson's practice, and he and Susan moved here to town, Susan was pregnant; the result of which expectancy turns out to be a retirement home administrator, but nobody thinks in hopeful youth of such dreary outcomes. Certainly not Susan, who for the most part stayed happily home while Sylvia, quite the old pro, became sociable for two.

Unlike Jackson, Peter specialized in criminal cases: shoplifting, assault, the very common break and enter, the very uncommon murder. Jackson brought home stories, interesting enough, of sisters and brothers wrangling over dead parents' wills, real estate deals falling disastrously apart on their closing dates—all the business of negotiating the town's competing losses and difficulties and griefs. That's what he most enjoyed during his three council terms, too—arranging alliances, he said, bargaining for middle ground, bringing opponents if not to accord at least to accommodation. While Peter—here was the difference, one difference—was more expert in confrontation. He handled the cases of violent, rampaging drinkers, men who turned to fists and even guns for their pleasure, drunken, drugged youths gone off the rails, sad housewives who shoplifted lipsticks and stockings.

Richer matters, in short.

Peter acquired—or arrived with, who remembers, who cares?—a dark tinge of danger himself. He also evidently found himself not compellingly intrigued by the domestic life of mother and squally infant; not enough, anyway, to prevent him from reaching treacherously for Sylvia late one Saturday night, while Susan sat home with Annabel, and Jackson went to get the car from the country club parking lot, and Sylvia and Peter waited together for him. "You're so *alive*," Peter whispered into her hair, standing behind her with his hands bluntly placed on her breasts. Fingers circling her nipples. "I want you." Oh *yes*. She leaned back into his body, harder and more narrow than Jackson's. He stepped aside, and then climbed innocently into the back seat when Jackson appeared with the car. A courtroom trick, probably, knowing how to give nothing away.

Imagine being wanted. Again. Like that. In that misting, shuddery way.

There are always places and ways. False appointments and meetings, long country drives as well as the reliable, thrillingly tawdry ABC Motel—wouldn't it be funny if she and Peter crossed dimly lit paths in the parking lot with Greta and George? Wouldn't it be awful to think they were ever in the same room?—although now that she's had the thought, it seems all too likely. The ABC wasn't large.

If she chooses, Sylvia can see particular moments quite clearly, but retrieving a feeling, an actual emotion, is often a different matter. Events that once must have been brilliantly coloured and sharp-edged are now grey-shaded and wavery, and it's hard to know if that's a decision or just what ordinarily happens to people in time: a normal fog of dispassion that rolls in with the years.

She might do better with these particular memories if she and Peter had ever spoken of love, but they didn't. What an absurd organ the heart must be. In those months of Peter it was steadfastly clear to her, as sometimes happens in these situations, a good news–bad news equation, how very glad she was to be married to Jackson; what a compassionate, smart, upstanding man he was; how many reasons she had, in fact, to love him.

Ironic in its way, then, to find herself pregnant. "Oh Jesus," said Peter. "But okay, we'll get you fixed up, there are places and ways. I'll arrange it." He would "even," as he said, pick up the tab.

What a prince.

If he hadn't been so quick off the mark, so tactless and presumptuous, she might well have made that decision herself. Instead, contrariwise, "Please, sweetheart," she whispered to Jackson, urgently placing a calculating hand on his penis as he read beside her in bed, "it's been such a long time, and I miss you." Desperation can be staggeringly ignoble. How touched he was. She thought of his sweet, startled pleasure later, not at the time.

And Susan? No problem there, poor pudding occupied with Annabel and as content, it appeared, as a clam.

The only lingering, indeed permanent, problem is a whole lifetime—Nancy's lifetime—of lies.

"Finally," Jackson said gratefully, admiring Sylvia's burgeoning breasts, touching her belly, resting his head there. Listening, he said. "I love you. I'm so happy, you can't imagine." No, she could not. "I love you, too." Which was true.

Susan said, "It's great Annabel will have a new little playmate. Isn't it, Annabel?"

It's been interesting in recent years to read how much more uncertain parentage there is than most people have dreamed. No wonder men everywhere on earth go to such great, gruesome lengths to keep a tight grip on women— they're right, often enough, to be suspicious when it comes to paternity, when even ape females find sly ways to slip away from their mates in search of whatever apes yearn for—fresh evolutionary blood in the clan, or just a pleasing change for themselves. At any rate, it seems genetic testing has come as an alarming development to a good many mothers with secrets.

Whereas Sylvia only had to worry about who her child would resemble. What if Peter's features were clear in its face? He had brown eyes, for instance, whereas hers and Jackson's were blue, which meant there could be trouble the moment the infant opened its eyes.

But Nancy was, as everyone said and still says, *the spitting image* of her mother.

What else should Sylvia have done, she'd like to know? Thanks to her brute will, which Peter called, for a time bitterly, *wilfulness*, two families and a law firm survived. Mother baboons do exactly the same. Jackson was thrilled to have a child to dote on at last. He held Nancy close. When Sylvia fed her, he watched the two of them with the widest-eyed reverence: Joseph, observing the Madonna and child.

Just as deluded, but just as entranced.

Peter, undeluded and unentranced, seemed angry in a thrumming, under-the-surface way when he saw Jackson carting Nancy around, but he didn't embrace her himself. With Annabel he made a show of jovial fatherhood, riding her about on his shoulders, tickling her. Annabel on Peter's lap wore what Sylvia considered the smug expression of a triumphant seductress.

Well, it was a complicated stew of one thing and another. Jackson and Susan, like children, were the ones who got to be blissfully ignorant; or at any rate ignorant.

A further helping of stew appeared a couple of years later, when Annabel had a baby brother, also named Peter. It was unreasonable to be wounded that his father was so cavalier about the purposes to which he put his body, but Sylvia was wounded anyway. Once, a rare shared babysitter held the fort while Jackson and Sylvia, Peter and Susan attended a cancer fundraiser. "I guess," she told Peter as Jackson and Susan took a turn on the dance floor, "I guess we'll just have to hope Nancy and young Peter don't fall in love when they grow up. We'll have to guard against incest."

"Syl!" How easily appalled he could be. Not a very *bright* man, really—it seems doubtful he could have been as good a lawyer as Jackson and he both claimed he was.

Jackson was altogether the worthier man; as no doubt Susan was the worthier woman. Also, all their children were worthy. Nancy in particular was fearless when it came to hurling herself off the porch or pelting over the lawn or diving, literally diving, into swim lessons. Obviously she felt safe. She *was* safe. Sylvia was a good mother, Jackson a most loving father, and Nancy had every care and advantage. "What a lovely, smart child," people said.

Lucky, too, and thoroughly indulged, unlike the poor dire children of Ruth's experience—what makes Nancy think she's entitled to tend her fury so very diligently for so many decades?

What made Sylvia think she and Peter could without consequence take another few runs, a dozen years after their first round, out to the old, reliable, unimproved ABC Motel?

As she recalls: a woman in her forties in those days (no doubt not any more) could easily feel her life on the slide; in the sense of, who would be interested? Not even Jackson— busy with his practice, serving his third and last term on city council, devoted to Nancy, kind and respectful toward Sylvia but less noticing and appreciative, or so it seemed to her. Whereas there was Peter, still lean and thriving. Still steamy. And indicating his own refreshed interest with significantly long, languidly wicked glances, and a hand that lingered on her rear end, camouflaged (she hoped) by the crowd as the four of them left a school concert in which all their three children performed, none brilliantly, in their respective class choirs.

Oh, she should have taken up a hobby that kept her hands busy; learned perhaps, like Greta, to endlessly knit.

Back at the ABC, never mind she was in her forties, they were careful about birth control. There could still be that way to be caught.

And there were corrosive, shattering ways.

Nancy was thirteen the autumn evening she turned on her mother in the kitchen, as Jackson watched TV in the living room and Sylvia washed the dinner plates and Nancy dried them, and said in a voice that came strange from a child, "I saw you today."

Sylvia damn near dropped a plate. She tried to remember what, exactly, Nancy could have seen: tender or quick, passionate or perfunctory, hands where? "What are you talking about?" The best defence being instant offence.

"You and Mr. Walker. Out at the ABC. You were kissing. Before you got into your cars."

Oh shit, oh Jesus. "What business did you have away out there?"

"We got out of school early and me and Samantha went riding our bikes out on the highway. We both saw. It was really embarrassing."

Even worse. Terminally worse. If Nancy's friend also saw, word would be flying among the children and soon, if not already, to their parents. All that tricky, inconvenient, exhilarating discretion blown up in their faces. Peter's lively, desiring face. "Does Dad know?" Nancy's face, too, was changed: on some cold and unfamiliar middle ground between child and adult. And how about Sylvia's? In the unmerciful light of the kitchen, its secrets would be as clear as the puckerings of skin at the sides of her eyes. *Laugh lines*, Peter called them; as if she were a woman of constant amusement.

"There's nothing to know. You have no idea, Nancy."

"I *saw* you." Nancy's voice quavered, near tears. Sylvia thought, *I should put my arms around her*, a child in such evident pain, but she was also aware that tenderness could trigger a tempest, which would draw Jackson's disastrous attention. So she didn't. She should have, of course. A difference might have been made, Nancy salvaged. A moment forgone.

"Go to your room. I'll come discuss this mistake of yours when you've calmed down. Now, go. Right now." She has to confess: watching Nancy stalk from the kitchen, she stared hatred into her daughter's departing back. Her eyes contained knives.

Children know things, even when their backs are turned. This is what turns mere soap opera into an epic poem, some days a *Guernica*.

Possibly priorities do, as well. The power, the sheer electrical surge of her need to save Jackson, her home, her whole life, nearly knocked her flat. She phoned Peter. "I'm sorry to call you at home, but we have an emergency."

"Oh hell, what kind of emergency? I can't get away."

"You don't have to, just listen. Nancy saw us out at the ABC today. And she was with one of her friends. I doubt she has the stomach to tell Jackson, but other people know now. That's why I'm calling, to see if you have any bright ideas. Is that enough of an emergency for you?" Honestly, she couldn't help that last sentence.

There was a long silence, although she could hear his deep breaths. Then, "Oh shit fuck goddamn cunt bloody goddamn fucking cunting hell."

How attractive. "I gather you're alone."

"Yeah, but I have to go pick up Susan and the kids from the movies in a few minutes."

"Then don't let me keep you. I thought you might have a suggestion or two, but I guess all we can do is hope for the best."

"And what the fuck would that be?" As if he blamed her, the coward. Again. "One thing's for sure," he said, "the two of us, that's got to be over."

Oh, honestly. "No kidding."

"And you'll be careful? No phone calls or the four of us getting together, no dancing, nothing, right?"

"When do I ever phone you, besides tonight? But we can hardly cut off contact. We didn't before, and we can't now. It's not just you and Susan who are so very attached, you know. So are you and Jackson. Anyway, she would notice and so would he, never mind everyone else." Once again: how good a lawyer could he be, thinking so slowly?

"You're right, you're right. We'll just have to be totally careful and cool, can you do that?"

"No problem. Really. Goodbye, then. Good luck."

A pathetic, clumsy, hostile farewell, yes; fortunately no emotion, even nostalgia, survives contempt for very long.

Upstairs, still wary of touch—afraid to touch, really— she explained to Nancy that Peter and Susan had had a misunderstanding, and he'd asked her advice, so they'd met to talk and all Nancy'd seen had been a friendly hug and kiss of gratitude. She said it was a private problem in his marriage that Jackson didn't know about, because he and Peter didn't like personal things coming up in their prac- tice, but that it certainly didn't mean anything between her and Peter. He'd asked her advice, she told Nancy, because she was Susan's friend, not because she was his. She said it was a shame Samantha had seen, because it would be cruel if something wrong and hurtful got back to Annabel or young Peter, so maybe Nancy could straighten her friend out. Carefully. So the situation didn't get worse. Oh, she piled it on. Nancy should have believed her, but consider- ing that Nancy is now half a century old and still cold and unkind, it seems she did not.

Still, she never told Jackson. Always quite a daddy's girl, protective that way.

As he deserved protection. Sylvia is embarrassed, even alone, to find tears in her eyes. Getting soppy in her old age.

Sylvia, who can no longer quite bring Peter's features to mind, and who sees Susan's each day in Annabel, and whose own bones have replicated themselves in Nancy—Sylvia sees Jackson's lost face, young and old, in photographs and in memory. Love, companionship, affection, familiarity, respect—what a compelling gravitational force they exert. With silence the payment a person makes in return.

When Ruth reads out her awful stories, does she ever wonder what those torturers of hers tell their wives and children when they go home from their long days of rampaging with guns, electrodes, waterboarding and rape? Sylvia bets they say whatever keeps the family together and brings comfort at nightfall, and if that means strains and silences, well, they'd be disastrously worse for the telling of truth.

Keep up a good front and a strong spine—how's that for another compelling gravitational force? Ruth tells of being a gymnast, long ago. Perhaps that has encouraged her to disregard gravity now; although it could just as easily have done the opposite, really.

Like mistaken fatherhood, death too happens in sly, sliding, possibly merciful ways more often than people think. Or so Sylvia has read, and there's no reason it wouldn't be true.

Somewhere in the Idyll Inn there may be people with straightforward lives they've conducted strictly according to Hoyle. Judging from the record so far, it doesn't seem likely—there must be many other misadventures and crimes lying tucked under prim double-bed blankets. Still, Ruth isn't necessarily wrong to imagine she's put her finger on a couple of people of vast flexibility; like Sylvia, who has done and not done what she has done and not done, and may be capable of far more—right this minute, even she cannot be sure.

17

SMARTER THAN, SAY, YOUR AVERAGE
NEANDERTHAL . . .

*T*HE MORNING AFTER is as jumpy as a blind date: feeling each other out, sizing each other up, cautiously wondering if there's any future in this.

Not for Ruth; so she says.

In George's room Greta and Sylvia apply themselves, not very vigorously, to George's limbs. Only he slept well last night, securely tucked in by Diane, that nice girl, and comforted that in the end he must, after all, have misunderstood what Ruth said, and then whatever Greta was muttering on about when she took him back from Sylvia's deck to his room. There are times when it's not unpleasant to suppose he mishears—what he recalled was so impossible that it could be nothing to stay awake over, pending all coming clear, or just going away.

Greta slept for a while and then kept waking up startled. Each time the awakening was anxious, and she felt a little bit ill. In darkness the mind is too open to strangenesses that would not arise in the light. Last night her mind held for a

few seconds after each waking such unhappy pictures, like
ones that have not come to her for many years, of an old
country and lost people that in the day she would be careful
not to see, and even after they flickered and faded, as pictures in dreams can swiftly do, their sadness and their unease
cling, they have seeped into the day.

If the pictures were not of Ruth or to do with Ruth, they
must nevertheless be the fault of Ruth. For bringing
unhappy ripplings into the heart. For raising distresses that
should not be raised. And questions. Such as whether such a
thing as Ruth asks can be true, and more than that, whether
it can be done. There are certain words, too. Such as *sin: the
breaking of divine or moral law, especially by a conscious act.*
Such a short, very large word. How many sins are there—an
endless number, it seems—and how are they to be compared
to each other? How are they also to be compared to the
good—possibly, how is mercy to be weighed against murder?
Is *murder* the word? It seems to Greta it should mean there is
an unwilling, resisting, taken-by-surprise victim, not someone who has made a request, but she could be wrong.

"Shall I read?" Ruth asks, newspapers ready beside her
on George's coffee table.

"Oh, not today, I think," says Sylvia, who also slept badly.
"It's a little hard to spare much interest for the outside world
when we've got a fair-sized elephant right here in the room."
She sounds as if she blames Ruth. So, to be honest, does Greta,
although she's unclear why Sylvia speaks of an elephant.

Sylvia's tone softens. "You know, I have to ask, is it an illness?" By her current standards this is cautious and tactful,
leaving the *it* hanging absent its antecedent; which would have
to be the cause. The blunt *death*. The unfathomable *desire*.

Of course they are unhappy and troubled, and of course they want reasons, and Ruth has a laundry list—let them count right along with her, this in the dubious hope that their arithmetic and hers will arrive simultaneously at the same uncomplicated total. "No. I could lie to you, but as far as I know I'm not particularly ill beyond osteo and its effects, so I'm not trying to beat a terminal clock, if that's what you mean. Actually it's partly because I'm *not* sick, and I don't want to be, either."

As if anyone does.

"Look. Sometimes I see shapes and colours that I know aren't really there. I think that's just because of a new drug my doctor is trying, but in a way it's also how I tend to see life: in a big curve, like a rainbow. It starts with an arc that shades upwards for a while, and then it goes along with bumpy patches but more or less nicely flat and pastel for quite a distance, until it begins heading downward. It declines and turns grey. And I don't want to decline past a still fairly good, reasonably bright end point. As it seems to me too many lives do. As we can see here every day, with one person or another going downhill. So I want to grab the moment while I'm right between what's worthwhile and what's not."

On those grounds should they all die, for heaven's sake?

"I'm not personally particularly depressed or unhappy. I've had all the love I could bear, and I'm glad every day for every colour and sound—well, most of them—and for the Idyll Inn and being taken care of in all the ways I expected when I moved in, and for some of the people, like Diane when she comes around in the evenings to help, and for all of you, too. My friends, I feel."

Never mind that there appear to be penalties for being Ruth's friends. It's not Sylvia's fault, or Greta's, or George's, that they're in the awkward, at best awkward, position of either defending life or having to consider helping to end one. Ruth gestures at the newspapers. "At the same time, I guess you could say I've given up on anything getting better, and I'm not interested in watching while it only gets worse."

"What's the *it*?" So George isn't the only one who isn't getting what's going on, and at least Sylvia puts the confusion into clear words: What can Ruth mean?

"I mean, look at this day."

Yes, so?

"This heat."

Again—so? When Sylvia stuck her head out the doorway to her deck after breakfast, unlike yesterday the air was already stifling—so much for gathering out there later in private again. Such heat is good for arthritis, bad for breathing, and generally speaking people choose breath over pain relief; Ruth being, by her own account, an exception, evidently.

"Well, we know all these things, we keep reading about them. A day like today here. The whole upheaval of the earth."

"You're talking about *climate* change? As a reason to *die*? For God's sake, Ruth, we're *old*. What's that to do with what's left of our lives?"

"Not much personally, I guess. Except," and Ruth smiles very briefly, "for being glad we have this excellent air conditioning that's part of the problem. But climate is just one example."

"Of what?"

"Of how stupid and destructive people are wherever you look, even just outside, into the air." Now it's Ruth who sounds angry. "We can think we're doing good things now and then, but on the whole we're not. On the whole we're wreckers, we're a ruinous species, and I'm tired of it. Just tired."

She doesn't sound tired, though; she sounds rather energetic, rather impassioned. In a funny way pleased, as well.

It is a way of seeing that perhaps comes from knowing too much, is that possible? So much Ruth reads to them, so many disasters and cruelties that Greta, for one, has not previously had time for, or she has had time but not a desire to know, and is this not in the end for the best? Knowing can lead, it seems, as with Ruth, to despair, but despair must be a battle, not a giving in. Despair is how Greta and Dolph came to land in this country, a long way, an ocean away, from hunger and guilt. Two of her older brothers, and her father and Dolph's, wore uniforms, but they must have been only soldiers, as men had to be, and she would not believe they were ever bad men. But afterwards, in the shame, everyone suffered, wicked or good.

"This is a hard place now," said her mother, who once had been plump. "We will find a way to help you to leave." And so they did. And Greta and Dolph did not look back; would not. Except sometimes in small dreams, which cannot be helped.

"How can you think this?" Greta hears her own voice lifting and vibrating with, nearly, fury. "People *work* to live. All those you read us of, in starvation and war and illness, they will endure anything to be alive. They do not give up. We do not give up. Even without hope, we do not."

She of all people should not have to say this to Ruth of all people.

In Greta's mind's eye, too, is Dolph, arms eternally flung upwards behind blank grey silo walls, helpless under the weight of feed corn pouring down—Dolph desperately drowning, struggling to live.

There is also a young woman alone in a strange land, rising every morning to care for her girls and search for work, and finding work, and raising her girls. Badly or well, *going on.* "It is our *duty.* We *must.*"

Greta's face has gone cherry red, and there are big fat alarming tears in her eyes—what if she has another heart attack, what if Ruth inadvertently kills someone else? Even so: "I don't mean to argue, Greta, but duty to whom? Who says we must? And I'm not the only one. I read about a woman, quite famous, who did exactly what I'm proposing for no obvious reason except she felt finished. Although she didn't have osteo, so she managed it all by herself." Then go ahead, why drag them into it? But nobody says that; not right now.

There is again this, too: that if Ruth had people to love and be loved by, if she had children, grandchildren, she could be upset about what lies ahead for them, as Greta can also be, now that she has heard so much on these subjects, but she would never be able to cause such an injury to loved ones— no. And so how sad for Ruth, to have no one like that.

How light, also; how freely Ruth must feel herself able to fly off the earth, without love and duty holding her down.

This is also not something to be said; except by Ruth, it seems. "I realize I might feel differently if I were wondering if a child's marriage was going to hold up, or a grandchild would ever get a good job or have a healthy baby—that personal sort of care a parent would have. Not that I regret at all not having those particular ties. Although if Bernard were alive, it'd be different. Whether he was well or not, I couldn't—wouldn't want to—abandon him. But I have none of those pulls. All my work is done, and there's also nothing more to be loved, and even if there were, I can't feel any love in me to give. So I'm finished. But what I do have is the luxury of my own choice."

Does choice go so far? Is this a moment to speak the word *sin?* Perhaps not. Or *despair.* Only listen, listen. To Ruth saying, "I understand you've got all sorts of reasons for living, Greta, your own desires and your daughters among them. But we all die at some point, every blessed one of us, so why not consider when that point could best be? It's not as if thousands and thousands of people don't die every moment from every imaginable cause—disease, carelessness, cruelty, just wearing out—we're as disposable as ants. Maybe special ants, maybe not, but in any case, in a million-stars-in-the-sky, million-grains-of-sand-in-the-desert way, a death is only one more small thing. As am I, really. Even when death isn't easy, it's completely ordinary and normal."

Normal, yes; ordinary, no. Even Greta understands that difference. How dare Ruth—what?—*betray* her cherished humans in this way? People are not stars in the sky or sand in the desert, how can Ruth especially, who seems always touched and troubled by indignation and sorrow, think such a thing? This is an unwillingness to go forward, an emptiness on such a scale that there is no answer to it that Greta can see. In fact there is a terrible absurdity—*absurd: ridiculously unsound, without orderly relationship to life, lacking reason or value*—to this whole conversation.

"And think," Ruth is going on, "of the amount of death we're all already responsible for."

Oh honestly, that's a bit much. "We're hardly experienced assassins, Ruth," Sylvia snaps.

"Maybe not directly, but nobody's an innocent, either. We use the oil that people are killed for, we wear jewellery that miners and child soldiers die over—why, there's been blood all over our engagement and wedding rings forever. Mine too, I realize that."

Greta considers her silver bracelet with the engraved twining vines and two tiny diamonds, that gift from a grateful jeweller at a time, and a shabby ABC Motel place, when she was dying a little death of her own. But in comparison to what Ruth speaks of, that hardly counts.

"Coffee, tea, sugar, the fruit we keep in your fridge, Sylvia—farmers starve in other countries, and lose their land, and children die from crops being sprayed."

"My goodness, that's quite a list. Is there anything left we might still enjoy?" Sylvia sounds angry and amused both.

"Shoes," George says suddenly. "Shoes," he repeats. He means, if he could say it properly, cheap shoes people buy, the ones that come from countries where people work for slave wages and get mutilated by machines and burned up in locked factories in the manufacture of bargains—those people die, and his business where shoes are not shoddy and cheap dies too—he would never be able to say all that, so he just says, "Shoes," for the third time, and bangs his right fist on the arm of his wheelchair.

They leave the usual pause to allow him to imagine they

have any idea what he's talking about. "Yes," Greta says finally. "You are no doubt right, George."

"Damn. Don't." Patronize him, he means. Pat him on the head like a child.

Should he have died on the floor of his kitchen? If he'd known then what he knows now, would he have let himself go?

He thinks not. Even as things stand, he would not.

But he can almost see why a person who's not like him might.

Why shouldn't Ruth get what she wants? Somebody should.

He remembers a story Ruth read to them—yesterday? months ago?—about a feeble former South American dictator, elderly, their age, charged at last for a few of his many long-ago crimes: opponents attached to electrodes, deprived of food, water, sleep, warmth; women subjected to particular torments as, Ruth pointed out, women always are; and, an unpleasant twist new to George, live, struggling, bound prisoners tossed from helicopters to, far below, wherever they landed. Because he was feeble and old, the newspaper said some people thought he should be left in peace with his infirmities and, if such existed, his conscience. And Sylvia laughed in that barking way of hers, and said, "See? If you live long enough you get off the hook for *anything*. Isn't that insulting? If I were him, I'd be furious. I'd want to hurl somebody right out of a plane."

Ha ha ha. But maybe that's the kind of thing that made Ruth think they too could do anything and still *get off the hook*. That they'd help her because they're old and she's old and nobody would notice or care.

"My point," Ruth is saying, "is that what I'm talking about is just more immediate than some of the things we're already responsible for. Only one step past knowing."

"Rather more than a step, I think." Sylvia, chilly.

"You know," as if Ruth didn't hear, "there was a time when I assumed human nature had to be on an upswing, give or take the occasional genocide, the kind of mass insanity that causes a holocaust." She glances at Greta, then away; ordinarily she wouldn't make such a reference. "But mainly I figured that in the evolutionary nature of things, humans had to be improving. Now I can't imagine why I thought any such thing. Now I think, no, we know more—we can know practically anything we set out to learn—so in some ways we're smarter than, say, your average Neanderthal, but we're no better. And there's nothing better to look ahead to. There's no chance of a magic moment when people will realize they could stop causing grief, there'll just be the same old famines and slaughters and, okay, some rescues and acts of generosity here and there, on and on. Nothing, nothing at all, will ever be new, except perhaps in the details."

As if everyone is so wicked. What about goodness, the good acts people perform, their goodwill, is that nothing? Why, some people give their whole lives to goodness. Not Greta, of course, and not George or Sylvia, either. Maybe that's why Ruth thinks they'll help.

"So as I say, as you see, I'm just about done. Nearly out of steam. I'm not depressed in the ways doctors talk about, and I don't actively hate my life—in fact it's quite lovely much of the time, and even especially lovely these days, with a deadline coming up, as it were, and there's a great deal I'm fond of, including you three. I realize it's unusual to feel this is it, but I assure you, it isn't unique. I want to be clear, I wouldn't like any misunderstandings."

They're four people in a room; of course three of them aren't going to entirely hear what Ruth must think she is saying—how could she have spent a lifetime with other human beings and still, even now, not know that? Even a golfer, a bridge player, a board chair, much less a mother or a father, knows more about misunderstanding than that. Still, no point saying so if Ruth is as finished as she says, with no more to learn. "Tell me," Sylvia says instead, "did you cultivate Greta and George and me because you thought from the start we'd be likely candidates? Was there something when you first clapped eyes on us that made you say to yourself, *There's a bunch of killers, if ever I saw a bunch of killers?*"

Even with its morsel of truth, that's just crude. "If you remember," Ruth says, "we drifted into the lounge at roughly the same time that first week, no mystery about it, just serendipity. But now there's nobody else here I would trust to ask, and we've shown how we'll look after each other, as best we can."

Sylvia wasn't a lawyer's wife, or for that matter a lawyer's lover, for nothing. She wouldn't have minded being a lawyer herself, come to that. "So just to be straight, you're reasonably pleased with your days and your friends, you're not depressed, but you're discouraged by human nature, there are wars, lies and tortures, and enough carelessness and greed that the earth itself is on its last legs, and you can't see anything getting better, if anything only worse, and you've decided you're done, finished, ready to shuffle off this mortal coil altogether, preferably with our help and at least in our company, because even if just about everything else on earth is doomed, we are friends—is that a fair summary, do I have it right?"

Ruth frowns. How fierce Sylvia sounds. "More or less." Less, really.

"Then I'd have to say that's all a pretty big crock, wouldn't you?"

18

NOT AN IMPOSSIBLE ACT . . .

A CROCK. RUTH SMILES AT THEM, then stops smiling.

What a liar she is.

No, only an incomplete teller of truth; presumably a lesser form of fraud. Technically, catastrophe on every conceivable level should be sufficient, shouldn't it, to an aim which in that light might even be self-sacrificing and noble? *Noble*, however, is not one of the words springing so far to anyone's lips, nor, unfortunately, is *sufficient*.

So call it half a crock. The rest, the part Ruth has left out, is something else entirely.

The trouble, one trouble, with what she has not said is that words spoken aloud can be much like a foot placed slightly wrong, weight shifted slightly to one hip rather than both, one shoulder raised slightly higher than the other— she could easily send herself crashing. Even now, that would matter. She would like to leave, if possible, in fairly composed fashion, not flailing through air.

The most important thing in the end, any end, is to know a person has done the very best she knows how to, and could not have done more. At least twice, though, Ruth has allowed desire to overwhelm duty. Once was when she was very young and chose tumbling and vaulting over her parents' fears for her bones.

Bernard was her second. He can still send her flying.

When he knocked at her office door, she looked up from her desk to a pleasant-featured, medium-sized, round-faced, blue-eyed, blondish, freckly man, close to thirty, as she was herself. She was disinclined to welcome this new colleague, since she was disinclined to share her office. Certainly there was little sanctuary at home, where Ruth now cooked the suppers for her parents, watched TV in the evenings with them, played rounds of cribbage or hearts. She wasn't the only daughter in town who'd deferred life in the interests of parents (sons rarely deferred anything, and if they did, they tended, she thought, to be strange, pitiful men), and the tight tweedy lives of those daughters were not reassuring; were, in fact, as disheartening as just about any sadly mistreated child who might crop up in Ruth's work. "I feel bad you made such sacrifices for us," said her mother, and Ruth noted the past tense: case closed. She no longer spoke of someday returning to another life, having seen their fluttering panic, and tried not to dream of it, either.

Once, they'd been good at survival: a lesson in holding a portion of courage in reserve, since it seems the need for it arises at any time, right up to and including the end.

"Hi," Bernard said from her doorway. "I'm sorry about this. I bet the last thing you want is some stranger suddenly taking up half your space." She stopped frowning. "I hope you like coffee. I brought us both some, in hopes it'd make you think well of me anyway."

So it did, somewhat.

He too was to work with the fractured, but unlike her had deliberately sought out this small city after several years of doing similar work in a large one. When he spoke of the beauties he admired and looked forward to exploring in surrounding nature, the rivers, rocks, lakes, fields and woods of the region, she took him to be one of those naive urbanites who considered rocks merely romantic. When he said he figured opportunities would be greater here than "getting lost inside a bigger bureaucracy," she was relieved to hear hard-headed ambition. "There's more management layers back there," he told her, "which slows down the decisions, and you know, bad things can happen to kids while you're waiting."

Apparently one or two very bad things had happened, it wasn't just the splendours of rivers and woods that brought him to her door. Nor was it only an ambition to be in charge, although eventually he was, which by then was both more and less awkward than they might have supposed. Like Ruth, he was burdened in his work by single-mindedness. That toddler who'd been plunked on a hot stove-top by her mother's boyfriend?—Bernard was as fierce as Ruth, in agency meetings and in court, about keeping the child from being returned to what had passed for a home. She thought his fervency brave considering his ambitions—zealots don't get promoted—but when he was engaged in the fight for a child's well-being, his whole body seemed to rise up and sharpen, growing bony and tense, a dog on the scent transformed from roly-poly puppy to lean, hungry hound. To have this ally . . . Ruth began waking in her pink-wallpapered, white-trimmed childhood bedroom each morning keen to be up and out, trading cases and stories and coffees, giving advice, offering tactics. What had made her think she did not need help, and could go on unsupported?

Plus he asked how she was, what was new, how her parents were doing. He mentioned it when she got a haircut, or a new dress. He paid *attention*. He fell into her life like, oh, something hard and feathery both, and she found herself moving again like a gymnast, with a rediscovered once-upon-a-time, look-at-me grace.

Until out in the parking lot on a spring after-dark night, about to head home, Ruth to fragile parents, Bernard to solitary apartment, he caught at her hand instead of waving good-night, and pulled her closer, and bent, and they kissed.

She'd forgotten lips. She'd forgotten shoulders, a body. "Should we?" she asked nevertheless; was this wise, she meant, for two people working together?

"We should. Definitely we should."

With this, so simply and swiftly, she acquired brutality—the second time desire overwhelmed duty. "I'll be out," she told her parents as she settled them in the living room with the TV after dinner. "But I won't be late, don't worry." How, after all, could they stop her, those two little people?

As long as she didn't look in their faces, she was free, for a few hours, for regular life, the kind regular people conducted. She imagined this must be something like an animal—a chipmunk, a bear—emerging squinting and blinking out of dark hibernation into the light. Because in the company of Bernard, even this familiar town dazzled; something of a miracle. They went to movies and held hands and went afterwards to the customary Ritz on the main street for coffee or, in the backroom bar, for a drink. Bernard packed picnics and they drove to beaches and parks where, he said, he enjoyed hearing of Ruth as a child in those same unaltered places, with her since-much-altered mother and father. She showed him the side-by-side clothing stores they had once run, where she'd played among the long legs of customers. They walked around town in the evenings looking into open-draped windows, glimpsing lives, pausing on sidewalks to remark on people's choices in art, pointing out good taste, making fun of the bad. They talked about cases and work, and their histories and ambitions; about how they had been when they were young, and how they had changed. They cooked late-night meals together in Bernard's apartment. She picked up, and put down, photographs of him with his family: a mother, two older brothers, all living far away on the western edge of the country, and a father, already dead. "I left by leaving," Bernard told her, as if that was the only way it could have been done. He called his mother "a hard worker—well, she had to be." He didn't care for his brothers. Once he'd been engaged, "but we found we were too different. For one thing, she wouldn't move." For another, and another? He didn't say, and Ruth admired his reluctance to discuss that other woman's shortcomings. For her part, she could tell him she'd had three boyfriends, lovers, in her years away at university, but was free to be similarly close-mouthed on the details. Which anyway were long past and didn't matter.

His apartment was not only a location for food and talk. It was where they grew acquainted too with how well her body retained the powerful and flexible qualities of the gymnast, and how receptive his was to experiment and delight. How lightly the word *love* is thrown around. *I love your dress, I love spinach, I love my child.* Love is a radiation. It alters temperature, vision, every cell of the body.

Children weren't the only people whose lives Bernard saved.

They had their brief, unceremonious wedding within a year of her thirtieth birthday, Ruth in pastel pink suit, Bernard in then-modish charcoal.

And two mournful witnesses. "I'll come by every day, I promise," she told her mother and father when she and Bernard pooled their resources and bought their small house, "but we need our own home." At some point, *sauve qui peut,* as Sylvia no doubt would say.

A decade after his first, her father had another big heart attack, except this one killed him in a moment of sliding sideways in his recliner. Ruth thought—she thinks—what a reward and relief it must be to die in a sudden, unprepared instant. Like that, or in a head-on high-speed crash on the blind brow of a hill, with only a single last horrified thought; maybe just a single last horrified view, no requirement to rise, or not rise, to an occasion from which there is no possibility whatever of rescue. *Daddy,* Ruth thought at his funeral. Her father looked almost young; healthy, even. Ready to leap up and start his whole once-brave life all over again. What had happened to that? How she wept.

So did her mother. Who, no less helpless and lost as a widow, eventually moved in with Ruth and Bernard, who was more patient than Ruth always managed to be. Her mother got cancer—breast, then lung and liver—and went into hospital and finally died. Bernard embraced both the dying woman and Ruth. These aren't tendernesses that pass from the mind, they are not small, forgettable gestures. Sylvia, who of course knew Bernard, if only in passing, said once, hearing some of this, "He sounds quite the saint."

Ruth found her tone offensive. "He was a damned kind, smart man," she snapped. With his freckles, his soft flesh, his round face and good heart, Bernard, she could see, was not the type of man Sylvia would have been drawn to; nor prob-ably Greta. But men like Bernard try harder than those who can rely largely on their skin, bones and charm. "He was sexy, too," Ruth added. "Very creative and clever. Totally satisfying." Take that, Sylvia Lodge, connoisseur of bad and good men.

She would always be fierce on Bernard's behalf; as he would be on hers. A marriage is bound to be mysterious. Hers was certainly different from Greta's cut-short one, and Sylvia's come-and-go one, and who knows about George's? The point now is that from beginning to end, one way and another and by one person and another, Ruth has been luxu-riously, thoroughly loved. And she has repaid, if not per-fectly, as best she could, in as many ways as she could. And love is not an unmixed blessing. Its loss and absence can in some circumstances feel startlingly free, quite a relief.

What can she say, as Sylvia and Greta work away at the exercising of George's limbs, pushing and pulling, so they'll *feel* Bernard? Without dangerously feeling too much herself, can she make plain any of the thousands of individual moments of joy? Can she speak about the smooth skimming of her hand over his body, soft as skin cream? Of the deli-cious, remarkable splendour of the rising penis, which any-way they must know? Of tracing moles—two close together

high on his left breast, three on his shoulder blades, one
on his left buttock, round and readable as Braille—and of
adding up a confetti of freckles scattered top to toe, back and
front, infinitely uncountable? How about the two of them
after a hard winter storm, out shovelling the driveway
together, lifting and lowering, lifting and lowering, growing
warm and humid under their woolly hats and puffed jackets,
pausing, laughing, taking each other's hands and throwing
themselves backwards into the snow, creating a single
multi-armed, multi-legged angel? Or Saturday afternoons in
the kitchen together—how he enjoyed food, how securely
stocky he grew—making salad dressings and pickles, mixing
cookies, baking a cake? Sunday mornings in bed?

Or weekdays in the hard labour of salvaging children?
When Bernard became her supervisor at work, things were
sometimes tricky between them, with some matters they
each couldn't discuss—a difficulty she might have with a
colleague, a budget dilemma that had to stay at his desk, and
of course there was the particular care to be always profes-
sional on the job. Bernard used to say, though, to everyone,
not just to her, "Our job is the kids. If we keep our eyes on
that ball, it's hard to go wrong." Mistakes might get made,
but he meant that they shouldn't be made for wrong reasons
like office politics or bad moods or personal problems or lazy
days. It was always "consider the kids."

Greta asked once, in that context, "But did he also not
want to have children?" apparently never supposing that was
a very rude question.

If Greta hadn't had children, she would probably have
gone back home to her family when her husband was killed,
and then she'd have had an incomprehensibly different life

and would now be an ocean away from the Idyll Inn. It really doesn't do to imagine alternative lives. "We liked what we had," Ruth told her. "Remember, we were in our thirties when we got married. Obviously that's not too late to start a family, but by then we didn't want to mess up what we'd finally found. Our own families weren't entirely happy, and we wanted to do what *we* wanted, not have to look after anyone else any more."

A blessing still. How can parents, grandparents—Sylvia, Greta and George—not be in a pure panic when fresh catastrophes arise all the time, and unforeseen dangers; when antes keep getting upped, further extraordinary shocks and deprivations soon lie ahead, and who wants to leave loved ones living on into all that destruction and turmoil?

Who wants to live into all that destruction and turmoil themselves?

Ruth tried that argument, and Sylvia called her bluff. A *crock*, as she put it. Although it's not; not entirely. But Ruth sees that before they're done, she's going to have to dive right to the bottom of the pool. Well, she knew that. It's a deep one. Might as well be now.

"You know one thing I miss? The aftershave Bernard wore, from the first day he appeared in my office till almost the end of his life. I'm glad nobody here wears it. I'd hate to smell it on anyone else." She's susceptible to scents anyway. If she concentrates, her mother's bath powder can be resurrected as a floweriness trailing through evenings. Or there's the city-stink, sharp and metallic—the smell of freedom— when she and Bernard took off for a weekend. The tang of warm flesh, too, in the night—oh, that can still make her reach out.

One of the risks of remembering. There are larger ones.

They had six, almost seven, precious post-retirement, pre-cancer years. Some couples find it difficult to be suddenly around the clock in each other's company, but she and Bernard were accustomed to that. The only shock was in absence: of schedule and duty, of colleagues, of children—the whole great weight of care. Bernard took up gardening, which Ruth was pleased to admire. Her osteo, growing worse and more painful, made it difficult to travel far, but now and then on a morning whim they could take off in the car for a day of galleries, museums, streets elsewhere. Their excursions had to be modest, given the small pensions earned by those who try to do something good. "Maybe in our next life," Bernard joked, "we'll get to a few of the exotic spots on the planet." They had their magazines and newspapers and books. "Listen to this," they said, any hour, any day, "Look at that."

It's possible she romanticizes life with Bernard, making the best of their times. No harm done if so, surely? Or as Sylvia says, "Memories—entirely portable, and they don't cost a dime."

Or they may cost a great deal.

When Ruth said, months ago, "Cancer," she knew that Greta and even George, but particularly Sylvia, would understand that she was saying, and not saying, that Bernard died hard. That day by day he diminished, grew gaunt and exhausted, until he didn't look like who he was any more. He went bald, of course, which was no great loss, and three times called Ruth "Mommy," which was. Ruth sat with him, sang to him, talked to him, turned him, massaged his strange, thin new skin with unaffordable creams, fed him as best she could, loved, cherished and obeyed him just as well as she could.

Lucy, his oncologist, having promised that these days pain could almost always be kept at manageable levels, stepped him up, up, up from one drug to the next, reaching eventually what she called "a kind of meta-morphine." Of course there were losses under the influence. "Some aware-ness goes," Lucy admitted. "Some degree of comprehension of what's real and what's not. But the goal is to not suffer." As if distortion and unreliability of perception were not themselves a form of suffering. Moreover, they cost time just as time became a most urgent commodity.

On good evenings Ruth perched beside him in bed feed-ing him small sips of Scotch, for which he retained an unlikely tolerance. "You shouldn't mix alcohol with these drugs," Lucy warned, but who on earth cared? What possible grim difference could a few sips of Scotch make? Doctors were funny. Ruth told Lucy so, and Lucy winced, shrugged and then also laughed.

But here's what Ruth has to say now, more foolhardy than any high-flying with rings and uneven bars. "In the end, I sped him on his way. It was simple, and it was hard, but I did it."

Instantly she feels the oxygen departing the room in one big, fast whoosh. *Oh,* say three silent mouths.

Life, it seems, never runs out of shoes to drop. Suddenly, if they've understood her correctly, Ruth is as extreme in her way as a terrorist; certainly as Art Fletcher with his two whirling knives.

Has she gone too far? Trust grows at its own pace; it's rather like cancer that way. "He asked me, if I loved him, to help. He begged. I could see death was coming, but so cruelly. There was nothing that could ever help him again, except me. So I did. And I can't be sorry, except for not being quicker about it. But once I got up my courage, well, I still believe the very best I could do, and *did* do, was to love him to death."

Everyone is so still, so gaping. "Honestly, George," she says, because he looks, or half of him looks, more appalled, or perhaps frightened, than the others, but more because the moment needs lightening and that has to be up to her, "don't worry, it isn't a habit, it's not going to be catching."

Oh, ha ha ha again, and that's not it. It's that never mind how frustrated and unhappy and angry or even confused or teary he gets, never mind how he longs, and on a strong day still aims, to be restored as a man who can do any damned thing he wants, and never mind that he keeps falling short and once fell right over, George refuses *dead*. People die—how many funerals has he been to?—but "Life," he says loudly; meaning urgent necessity, the very opposite of unthinkable absence.

Good news stories, not only terrible ones.

"I know, but there it is. But I'm sorry to have upset you."

Upset. How mild. Sylvia is dumbfounded; she stares—who would not stare?—and what she sees is a strain and stretch in Ruth's face that maybe comes not only from the bravely borne, persistent pains of osteo, but from the act behind this extraordinary confession.

Then what strain of secrecy does Sylvia's own face contain?

But perhaps she's making things up, now that she knows what she's looking at.

There's Jackson fading and failing, although toward the end in the hospital and not in her hands. "How?"

"He was very weak." No, Ruth will not weep. She can feel weeping, though, in the fragility of her hands when they had to be strong, the ache in her back, the anguish of her straightened arms resisting resistance. "I took a pillow, and I smothered him. It's a method that isn't always unkind."

Any air that's begun seeping back whooshes again out of the room: a sick, frail man held down, this little gnarled woman bending over him with a pillow—one whisked from under his head? With or without pillowcase? George starts to cough, something's caught in his throat, and he can't stop till Greta pounds his back lightly, then moves her hand in circles a few times as if gentling a baby. When he's calm, she sits on his sofa, behind Ruth still perched on his coffee table, and reaches for her knitting—maybe it looks bad but she *needs* this—and *click, click, click*, the tiny, slow, percussive sound, which some days is as maddening as jackhammering, grows into the rhythm of breathing. Which they are all doing still, in and out, in and out; and are aware of doing, which of course isn't always the case. "Treatment?" she asks. "Were there not more ways to be tried?"

Again it's probably only Greta's sometimes clumsy use of language that causes this to sound like a reproach: as if Ruth and Bernard didn't bother putting enough effort into saving his life. For all of them, not just Ruth, these must be heightened, prickly moments. "Yes, he went through the whole smorgasbord, but it didn't work, and Lucy was wrong about the pain, and he didn't deserve that. Nobody does.

"It's what he asked for, and he only had me, and it still seems to me that the least a person can do, and sometimes the most, too, is just exactly what someone else wants."

Surely it's more complicated than that.

"Please, I'm counting on you all to not tell a soul."

What's done is done, and they do look after each other, when that's possible. No one else will, not day after day, voluntarily and not as a job. "Of course," Sylvia says.

"Thank you. I hope you understand that I haven't told you out of some kind of guilt I can't bear. I've told you because I want you to know it's not an impossible act. I realize you couldn't do it for my reasons, for love of someone in Bernard's sort of misery, but you know, maybe from affection? Respect?"

No one has an answer to that. "I think," Sylvia says finally, "we can at least guarantee we'll be thinking about it."

Will they, won't they, will she, won't she—never mind that it's still summer, how chilly Ruth feels. And yet she hasn't, after all, lost her balance, she hasn't fallen or flailed. That's good to know.

On a black unstarred night, sharp and shocking headlights shoot over the rise of a hill. Sudden and merciful. Can she do this? Ruth thinks so. Just another heart-lifting grief; also good to know.

19

AT THREE IN THE MORNING . . .

DRESS FOR THE MIDDLE OF THE NIGHT in an Idyll Inn corridor is necessarily informal. Pyjamas, nightgowns, robes, fuzzy pastel slippers and plaid hard-soled ones may not rise properly to the occasion, but like fatigues on a battlefield, nightwear is good camouflage.

If discovered, they're at least in unsuspicious, appropriate uniform, and if undiscovered, they're at least comfortable.

Robes have pockets, too, which are handy.

Considerably less relaxed than their clothing is what's going on inside. Three busy hearts leap and bang. Legs are wobbly, hands a bit shaky, flesh feels fragile. These pyjamas, nightgowns, slippers and robes are warm, but the skin beneath is unfairly goosebumpy, shivery.

They are exceptionally alert to how warm, precious and vulnerable a body can be; and how quickly it can be none of those things. This is a mystery, although not one they're likely to solve. It's magic, too, although none of them would say at the moment that it feels like magic of any good kind.

Just abracadabra: now you see, now you don't.

20

WHAT FRIENDS DO . . .

*W*HAT RUTH WANTS: "My time, my place, my way."

And who wouldn't like that, but in the statistical scheme of things what are the odds of a made-to-measure leave-taking? Some people die in plane crashes, some from gunshots, some of disease, some falling downstairs, some of exhaustion or hunger, some tidily of old age in their sleep— who's to know? Who does Ruth think she is?

She thinks she is someone who has decided that *my time* will be her seventy-fifth birthday, now four long, very short months off, "a pre-dawn celebration, only without candles and singing"; *my place* will be her own Idyll Inn suite; *my way* swift suffocation, with the aid of a little minor equipment, at the hands of her friends.

She admits the timing is pure sentimentality, the location for optimum convenience, the method merciful as can be. Well, she's the expert. "Bernard and I made do with what was at hand, but I've had lots of time since to do more research, and it turns out I was more or less right in the first place." So she says.

"There's no way that's both easy and foolproof"—is she calling them fools?—"but I've looked into the options. My birthday's in December, so if the weather co-operated, I could sneak outside and lie down to freeze in a snowbank. I understand it's not a terribly uncomfortable way to go, at least not after the first while, but it strikes me as, oh, too desolate. Plus, there's that first while. Or unco-operative weather, no snow.

"You'd think an overdose would be peaceful and reliable, but apparently drugs are hard to calculate, never mind that it'd be hard to get my hands on the right kinds and amounts, and I wouldn't want to harm a doctor's career. In any event, it sounds very easy to go wrong and wind up sick or brain-damaged or crippled. More so"—she smiles—"than I already am. Crippled, I mean, not brain-damaged. I don't think I'm that."

Something must be wrong with her head, though. "I see your eyebrows, Sylvia. Nice of you not to say what you were just thinking."

It was, wasn't it?

"I couldn't possibly manage to hang myself, and you couldn't help—even professionals with all the right equipment seem to botch hangings. If we had bathtubs in our suites instead of showers, I could slide into a bath and slit my wrists—I gather really hot water dulls pain and makes blood flow faster, and then, too, a tub contains the mess. Otherwise some poor soul gets stuck with a nasty cleanup, which is just selfish and rude. But the therapy tub here is always either locked or supervised, so that's out.

"A gun makes a big mess, too, even if I could handle one, or even get my hands on one—it's not as if I could add a pistol and ammunition to Diane's shopping list. So it turns out that the best way is only a few steps away from what happened—what I did—with Bernard. For him." She cannot say *to Bernard*, since he had his own desperate voice in the act. She cannot also reasonably say it *happened*, as if there were no agent involved.

"It's practical, and surprisingly quick and apparently merciful. As I said, I've read about people doing it for themselves, but I can't get my arms up high enough, and if I could, my hands are too fumbly. But it'd be smooth enough with your help. Basically all it takes is a plastic bag, and just to make it easiest for everyone, some tape. Oh, and scissors for cutting everything away afterward. And that's it."

"Homey items."

"Exactly. Things any of us might easily have lying around."

Now comes the deep breath, and the hard, real part.

"The plastic bag goes over the head, the tape gets wrapped around the neck, and in a very short time that's it. Maybe only a few seconds, since I'm not very strong." Ruth means that despite her best intentions, her body could well lash out automatically in its own defence. Bernard's—but that's nothing she thinks about. "You'd have to be, though. Strong, I mean."

This is unspeakable. Although it seems that it's not.

"It's also a method that's not likely to be noticed. So nobody'd be in trouble, believe me, I know. You'd snip the tape free and whisk the plastic away and that'd be that." Well, not quite. There'd be the morning to face.

Not for Ruth.

"And who else could I ask?"

Who indeed? Isn't that sad, that she only has them.

Except, in the unlikely event that Sylvia, Greta or George came to such a decision, who could they ask? At the best of times children have limits. As far as George can see, Colette has neither the time nor the will for grand acts of engagement, much less for something like this. Greta's girls are too tender-hearted toward her, and too respectful, and Greta would be too tender-hearted and respectful toward them to ask. Only Sylvia's Nancy might come through for her mother, but then it'd be for distinctly wrong reasons. And Sylvia too wouldn't ask, not altogether from pride, but because there'd have been no point keeping certain information from Nancy all these years, then requesting of her something even more shattering. Ruth can be brutal about this if she wants; a mother, even Sylvia, really cannot.

Still, every life, and every death too, should have a witness. Not everyone gets that. Maybe it's lonely to be Ruth, with no one but them to ask her great favour of, but it seems that in her place, with her desire, they'd be just as alone.

"I expect it sounds pretty strange," Ruth says, "but finally discussing it makes me feel lighter. Not insubstantial, but light." There's no arguing with that, is there, no logic to weigh against lightness? Nevertheless. There have to be limits to what one person can ask of another, as well as to what any person will do. What they need to figure out, and this is most unexpectedly interesting, is exactly where their limits, separately and together, will lie.

Ruth waits, Greta knits, George half-frowns, Sylvia looks almost angry. But they still have four long, very short months, so—they will see.

21

WALKING DOWNSTAIRS IN THE DARK . . .

*I*T'S SAFE TO SAY NOBODY LOOKS AT RUTH quite the same way any more. George is leery— although pleased by the word *leery* returning out of the blue—because never mind she made that crack about killing not being a habit, and never mind she's the one who kicked off his rescue when he took that topple—if she got it into her head to do him harm, who knows where it might end?

Not that she would, that's a crazy idea; but even so, there are times when the others are busy or out and Ruth suggests wheeling him around to the dining room for an afternoon concert—it's not so comfortable any more knowing she's right there pushing, behind him.

Other than that, he's going to flat refuse to think about what she's been talking about. It's beyond him, and anyway, if he hasn't done it to Alice—for Alice—why would he help do it to—for—a woman he's only known a few months?

He could have done it. When Alice, brain being ravaged, memory blasted, begged for help back when she still had the words, he supposed what she wanted was to be freed and restored, which was out of the question. Even if most days hope is hard, though, and some days impossible, it doesn't mean anybody wants a pillow mashed down over their face, does it?

How about if they were reversed, would sweet-faced Alice be sitting here confessing to putting him out of his misery? Not much is impossible in women's hearts, and vengeful women have long, detailed memories; except, as with Alice, when they have no memories at all.

When Colette was here—when? A long time ago, wasn't it?—and visited her mother, she reported that "Mom hardly ever gets out of bed any more. She doesn't even know who I am. It's just tragic." He could see she'd been crying. When she asked why he didn't go to see Alice, and he said just "Too hard," she frowned, but he meant any number of things he couldn't put into words, including but not limited to the real horror of what a once-familiar, mostly gentle human can come to. Alice's absence wipes out decades. She's immune to every moment of their lives, good and bad. She takes the ground of history right out from under him. "Too hard," he said, and Colette had such a look.

He could sit beside Alice. He could even hold her papery little limp hands and say anything.

But moods come and go. Feelings and impulses. Same with Ruth, probably. Hopefully.

It would be ludicrous to be frightened of Ruth, but to be honest, Sylvia is also uneasy. True, Ruth didn't precisely cause her husband's death, that was the cancer, but she sped him along, she did do him in. Someone she claims to have loved that much. With her own two hands, and without leaving a clue—Sylvia catches herself staring at Ruth's small sedate fingers holding a newspaper or a cookie or teacup and—imagine!

Sylvia regards her own hands: longer-fingered but gnarled, wrists and knuckles lumpy and ugly. Ruth's desperate circumstances—her husband's desperate circumstances— are sadly common; one view might be that Ruth, unlike most people, simply rose uncommonly to the occasion. Whether because Sylvia cared for Jackson too much or because her care was insufficient, she was not so brave. On the other hand, who knows exactly what a man means when he's crying out for the blessing of *help?* Or whom he's addressing? Ruth may have misinterpreted. Or Sylvia did. Or they both did, or neither.

In any case, if what's done is done, equally what's not done remains undone forever.

By the end, Jackson's hands in hers were so birdlike that they caused no distress at all to her swollen ones. He drifted away but it was no peaceful push-off from shore, and if he was waving, it was a frantic semaphore and she only waved back, didn't offer even a rope.

People don't offer ropes and rescue. Who would dare?

Ruth would.

At his funeral Sylvia kept her grief to herself. It was nobody's business. Anyway, Nancy made enough of a fool of herself for two people; might as well have been naked, with all the wailing and weeping. For the wrong father, of course.

Or not.

"Aren't you sorry at all?" Nancy demanded.

"Of course I am. He was a very good man." Sylvia could have said the word *love*, more than true, but did not. Like

tears, that was private. Nancy considers her mother unsenti-
mental and cold, and how would she know otherwise? No
wonder she chose a career as a trainer, working with bodies,
when she can have so little knowledge of hearts.

But how arrogant. What Sylvia really knows about her
daughter, a middle-aged woman conducting a life all her
own, is pathetically limited. And look at Ruth, for heaven's
sake—even someone seen daily, never mind Nancy, still
contains deep, unrecognizable pockets of mystery.

Sylvia herself does. Everyone must.

What might Jackson's have been? There are moments
when Sylvia is furious with Ruth. She would prefer not having these thoughts.

Still. Since she is having them, she's dying to chew them
over, hear what outsiders might have to say. Why not bring
up over bridge Ruth's history, and her desire? Without Ruth's
name, of course. Bridge is a smart game, and Sylvia's bridge
friends are not dim-witted, so they might not have stupid
reactions.

Or they might. Just as likely as an interesting discussion
of rights and duties when it comes to staying alive would be
a round of tightened lips to do not with cards, or even the
subject at hand, but with Sylvia having put herself in a place
where such a dismal form of madness can arise.

Sylvia still heads out doggedly to her long-standing
weekly bridge games with her long-standing bridge friends,
mostly widows like herself now, with their own sedately
tucked away tales. They are no longer the wives-of they
once were: wife of doctor, wife of high school principal; an
exception soft plump Mabel, whose parents owned the land
and buildings of a good many downtown businesses, and

raised her to a kind of creative idleness that kept her at home gardening and doing watercolours and reading and, yes, bridge-playing until they died and she kept right on the same way because, she told Sylvia happily, "It's such a nice life and I thoroughly enjoy it, so why should I go out and try to make it hard for myself?" A relaxed and somewhat enviable point of view.

Many friendships, it appears, are surprisingly circumstantial. No doubt the ones here are, too. Now that Sylvia has ensconced herself at the Idyll Inn, former connections stretch like elastic, like taffy, and even Mabel, previously so pleasingly impressed and easily amused, has taken on a thin air of superiority. Sylvia's own fault—she shouldn't have told the buttery story of Amy Perry and her arthritis cure, which, instead of being an entertaining anecdote about a retired librarian they all used to know, was heard as a downhill-skidding reflection of Sylvia's own alien circumstance. She knew better, then, than to mention Art Fletcher and his two knives. So of course she can't now talk about Ruth, even unnamed. Anyway, if she blabbed, so would whoever she blabbed to, and so on and so forth, until word inevitably returned to the Idyll Inn, to Annabel Walker, to trouble.

Well, bugger them. It seems that sometimes she doesn't especially like her old friends any more. Causing the diverting question to arise: can people still reasonably be called friends if a person no longer much likes them?

Loyalties shift, nothing new about that. And if she can keep her own gravest secret, she'll keep Ruth's if it kills her.

Funny, that. *Ha ha ha,* as George would bitterly say.

Greta too is thinking not only of Ruth but of George. What she thinks is that what followed him was so shameful that anyone, not least her Idyll Inn friends, would think worse of her than they ever could about Ruth: either what Ruth has done or what she wants done.

That it's funny, meaning strange, what is respectable—*respectable: honest and decent, having the qualities of fair social standing*—and what is irredeemable—*irredeemable: hopeless, absolute*, even if nothing is fatal.

That there is something very large about Ruth, and nothing like that at all about the fact that for Greta, when George ended, the ABC Motel did not.

She still even has a few pieces of jewellery from those days, although they are not real jewels except for that silver bracelet engraved with vines that meet at the intersection of two tiny diamonds. That was from an actual jeweller, which accounts for its semblance of quality.

The ABC with its musty carpetings and dusty pink walls and cheap blankets and the mildew around its windows, and the linens about which it was best not to think, its *seediness*—for much too long the damp, faintly rotting smell of ABC rooms signified to Greta pleasure and comfort. She finds it hard to picture Sylvia in that place, but she too knows it; even once, in the absence of George, made a joke: "It should be more widely understood that going to a substandard place means you're very likely with a substandard man." Although adding, "Sorry, Greta, I'm not saying George was substandard." And then laughing. "Necessarily."

But even Sylvia, who already makes now and then a sharp remark about Ruth's situation, would not be able, Greta believes, to make any joke about what followed George.

Those years, they are like walking downstairs in the dark: from luscious—*luscious: richly sweet in taste or smell*—

golden, hard-working Dolph to handsome, tender, weak George; then losing her footing and taking a tumble-tumble-tumble all the way to the crash and shock of the bottom.

Sometimes memory is blinding, like looking at the sun—best to keep moving, the head down, the eyes shaded. Greta supposes that this is why Sylvia speaks as she sometimes does, as her way of protecting the eyes. Greta too has practised this method and gift, but it must be that sometimes the unshaded eye, all on its own, turns toward light.

She had never, before the after-George time, lived with no other human around. There were mother and father, sisters and brothers, all that left-behind, out-of-mind noise and need of a household trying to be careful, safe and alive in turmoil and war. Then came the beauty of Dolph, and the over-the-ocean journey out of history toward the new and promising and not dangerous, and there were the girls, and all the noise and need of that household.

And then there was George.

And then there was not. All was finished, and it was scarcely bearable to go home after work, with the girls gone and no prospect of George again dropping in and out, coming and going. No matter that he was not, after all, any true measure of what they had called, for want of a better word, love. Skin was the object; skin and sound. In her apartment in the evenings, absent the very breathing of others, there were only her own sounds, specific and solitary, and what was she to do with her empty arms for the empty years of the empty rest of her life?

If she was angry with George for anything, it was for silence.

What people say about hearts being broken sounds like something romantic, but it is true: it is possible to have a heart that finally cannot be restored, and what is that if not broken?

Mourn and function at the same time, grieve and cope; she learned that from Dolph. Crack-hearted or not, a person must go about in the world, one hard step, then another. Only Ruth could think otherwise.

The first time Greta stepped into the Ritz restaurant on the main street after work was as brave as her first Idyll Inn foray—*foray: attack, raid or incursion*—beginning her way, once again, into the friendly or unfriendly unknown.

Many people went to the Ritz as businesses and offices shut for the day and for a few hours it became a community of downtowners. In the big bright restaurant room at the front, people gathered in red-cushioned booths for coffee, and teenagers, on their way to and from school and dances and movies, for fries, burgers and pop, as Sally, Emily and Patricia had each done, in the growing-up years before they left home.

And the Ritz had also a darker room at the back, with round wooden tables and wooden armchairs and brown panelling and a more becoming, dim light, which some people moved to for an hour or two or an evening of recovering from their days. A legal secretary who had consulted Greta at Alf Stryker's drugstore over blush and mascara invited Greta to join her in that room for a cocktail. The lawyer who employed the secretary arrived later for an after-work drink, the manager of the hardware store had business with the lawyer, a plumber had a question for the hardware store manager, a florist took advantage of the plumber's presence to ask about new methods of keeping his stock of domestic and foreign flowers refreshed—there at the Ritz, in its back room, it unfolded, were many men, those casually betraying creatures, who would buy Greta drinks, treat and compliment her.

Later they would stroke her like a rare cat.

Much in life can be explained. There are always reasons, recent or distant. In the end, however, it is unimportant whatever are the causes of mistakes and regrets. What remain are the mistakes and regrets, just themselves.

Lawyers—there were several, could one have been Sylvia's husband, another her lover? Surely not—a lawyer might be gifted with words, a plumber with hands, the jeweller with a secret desperate sentiment of his own; and was Greta not a woman still in her forties, with muscular legs, and luxurious hair when unpinned, and a body that was all lavish breasts and broad hips? Was her skin not still firm, were her eyes not clear blue and, most to the point, was her painful desire to be touched, and to touch, not profound?

Were there not more men than George, than even Dolph, who might love her?

Yes, yes, yes; but no.

In discreet, whispered moments plans were made, encounters plotted. Out at the grubby ABC Motel, Greta's hips proved capable of remarkable feats, her breasts demonstrated minds of their own, her legs shaped themselves into forms of amazement. All of this *thrilling*, all *delicious*.

These men, too, for these moments, helpless with wanting.

Not every man lived up to his promise, not all were appealing unclothed, not all were sufficiently sober or tender. A disheartening number were overcome by sorrow or guilt once they were done. They were all warm, though, and some were grateful. Thus a number of trinkets, including the silvery bracelet with its two tiny diamonds.

How many were there? A haze and a blur of chests, mouths, thrashing limbs. A kind of madness and fever, a time of profligacy—*profligacy: given up to dissipation and licentiousness*; not a kind, admirable word, but better than promiscuity: *miscellaneous mingling, casual, cheapened*, a word aimed, weapon-like, only at women. At her and her frantic longing to be not alone. Touch, sweat, voice, *contact*—all that was solace of sorts.

At the ABC, with its pleasures and awkwardnesses and shufflings and low-voiced dexterities, she was no one's mother or widow or clerk or, for that matter, true lover.

Still, eventually she had to go home every night. These were not men without obligations.

At home, there was no longer so much silence; instead a nervous buzzing of fear, a sizzle of wonderment: why was she doing what, once done, felt so anxious, why was she risking, what was the pleasure? Also, what if she was found out and talked about, and women, wives, spat at her in the street, or refused any more to shop at Alf Stryker's drugstore? There is more than one way to be a foreigner in a town. And if the girls heard—this too could happen, during one of their weekends visiting home. Many times Greta woke before dawn, eyes wide, sure she could not have been doing what she had been doing, determined she would not again—and then, like an addict drawn to needle or pipe, there she would be once more, twice more, many times more, falling into a soft ABC bed, a not entirely strange man's desiring hands anywhere that he pleased.

Hers too.

Nothing like Ruth, using her honourable, unashamed hands on one man.

A lawyer, plumber, real estate agent, electrician, hardware store owner—someone—rose from an ABC bed late one evening, and like an addict stopped cold by an unexpected, illuminating view of needle or pipe, Greta saw abruptly and with perfect clarity, even in the pink-shaded light of the bedside lamp, a crumpled-skinned man with small eyes and loose shanks and a pot-belly, a man of no consequence or beauty whatever. A man now in a hurry to shower—they all showered before going wherever they went, to their wives and their children and houses. And she turned cold. Her skin rose in goosebumps.

Home, she turned on every light. Now she was hot, and understood the words *burning with shame*. Patricia chose that moment to phone. "What's new, Mum?" she asked brightly. Greta scrubbed herself in the shower, then in a bath, lying in the tub feeling the water change around her from scalding to cool. So: the fever was broken.

Although she hopes he does not, George may know anyway. Men say things to each other; they are boastful. No doubt it is unkind to wish that if he ever heard rumours and stories, they were exploded from his mind by his stroke. Probably they were. He would have said some words by now if he knew, if he remembered. He does not often hesitate any more to be hurtful, or truthful. He would, she imagines, speak to her, if he spoke to her at all, as if in some way she had betrayed him, instead of the other way around.

Ruth and Sylvia too, they are women, they were married, and even Sylvia had only one lover. They would despise not a portion of Greta's long life, but Greta herself. So she supposes. But Sylvia is right that histories are well buried under decrepitudes—*decrepit: weakened or worn out by age and infirmity;* perhaps for Greta also under the knitting of scarves. In many ways, which may be good ways, they are not visible to even each other. Ruth and Sylvia, possibly George too, may think her placid, a good mother, and kind. As she is. But these are qualities that might cause them to think she is not very smart, and has not done more than she has already told.

Is it like that for them?

Not for Ruth; Ruth cannot have done more or worse than she has already told.

Companions gained late in life have not been *present.* They must take each other only on grounds of what is recounted, and then how they feel the balance and fit. Here at the Idyll Inn people see each other, as best they can without ghosts.

Without too many ghosts.

There is . . . Ruth calls it *serendipity.* There is also knowledge of what matters and what does not. Flagrant use of the body, Greta believes, that would still matter. That is why it is shameful.

Is it sin, also? Do sins not have to be shameful? Is what Ruth did a sin if she is not ashamed? Is what Ruth wants a sin if she is not ashamed, but Greta, George and Sylvia could be if they did as she asks?

Would they be ashamed? A secret is not always the same as a sin; shame, even a secret one, might not be sin either. It is a confusing language, this one, with too many delicate, difficult shadings. This is why Greta is sometimes awkward with words, which she understands is another reason she might be mistaken for someone not smart.

It is why, also, she prefers knitting in bold, clear colours, even if they are not always so pretty together. Something must be plain and straightforward. Warming, too. As if shame and sin can be tucked beneath a bright, plain, straightforward blanket of forgiveness and mercy, which, if Greta were a god and had such powers, like any good mother, she would make it be so.

22

GOD CROPS UP . . .

*G*OD CROPS UP.

Well, in the circumstances he has to, although ordinarily they'd be skittish about talk of religion. Political discussions aren't terribly difficult despite relatively minor ideological differences—at least nobody favours brutal dictatorships and everyone more or less favours freedom—and a couple of sexual revelations have come readily enough, albeit within strict private limits, but there's nothing like religion for revealing unnecessary, undesirable schisms. So generally speaking, it's a subject best skipped over in the cosy interests of calm.

It's not as if any of them has been among those regularly, and possibly fervently, climbing aboard the Idyll Inn van to head to various places of worship around town, which must be an unspoken sign of something right there. Now, though, skittish or not, matters of faith and belief have a direct bearing. There are certain prohibitions and punishments to consider, and as far as they know, no equivalent promised rewards, for fatally helping a friend.

Since Ruth's basically to blame, she feels responsible for finally raising the subject. This is made easier by the newspapers at hand in George's room on this September Wednesday morning, with Greta and Sylvia poised to launch themselves at George's limbs. Ruth never has a problem finding two usefully unpleasant stories to read them each day, and it's not much harder narrowing the unhappy field to this specific one. God may, as usual, be technically absent from the news, but religion is not.

"Okay," Ruth says, "listen to this." Three truckers have just blown themselves up in a village, wiping out dozens of people, mutilating hundreds of others. The villagers' obscure faith is evidently different from their country's main religion, some of whose members have taken radical offence. "Among other things," Ruth recounts, "the people in the little sect that got blown up don't believe in evil or hell. Or at least they didn't until yesterday. Now maybe they do."

She finds further potential in the business pages. "Here's a company that only hires what the owner thinks of as Christians. They all sing hymns at the start of each workday, and pray at the end. He says it's important to him that everybody believes the same way he does, so everybody has the same goals. God hears more clearly when prayers come from a whole bunch of people, and he says God is pleased by their faith and rewards him with profits. Apparently there are more and more companies operating that way, on those grounds."

"My God," Sylvia says. Then leans back from her ministrations to George's left arm and laughs. "My God," she repeats.

"Indeed," says Ruth. "My God." Then: "You know, I wasn't raised religious at all. In fact, my father had a bitter sort of joke when I was young. He'd say, 'If we're the chosen people, I wonder who we could tell we'd just as soon not be chosen?' He'd say, 'We've already had quite enough of God's attention, thank you.' Which was bold of him in a way. That was long before he wasn't bold any more.

"But the stories were a different matter. My parents were attached to those and made sure I knew them. My own name was a favourite—they probably thought *Ruth* would result in an unusually loyal daughter, which was clever of them. And I remember being absolutely horrified by the Abraham story—I've even wondered if I chose my work partly because of him. That he would agree to slaughter his little boy to prove himself to a god who could even dream of demanding such a thing, and never mind rescinding the order at the last minute—even when I was a kid I thought, there's a god who's just power-mad and sadistic. Exactly the kind of parents, God and Abraham both, who shouldn't have children, and if they do, they're just begging to have them taken away."

There. If there are any especially vehement views in the room, that should lure them into the open. But Sylvia just suggests mildly, "Moody types?"

"At best, moody. These days they'd both be in for years of therapy, and on pretty strong meds to boot." Even if laughter is of the cautious *Just kidding, God* variety, it's an encouraging sound. "What about you, would any of you have religious hesitations?"

About her desire, Ruth must mean. But—*hesitations?* Hesitation's the least of it. In wedding ceremonies, there's the part where observers are invited to speak up if they know of an impediment to the joining up of two souls. "Is this an inside-out version of that?" Sylvia asks. "Whether we see impediments to the unjoining of one soul?"

That is clumsy and scarcely amusing. Greta is not so brittle. "I grew up in a church," she offers. "Not a fancy one, only small. As," and she glances at Ruth, "our village was small, and far from where important events were decided."

Every Sunday they went to the plain, square-built wooden building, Greta and her parents and sisters and brothers almost filling a pew. Later it was where she and Dolph married. Scents of wool suits and print dresses, the smoke of candles, these rise hotly up. Also a picture of an elderly god—her age now?—observing from far above, and all the time judging. Frowning. "This is childish, I know, but pictures from childhood, they stay in the mind."

Two opposing things happen now: Greta's eyes narrow fiercely, but her shoulders drop, and she lets go of George's right arm. "Then Dolph died," she says, as if these are the only words needed, although they are not. "I asked over and over why this should be, how a god could do this, so heartless and cruel. There was a great noise in my ears and I could not hear an answer. And then I thought, How could there be a good answer? I was taught God is stern but always just, and that we cannot always see his greater purposes but must trust in him. Trust that Dolph died, and so badly, for a just reason with larger purpose? No. No. So I understand then either a god is not there and I have cried out to no one, or he does not care anything for us, and we are like my girls' dolls, which some days are cherished and other days broken. And finally I think, whatever is the answer to this, it does not matter. Because I do not forgive."

Those last words are steel. This is a great surprise: their even-keeled, no-conflict, knit-onward Greta doing battle with God? Saving her wrath for the very big leagues? That's impressive. "And yet the first pictures—I see sometimes meeting in heaven with all my family. And Dolph, even though it is a long time and he was so young and I am so changed, how would he know me?" She shrugs. "But I do not think any more that those pictures are true."

"Heaven," Sylvia inquires, "as family reunion?"

She sounds teasing, but Greta says, "Yes, like that." Her jaw tightens. "But no God. If he exists, he has made too much wickedness."

Sylvia and Ruth may be startled, even shocked, but an ancient grievance has flickered in George, in the form of Greta's dead, sanctified husband, whose existence and absence years ago haunted worse than Alice's, even though Alice was waiting at home, a living reproach. It's tough— was tough—measuring up to the dead.

Put it this way: if George had died, Greta'd have been sad and maybe peeved, but she wouldn't have to be popping one of those pills she takes those rare times when she gets too upset. She wouldn't have gone into a rage at the Almighty.

Would Alice?

Say heaven was a reunion, the way Greta says—Alice would be restored and there they'd be, the two of them strolling past Greta arm in arm with her *beautiful* what's-his-name—oh yes, he remembers *beautiful*—nodding discreetly as if they barely knew each other. Then there'd be Greta's big foreign family gabbling away on a big family-sized cloud, while he and Alice were stuck off by themselves on their own little wisp. All the careful dipsy-doodling, it'd be like the fast-footing of learning to dance. As a boy, George was clumsy. He's clumsy now. But for a long time he was graceful. Maybe he'll be graceful someday again, and Greta will be lithe and smooth and not angry, and Alice will be sweet as well as meek, her old self.

Greta says God's decisions aren't fair, and it's true that whatever else he's done, George would not do to Alice what God has. Alice never did any great harm, and look what's happened to her—that isn't right. He hasn't thought of it this way before: that these kinds of things aren't only God's will, but God's fault.

Thinking about all this hurts. It gives him a headache.

Ruth can't expect to be in heaven at all, can she, with what she has done and then what she is planning? That's a shame, and it doesn't seem right either. Give or take this and that, she doesn't seem a really bad woman.

And what would Sylvia be like in heaven? Snotty, probably. A well-off woman with good legs and narrow hard-to-fit feet. Her husband, too, an important man with important feet, who wore either loafers or expensive shiny lace-up leather. Good quality, good taste. In heaven, would some people still get the highest, fanciest clouds? Here at the Idyll Inn, though, Sylvia's snotty enough, but not as snooty as he'd have thought. Probably in heaven all that kind of thing gets planed down and evened out anyway. Once, he made a dollhouse for Colette. The feel of the plane in his hand, the satisfactory curlings of wood peeling away, rounding off sharp edges and corners, trying to make sure she couldn't be hurt—that was nice.

What are they talking about?

"You're exactly right, I think, Greta," Ruth is saying. "Maybe we're not experts, or probably even particularly good amateur theologians, but it's always the question, isn't it, however many fancy words get built up around it—that if there's a god who made and cares for us, how do we account for evil and cruelty? I know there's no end of different answers, but they always seem to me on wobbly ground. Faith in some ineffable mystery or nondescript love—what sort of creator punishes his own creation in the staggering number of ways most creatures on the planet are punished every day of the year? As you say, Greta, that's not likely a god we'd care for. In any event, there's no family reunions for me, I'm afraid. I would love to see some people again, Bernard especially, but what I believe is, when it's over, it's over. Dust and ashes. And I think I'm content with that, I really am."

"We seem," Sylvia says, "to be disposing of God rather snappily, aren't we? Although I guess that's all right as long as lightning bolts don't flame down our way."

"You're a believer?"

"Well, you know how much trouble I have with authority. Anyone's, really." So the answer is no? "And then, if you're raised Christian—Protestant in my case, like you, Greta—you stumble into all those discrepancies between the Old Testament God and the New Testament one. That, at least, is a problem you don't have, Ruth. All you have to worry about is the old one, and he's more realistic in a way: all those whimsical cruelties. In ours, God's also supposed to be love, which as we've noticed is not exactly common on the ground. Those stories you keep reading us, Ruth"—so after all, a harsh and steady diet of unhappy news has its intended effects—"never mind our respective dead husbands and whatever other troubles we've had—none of it strikes me as remotely affectionate. Love can be terribly hard, but it shouldn't be cruel." Oh, really? "Not gratuitously, randomly cruel, anyway."

Sylvia's eyes often soften when she's about to speak of Jackson, so the others aren't surprised when she says, "Jackson and I used to talk about this sort of thing, especially when he was on city council. What kinds of systems people devise for rubbing along together without doing much harm, how there have to be compromises, but how one way or another we try to work out laws and agree to educate people and treat illnesses and so on and so forth. And how we do that for each other, but really in our own interests too—for peace and safety and a reasonably comfortable, intelligent, friction-free existence. Simply because it makes practical sense to do well by each other as best we can, not because there's a god saying do this or do that. Especially when, as a matter of fact, the gods people listen to seem fond of the worst, not the best, people can do.

"In his practice and on council, Jackson would say, 'Impatient, raw people with impatient, raw ideas, they're a terrible trial.' Including particularly the ones who brought what they thought God would want into the picture—quite amazing how often they assumed God would want to be punishing this or that, or laying down rather arbitrary, harsh rules. Of course one could never say that in public. It would have been a sure way to ruin his practice, not to mention lose an election. Although after three terms he gave up on politics. It took far too much time, and he found he wasn't ambitious that way. He wasn't godlike at all, when it came to rejoicing in power."

What are the odds that all four of them—or perhaps three, since it's hard to tell if George has actual views—are skeptical, if not entirely disbelieving, when it comes to the nature, the very existence, of God? Long odds, one might think, but one might well be wrong, and moreover wildly presumptuous. No atheists in the foxholes? "In fact, I imagine that's where one might find quite a number," Sylvia says. "And you know what?"

"What?"

"I have to think that as a god I'd do much, much better. I expect you would too. So would any of us." Except maybe George, who's not really in any kind of shape for divinity.

How they laugh: so easy to picture Sylvia playing God.

But also how brutal Ruth's friends can be. How crisply and personally they speed through millennia of theory and thought, disputation, raucous certainty and fierce doubt—how alarmingly angry they can be, as well. Ruth can't help feeling a tingle, a touch of unease.

Which must be silly.

Less silly, though, in the middle of the night, that eerie, wondering hour—is this God's loud, unmerciful voice? They're each wakened by shockingly close, immense booming thunder, and lightning so near it lights up their rooms—a prompt, powerful response, if that's what it is, to Sylvia's daylight jibe about lightning bolts.

It takes a few minutes to settle the nerves on that score.

When the thunder and lightning shift southward, they're replaced by a howling wind and harsh drilling of rain. This is a storm that makes windows rattle in their frames and strain against the pressure to crack and blow inwards, scatter broken glass and debris across bluey-grey carpets and into the seams of elderly furniture. Which doesn't happen, but still, the wind is ferocious as it whistles around

corners, and there are long periods when the rain sounds like
bullets.

Some of the more innocent Idyll Inn residents are pleased
to know there are destructive forces just outside the walls from
which they're nestled away, safe under blankets, with help, if
help were necessary, that would come on the run. This has
not always been the case. One benefit of living in a place like
this in old age is that in earlier times elsewhere, they've been
responsible for the safety and comfort of others, and now they
are not. Nor do they have to concern themselves with the
cleanup. At daybreak everyone is astonished by the view that
comes with the light: an angry, grey, choppy river bedecked
with stray branches, as well as a random lawn chair caught on
the shore, half in and half out of the water, tipped as if a surprised occupant has been carelessly swept away; and gaps on
the distant hillside where aged trees stood yesterday, and
flashing emergency lights where limbs weighted with leaves
have toppled over road, through roof, across car—this is by no
means the worst storm that has ever blown through town, but
it's definitely a dramatic event, and better than morning TV.
At breakfast, residents point out to each other the river lap-
ping at the top of its banks, and sky the dull silvery shade of
pewter, threatening more to come—whatever the weather is
doing, it's doing it fast. Rapid change is what causes storms.
Or "You don't think it was God, do you?" Sylvia whispers,
passing Ruth's table, and in the light they can smile.

Staff are working short-handed. Several have called in
unable to get to work—driveways and streets blocked by
fallen limbs, roofs damaged, one car windshield broken.
Annabel Walker, though, arrives early, on foot, and is helping
out by getting some residents dressed and handing breakfasts

around. "Everyone has to pitch in," she calls gaily. Even so, the meal takes longer than usual to cook, serve and clear away. Many of the residents, awake half the night, are moving more slowly than usual too.

A relatively minor crisis that doesn't have to be actively dealt with—it's pleasant to feel somewhat under siege with, really, none of the downsides of a siege. Certainly there's no dismay when Annabel announces, "I'm afraid our mall outing this morning is cancelled. A lot of power is out, and quite a few streets are closed to traffic. I haven't heard yet, but if the Golden Cowboys can't make this afternoon's concert, we'll show movies in the library. I'm sure you all understand that these disruptions cannot be helped."

What should have been helped, obviously, is that a building that's been open for just a few months should not have a leaking roof, but inside the front doors, Annabel Walker has placed a bucket, which is fairly rapidly filling with the rhythmic plunking of seeping-through raindrops. "One last thing. We're operating on our backup generator, so please keep electricity use to a minimum until we're back on the grid. If you want to watch TV this morning, try getting together in the library instead of everyone turning on their individual sets. Let's all pull together, and hope everything's back to normal by the end of the day."

How rousing. Some spines in the dining room straighten: preparing for sacrifice. No TV in their own suites—all right, they can do this. "Damn, I believe that's one of my lawn chairs getting drowned in the river," Sylvia complains, peering out.

"Look on the bright side," says Ruth. "Without me around, you'd need one less chair anyway."

Honestly, it's scarcely safe to say anything when Ruth
will take advantage of just about every opening to adminis-
ter a nudge, a reminder, a hint—drip, drip, drip, like the roof
leak at the front door. Surely to God they don't have to talk
about death all the time; or life, for that matter. "Or," Sylvia
retorts, "I might very well want the chair for somebody else."
Ruth needn't think she's the end of the line when it comes
to new friends. At least acquaintances. Oh, who knows what
will happen? None of them got enough sleep. "Shall we get
to work on George? It doesn't look as if anything else much
will be going on here today. I don't know what you'll do for
bad news to entertain us with, though. Even the papers
haven't arrived. Still, maybe you can discuss from memory
the latest on the climate and the end of the world as we
know it. That certainly seems appropriate to the day."

From one day to the next, it's hard not to get snippy
sometimes. Knowing what Ruth wants, never mind doing
what Ruth wants, is a rather staggering burden. Although
quite interesting, too, and sparky to contemplate, in its
way—as with God and Abraham, there are vast mood
swings involved.

From George's room, which faces the parking lot and the
bulk of the city, they can see many more red and white
emergency lights flashing. "Listen to those chainsaws," Ruth
says, as Sylvia and Greta buckle down to the regular, possibly fruitful, possibly not, pushing and pulling of George's
legs, and she's right, the buzz is a constant white noise. "That
was scary last night. It's funny, though. After Bernard was
gone, I used to lie awake in storms worrying about the big
old maple in our backyard crashing down on the roof. Mind
you, I could lie awake fretting about all sorts of disasters back

then. At least I don't worry about falling trees any more, although I hope the young people who bought our place are all right today."

Ruth speaks of Bernard being just—*gone;* making the effort to suggest, to them and to herself, that his departure was as ordinary as can be. It's a fearsome effort, though. There's Bernard feebly bucking beneath her again, here's the terror in her own rigid arms.

She feels on occasion like a carny selling vegetable choppers and peelers: step right up, ladies and gentlemen, and watch while it slices, it dices, it decides and it chooses and in the end, look—*voilà,* as Sylvia would say—the perfect potato in the very shape and picture of julienned opportunity. "All those things I scared myself about—I wonder how much we haven't done, due to fear. Or the other way around, what we've done even if it's been scary. I've managed a few things like that, and been glad and proud in the end to have done them."

There she goes again. "I don't believe in regrets," Sylvia says. "Either way." She means that it does no good to second-guess. Make a decision, any decision: to marry, to have an affair, to love a husband, to keep a great secret for decades, to move here, to take pokes at Annabel Walker, or at God—for all she knows, agree to kill Ruth—and having made these choices, stick to them. Live with them, for God's sake. "In any case, I can't think of much that was especially major. I was afraid to water-ski but I did, and I guess I was pleased with myself, but that's not a big deal. I wouldn't spend time underwater, though, whereas Jackson and Nancy both loved it. Half our vacations were spent with them down at the bottom of one body of water or another, puttering around with the fish, and me on the beach in a chair with a book. Which was fine. I suppose I've missed a few adventures that could have put wind in the hair and a bounce in the step, but so what? I expect we've all been brave enough in other ways. I certainly have."

Brave is perhaps not quite the right word for what Sylvia did, but since nobody knows about Nancy's father, or at least her genetic father, no one can quibble.

And Greta? Courage isn't something she has given much thought to. Her boldest acts have been, like coming here to this country, carried out thrillingly, heedlessly, blind to danger or, like finding work and raising the girls after Dolph died, or entering the Ritz on the main street for the first time, or heading to the Idyll Inn lounge the first day on her own, done from necessity, without a real choice. She has welcomed certain occasions and risen to others. That is not nothing, but is it the same thing as courage? She thinks it is not.

As for George, he doesn't see the point of the question. A man can be scared or not scared, but either way it doesn't particularly matter in a real life where a person does every day what he has to do every day. Like running a store, or cleaning up the yard after a storm—he makes the decisions that keep a comfortable life going along, while taking whatever other pleasures and freedoms he can as they come up. He has never had to go to a war. That's where he imagines real bravery happens. Or rescuing a kid from fire or drowning— he's never done anything like that, either. So he's no hero, so what? He might have been, if he'd had to be. Although he guesses somebody brave doesn't cry at the drop of a hat, especially without knowing why. That hardly happens any more, but it can still come as a surprise to find a tear plopping down, and it blurs the astonishing view of Greta and Sylvia obvious at his feet, working his legs.

Truthfully, it's nice being a man among women again. Although it could be that just putting himself in their hands is brave enough these days.

Probably nobody kills, including in war, without being changed. Is Ruth brave, or the opposite? What should they call what she asks them to be?

Ruth notices everything. She has to. She notices Sylvia's shifts into irritation and back, and George's tear of the moment, and Greta's small frown. She notices, too, that her friends are surrounded by a wavery nimbus of brilliant red-orange; for once sharing a common colour—outrage? unity? fear? But this vivid arc, almost certainly due to her stepped-up anti-inflammatories but useful just the same, doesn't look fierce, only bright. Perhaps that is hopeful.

Lying beside Bernard when it was done, holding him— so swiftly a person departs.

Who would lie beside her?

There'd be no *her*. Just as, immediately, there was no Bernard.

Well, she can live with that. In a manner of speaking. She hears herself snort, as if she has turned into Sylvia.

"What?" Sylvia asks.

What indeed? "Look, it's raining again." So it is, in a gentle, pattering fashion not remotely like the fury that swept through in the night.

"God settling down, do you think?" Sylvia suggests, and she and Ruth smile, although neither Greta nor George can see why, exactly, and would wish for no further discussions of gods.

23

LITTLE COOKIES . . .

ITH AUTUMN, the leaves are beginning their creep from green toward orange, yellow, red and bronze, and some are already drifting to earth; tall riverside grasses are losing their vigour; Ruth-related discussions remain prickly and unresolved; and school has resumed, which means not only that the vacationing voices of grand-children and great-grandchildren have mainly vanished from Idyll Inn corridors, but also that residents have been volunteered for a grilling by students.

Or as Sylvia puts it, "Oh, for God's sake, now we're *projects*."

Which is to say that this afternoon a clutch of seventh-graders is pouring noisily through the front doors, notebooks in hand, forming up loosely around a teacher who doesn't look much older than they are. These will be the youngsters Annabel Walker announced at lunch would be arriving for a study of "cultural history." To which Sylvia remarked, not softly, "Loads of history here if anybody can remember it.

Too bad about the shortage of culture."

What fun.

Children of an age for seventh grade are not necessarily adorable. They look, the girls, anyway, far older than they are, and nearly, well, *flagrant* in their appearance. Many of the boys are still childlike, scrawny or padded in baby fat, but the girls wear sleek hair and tiny pants and scant tops that leave their navels exposed. Each table in the lounge, plus several in the dining room, gets one child. "Aren't you cold?" Sylvia asks the taut, black-haired little girl who settles at theirs. She has thin bare shoulders as well as bare midriff, and looks to be wearing lip gloss and eyeshadow. Are there piercings? Tattoos? What is she, twelve?

"No. Why would I be?" Children's instincts are sharp, that never changes; this girl looks Sylvia straight in the eye, defiant and potentially hostile. She sure wouldn't have done that at one time, but naturally in her view she's on life's upswing while Sylvia, on the downslope, is inconsequential and can do no harm, and like all these crumpled-up oldies is good only for answering dull questions for a dull schoolroom assignment. According to the newspapers, little girls this age are handy with blow jobs—*oral sex*, as the papers delicately express it; surely not on these little boys, but then, boys change suddenly. One minute they're children, next they're tall, filled-out youths, perfectly available for blow jobs from willing little girls out to prove their affections.

Sylvia would like to suggest that it would be a fine thing if girls understood better their authority, not easily won, over themselves—that sort of information should count as *cultural history*, shouldn't it?—and that deciding smartly in one's own best interests isn't a right to be thrown around, blown around, lightly.

Still, these children—what will their secrets be when they're Sylvia's age? Maybe they won't need to have any. Maybe they're becoming people who'll be able to say airily, "Oh, your father's not your father, but don't worry about it, he loves you, it doesn't make a blind bit of difference. You weren't a mistake, just the pleasing result of an experiment I conducted to remedy an outbreak of boredom."

Speaking of poor decisions about what should be done with a body.

Carpe diem, Sylvia believes, meaning among other things that the young must seize the day as selfishly and hopefully as the old. Perhaps the states aren't so different, despite—or because of—some obvious and mutual hostility. Sometimes, it seems to her, the old aren't just in the way or even irrelevant to the young, but are subject to an active kind of *anger* for being the future made flesh. And vice versa, she supposes—the old furiously resentful that the young are, in a quite different way, the future as well?

At any rate, never, never say anything resembling "These kids today!" That's so banal. Think of this as an opportunity.

Too late. The girl looks at Greta working away at this week's bright green-and-purple scarf, glances at George smiling in his off-kilter way, and having already locked horns with Sylvia, fixes on Ruth. "I'm Sharon," she says flatly—so unexotic and plain a name, her parents must have expected to find themselves raising someone rather less surly and bold. "So okay. I've got these questions I'm supposed to get answered, okay?" She waves a sheet of printed paper in Ruth's direction, pulls up a chair and hunches with her pen at the table. "So, like, the first one is, were you a pioneer?"

What? How old does she—does her teacher, who must have had a hand in this—imagine Idyll Inn residents are? Ruth considers her for a moment, then smiles. "Yes, I suppose I have been, dear, in my own way." This causes Sylvia to snort, and even Greta's lips tip upwards as she bends over her needles.

There are no inquiries into the nature of Ruth's pioneerhood; no details sought on any subject, perhaps just as well. Evidently this project does not require curiosity, only the ticking of boxes and the jotting, briefly, of notes. How far did you go in school (university); where did you grow up (here in this city); how many brothers and sisters did you have (none); what did your parents do for a living (ran clothing stores); what did you do for a living (saved children if possible, families as necessary)—not even this causes a nibble of interest. Perhaps young Sharon can't bear the faces she'd see if she looked up; or possibly she already knows something of what lies beneath the town's smoothed-over surfaces. Were you married (yes); how many children did you have (none); were you ever in a war (no, not directly); what's the farthest you've ever travelled?

"Oh, quite a distance," Ruth says. "Farther than most," and again Sylvia snorts, and again Greta smiles. While George is reminded what strange things women will laugh at. He'd like to be interviewed by one of these little girls, but at their table Ruth's the one. Maybe she looks like the friendliest and kindest—if only they knew.

There's something about him that scares children off. He's noticed it with other people's grandchildren and great-grandchildren too, how they won't come very close even when he beckons and smiles. What keeps them away? Maybe what he half-sees himself in the mirror each morning: half of him a kind of mask; a man only half-working. He'd like to tell the children he's just a friendly old grandpa beneath, just a man, but what fearfully clear-eyed child would believe him?

The little girl talking to Ruth—Alice wouldn't have let Colette out of the house that way, all bare bones and skin. She insisted Colette look like a *nice* girl. Respectable. Well, he wanted Colette to be nice and respectable too, only Alice was in charge of making her that way. This poor kid— where's her mother? Where are all the mothers, letting their daughters out looking like this?

Then again, Colette did grow up to be a nice, respectable woman, and fat lot of good it does him; or Alice, either.

"Clothes make the man," Art Fletcher used to say, measuring George for new suits, years before taking up knives. Now George wears his slippers and stretch-waisted pants— what sort of man do his clothes make him now?

When she was here, Colette bought him five new identical-except-for-colour pairs of these pants. "These should do you for a while," she said. He can hear again, although he would rather not, her high, jollying voice, all the bright questions that were no more looking for true answers than this Sharon girl is: isn't the Idyll Inn grand, isn't it nice to be among friends, isn't everything so convenient and pretty, aren't the staff just the kindest creatures on earth? Colette would not hear complaints, and by the time she left, with the embrace, the kiss on his forehead, the cheery "I know you'll do better, do please just try to be good," and another of her flashing little waves, he was exhausted; relieved in a funny way to return to his regular life. It makes him sad how Colette grows faint sometimes, in both distance and time. Now they get visitors like this girl, who could be Colette's daughter and his granddaughter, or even great-granddaughter, but isn't, and who is going down her list of questions, writing slowly, as if she's as unfamiliar with words as he sometimes is.

"What's the most important thing happened during your lifetime?" the girl asks finally, the last question reached, it sounds, with relief, the task of a dreary assignment nearly complete, escape from this creepy place and these see-through old people almost in sight.

So it feels.

But this could take a minute. Who would, or could, answer a question like that? "That's a tall order," Ruth says at last. "For one thing, I'd point out that my lifetime isn't quite over. And you know, different people would have different answers because there's so much to choose from. But barring something really extraordinary happening to change things during what you call my *lifetime*, I'd probably say all the many kinds of damage we've done to each other and the planet that are going to make your lifetime very difficult indeed." Ruth has, when she chooses, a sweet, glinting, old-lady smile. Sharon painstakingly writes down Ruth's words as if she has no clue what Ruth's talking about. As she probably doesn't.

She stands abruptly, in the same movement folding her single sheet of paper and clicking her pen closed. "Okay, that's all I need."

Oh. All right. "You're welcome." Ruth puts out her hand to be shaken, even though being gripped hurts quite badly.

She must be trying to make the child pause, teach her something; manners, maybe. "Take care, dear." The girl frowns. "Do please take care."

"Yeah, okay, sure," and she shrugs, turns away and walks off, with a little flick-flick of her low-slung rear end.

"My goodness," says Sylvia. "I wonder what she'll be like at fifteen?" That being roughly the stage when, in her observation, humans are at their most obstreperous and rebellious. *Obstreperous*, she explains to Greta: *turbulent; noisily resisting control.* "Although maybe, like everything else, that starts younger these days."

"Not my girls, so much," Greta says. Well, of course not Greta's girls, those perfect angels, all grown in their absence to archangel stature. Sylvia does try, though, not to roll her eyes too noticeably; one of her periodic efforts at tact.

"Yes," she says. "Lucky you."

Colette, like Greta's girls, would have been thirteen, sixteen, eighteen when George was leaving the house to meet Greta. He does not recall Colette being seriously rebellious or angry. He can hear raised voices, slammed doors, but that would be to do with Alice, not him. What was the word Sylvia just said? One that's too fat for his tongue, that's for sure.

"One does worry," Ruth says. "I wish they knew more. But she's still very young. And I suppose there's no particular reason she'd be more interested in us than I was, frankly, in her. I find I've about run out of steam for inquiring into the lives of children. Who anyway, most of them, don't need saving. They'll come through just fine."

No, they won't. Ruth expects these young humans, Sharon, have no idea, and no inquisitiveness either, never mind fear, about how strong and adaptable and stubborn and clever they'll have to be to survive. They'll certainly need to be a lot slyer and shrewder, smarter and more skilled than they appear.

They'll also have to not mind too much being poor, hungry, endangered, too hot or too cold.

On the other hand, she would not herself have dreamed, as a tumbling, springing girl, of the far more daring challenges she'd be required to rise to in time.

"I liked your answers."

"Oh, I could have said anything, she wasn't listening. It doesn't matter, although it does take some adjusting, when it used to be that for at least a few children, what I said could change their whole lives."

All right, maybe the girl was a dull-minded little cookie, but what a dangerous one Ruth is. Quite the dictator: changing lives, ending lives—it's not fair, George would say, that you'd never know from looking at the smiley, curled-up little thing what a dark-seeing woman she is. Is there a word for that inside-outside kind of difference? It'd have to be another big one, so he can already tell there's no way he's going to come up with what it could be.

24

AT THREE IN THE MORNING . . .

*L*ONGER BY FAR THAN ANY IDYLL INN CORRIDOR
is the vast middle-of-the-night chasm between word
and deed.

Or rather, words. So many of them spoken in recent
months, often enough in different forms and with different
meanings in different mouths, and including, but not limited
to: *struggle, guilt, sacrifice, power, extraordinary, precious,
noble, heroes, freedoms, rights, suffering, dangerous.*

Words trip over each other, they contradict and conflict.
They do not by any means construct a high, steady bridge
over the chasm to deed.

The most suspiciously alluring ones have been *mercy* and
grace.

It is easy to be seduced by beautiful words; perhaps these
three in the corridor tonight have been. They have, after all,
each been seduced by forms of beauty before.

In the middle of still nights, words resonate in even
darker ways than they do in the light. Tonight syllables would

ring out like bells, they would roll rumbling like cannonballs down the length of the hall.

This is why silence is best; except for the whispered *Courage* repeated once more: a teetering, makeshift footbridge carrying them across, one way or another, in the methodical direction of deed.

25

THANKSGIVING GOOSE . . .

$\mathcal{S}$IX MONTHS AFTER THE IDYLL INN OPENED its doors to residents with healthy incomes but varying hopes, despairs, abilities and infirmities, and almost a year after she was hired to guide the place into existence, Annabel Walker remains stubbornly buoyant. She even continues to speak, although no longer with her old insistent sincerity, of "our one big happy family," and either doesn't notice or doesn't care when this results in a certain rolling of eyes.

The point is, good cheer is good business. Word of mouth matters when vacancies arise. Annabel Walker's basic criteria for residents are, necessarily, security of assets and degrees of health or ill health. Beyond that, it's fingers crossed. Assessing for compatibility would be a luxury, and in any case that's hardly predictable. People she wouldn't have supposed would have a single thing in common will form their own impenetrable, inexplicable connections, it seems.

Turnover isn't brisk, but it's not exactly rare, either. There are systems for most eventualities, though, including for when somebody dies. Immediately an on-tap doctor is called to certify death behind the closed door of the deceased, a hearse pulls up during a time—meals are best—when residents are apt to be otherwise occupied, and zip-zap, the body is gone, and family members or staff get right to work packing up possessions and cleaning, while Annabel Walker surveys the waiting list. The aim is to keep disruptions to a minor shuffle and stir. It's not, obviously, that death and the subsequent appearance of someone new can go unnoticed, but it's pleasing to have a sensible process that makes transitions just as smooth and easy as they can possibly be.

Systems leave her freer to keep tabs on the inevitable glitches as they arise: the roof leak, for instance; a staff member requiring maternity leave; a resident reacting badly to new meds, or getting ill in a way the Idyll Inn isn't set up to handle. Some of the old are meek enough—or frightened, or ingratiating, or genuinely kindly—but by and large they have high expectations of what their rents buy them. Like instant attention. Some, never mind that they're now living with other people with quite different preferences, are under the impression they can behave any old way. Jostling at mealtimes a little too vigorously, say, to be first in or out of the dining room. Sometimes a quiet word works, sometimes makes no difference at all. One thing's for sure—if she ever imagined that the old would focus their dwindling time on approaching their ends with appropriate grace, she's been disabused of that notion. It's more as if they're trying to eke every last greedy morsel of service or food or goodwill out of each day remaining to them.

The essential trick is to keep smiling; keep them busy, as well, preoccupied with events, which is what Linda Swain's

for: organizing entertainments, although Annabel Walker
has to approve most of her plans. There are expenses
involved, and in the case of excursions, insurance issues—a
sea, all in all, of paperwork. Annabel also has to produce
detailed accountings of staffing, nutrition, expenses and
incomes monthly, semi-annually and annually for the management company, where she assumes somebody's paying
attention. Certainly she expects to account to the penny for
this weekend's Thanksgiving blowout, from the cost of table
centrepieces to the price of turnips and turkey. At least dou-
ble the regular number of meals will be served, since residents' families are invited to dinner, but it all falls into the
category of allowable expense, relatively cheap advertising
of Idyll Inn splendours.

   This isn't the kind of minor activity that Linda Swain
can handle and Annabel rubber-stamp. Everybody, top to
bottom, has extra work to do: planning and preparing a
traditional Thanksgiving menu along with the usual
attention to individual diets—low salt, low fat, no sugar—
and decorating the place with the grasses and gourds of
old-fashioned harvest-time, and making centrepieces out
of tiny corncobs and little baskets and strands of orange-
and-yellow-striped ribbons, a chore Linda farmed out to
one of her crafts groups with mixed, not exactly deft
results. For relatives, this will be the first big, significant
holiday since this place opened, which means not only
reunion but inspection. How are people holding up, how
may they be failing? Annabel Walker has advised staff that
they will need to be especially helpful. "There's a lot of
anticipation and stress when families turn up, and I want
everyone to go the extra mile. We want our visitors to

know their loved ones are well looked after and happy, and that no one goes around with things like draggy hems or unbrushed hair."

Beyond that, it's up to the residents to choose their own public faces, preferably of competence and contentment. And she has to hope no one brings loud family grudges to the table; or new grudges against the Idyll Inn, for that matter. "Just keep smiling," she has counselled her staff. "It makes a difference to how people behave."

Easier said than done. There are also those without visitors to take into account: residents whose relatives are too far-flung to gather, or at least to gather here; those whose families don't make a big deal of the holiday; those without families at all. George is among them—"I can't, Dad, I've already made the trip twice," Colette tells him—and so is Ruth, who says, "We'll eat together then, shall we, George?" Which is kind of her. And she can't do him any harm with so many people around. Anyway, it's not as if she loves him, and according to her she only puts pillows over the faces of people she loves.

Two of Greta's three daughters plus a granddaughter are coming. Even Sylvia's Nancy is to arrive in town the night before, and will stick around till after the dinner. Sylvia has been surprised by how much this pleases her, even knowing that, come Nancy's actual arrival, abrasions will arise as they always do. But Sylvia's determined to try; just as she's recently been trying to keep both the handy but evidently confusing foreign word, and the negatively clever remark, from leaping automatically to her tongue. She estimates that she succeeds maybe a quarter of the time, and is rewarded by an occasional large-spiritedness that feels vaguely familiar, as if it's something she once had, but mislaid, and then forgot.

Nancy too must be experiencing an outbreak of benevolence. When she shows up in the lounge, she even places warmish lips on warmish cheek before pulling up a chair to join Sylvia, Greta, Ruth and George. "Happy Thanksgiving," she says. "You look comfortable."

So they do, in their slippers, nightgowns and robes. The women, although not often George, have taken to changing early occasionally, especially if it's more convenient for staff, as it is on this busy weekend. With darkness falling earlier by the day, being wrapped in nightclothes feels cosy. "We old folks feel the chill," Sylvia says, meaning *we old folks* sardonically; Nancy's quick grin says she gets it. Does it say anything else? Briefly Sylvia puts a hand on Nancy's, then draws back in case she doesn't care to be touched.

"Nancy, how nice!" Ah, here's Annabel Walker, greeting Nancy like an old friend. "I'm so glad you're joining us. We're doing our best to make this a really festive weekend for everyone."

"So I see." Nancy nods toward the sheaves of fake wheat—real wheat would be messy—draped on the walls.

"I wonder if your mother and her friends would like to invite you to the dining room for our pre-Thanksgiving concert? We've got the Tonaires." As if they're special and not just regulars, a local male quartet in blue-and-white-striped jackets who sing a cappella.

"Oh, I think we can hear them plainly enough from right here," Sylvia says. "Too plainly, really. Nancy's always had such a good ear, and I'm sure you've noticed that at least one of those men keeps sliding off key. I imagine that's even more painful up close. And there's a repertoire issue—do you suppose they realize that 'It's a Long Way to Tipperary' thoroughly predates the most ancient among us?"

"Mother!" says Nancy; but does her tone not speak of private delight?

Annabel Walker sighs. "All right, fair enough, but don't you agree, Nancy, that it would be much nicer if people didn't wear their nightclothes when they're out in public areas like this?"

Nancy's eyebrows shoot up, just like her mother's. "Why would it be nicer? I'd have thought you'd be happy that people feel at home. I often get into my nightclothes the moment I get home from work if I'm not going out again, don't you ever do that?"

"Perhaps, but I think it's *especially* important here not to let standards slide, particularly with visitors coming and going." Poor Annabel, smiling, miscalculating her audience one more time.

"Seems to me if that's a problem, it's one for the strangers and visitors, not the people who live here. Who pay very well to live here, I notice. Personally, I wouldn't care to spend thousands a month to be told what to wear."

"Good for you," Ruth says to Nancy after Annabel has skittered away. "It's easy to see who you take after." Which creates a small, prickly pause during which Sylvia does not say, *And thank God for that.* Nor does she say, and never will, *If you had a proper chat with Annabel Walker, Nancy, you'd be surprised by how much you have in common—mostly those feeble paternal genes you have no idea you share.* The greatest kindnesses and generosities may, in a surprising number of circumstances, lie in absolute, bitten-lip, no-matter-what silence. In terms of motherhood that may be a pitiful gift, but it's the one Sylvia can give over and over.

Perhaps she deserves some kind of maternal achievement award. She'd have to get in line behind Greta, of course. She should ask Greta if her gifts to her miraculously, legendarily trouble-free daughters include keeping secrets from them. Well, besides George. Otherwise, probably not. "Join us in a glass, Nancy?" she says instead, rather bravely, considering that when it comes to her mother, Nancy can demonstrate a strikingly pro-temperance attitude.

Not this time. "Sure, I could use one after that drive."

"Are you feeling all right?" and really, Sylvia doesn't mean that unkindly.

"Why, don't I look okay?" Nancy leans back in her chair. "I'm just tired. I was thinking driving into town about those Thanksgiving parties you and Dad used to throw, remember? Dad making a ton of Bloody Marys because he said a vegetable mix made it a harvest drink, and everybody getting pissed up before the turkey was anywhere near the table?"

"They were fun, weren't they?" Sylvia is rather struck in the heart. "We had," she tells the others, "friends in, along with almost everyone from the block. People brought casseroles and desserts, and I did the turkey and so forth, and as Nancy says, Jackson took care of the drinks. He'd mix the Marys in a big old washtub, so they always tasted of metal. We held that party for, oh, thirty years or so." Before and after Peter, children, various dramas, oh well.

"I guess—" as if Nancy's on a similar train of thought— "Annabel must think she can appeal to my better nature because we knew each other when we were kids, but even then we didn't have much in common. Well, except for our parents hanging out, I suppose." Was that a crack? Couldn't really be anything else, could it? Apparently she too can scarcely help herself. "Are those singers we're hearing her choice? Because you're right, they're pretty bad." A four-part distant droning of "Red River Valley" at the moment—*Come and sit by my side if you love me* . . . Perhaps suitable for Thanksgiving. Perhaps cruel. "Will all your families be coming?"

"Two of Greta's daughters, isn't that right, Greta? George's daughter lives too far away and Ruth doesn't have children." Sylvia says this as flatly as possible so that, she hopes, no one is wounded by absence.

"Where do your people stay when they come to town?" Nancy asks Greta.

"They share a hotel room, but I am not sure which one."

"There's not much choice, is there? Clean and dull, or not so clean and far too interesting." Another crack? "Actually, I should go check in before my room's given away and I have to hunt down one of the lively places. Thanks for the drink, Mother, see you tomorrow, okay?"

"You're welcome, and yes, I'll look forward to it." Tomorrow's going to be a long day, though, sustaining these modest courtesies while dodging the barbs. Watching Nancy walk away, Sylvia wonders if her daughter's too thin inside her loose mossy-green trousers and pale yellow turtleneck. Hard to tell, with someone who's always been narrow. "I think I'll turn in too." An hour or so of bad TV should put her nicely to sleep.

"Me also," says Greta. "I will want to be rested to enjoy tomorrow."

"Room," George tells her. Now why is he crying?

"All right, I can push you."

Ruth goes along too. How tiring people seem to find their own children—whenever offspring whirl through the place, disrupting conversations and rhythms, creating stirrings of discontent, grief, love, they leave behind when they go a foggy residue, a grey forlornness. Now here's George, even without his Colette, tears glittering like mercury beads and wrapped in rough brownish grey like a monk. Greta appears outlined in bright purple but with shadows of someone leaner and tougher, like an old, stringy turkey, camouflaged behind her plush frame, while Sylvia, surprisingly, bears a sad sort of soft blue like a shawl over her shoulders. When Ruth mentioned her mildly hallucinatory visions to her doctor, he asked if she found them distressing. Good question. "I guess I'd say they're disorienting, but basically beautiful. I wouldn't be concerned if I didn't know everything's not really surrounded by rainbows. As long as they don't mean I'm having a stroke or going insane, they're mainly just interesting and pretty."

The one person around whom she never sees extraneous colours is her own self, in the mirror.

By mid-morning the next day, the scents of spiced stuffing and turkeys are beginning to drift out of the kitchen, along with an exuberant clatter of pans. Early on, too, residents begin the anxious wait in their suites, the lounge, the library, right at the front doors, already in their best dresses and suits, watching the time, watching the time—at the Idyll Inn, weeks and months may flicker by lightly, but expectant minutes and hours are an eternity.

George wonders if he looked as pitifully eager, waiting all slicked down at the door for Colette. Don't these people have any pride, don't they have lives of their own? Oh. That rings a bell.

When two of Greta's daughters and the granddaughter roll through the front doors, Sylvia says, "The Valkyries have arrived," as if they come girded for opera. Then Nancy appears, and she and Sylvia vanish into Sylvia's suite. As other people bring their embraces and words of affection, it gets a lot like moving-in week, with all the gabbling and hustle, except that nobody's carting furniture around or hammering pictures on walls. Even the tensions are back, in the cries of "You look terrific," and "How are you enjoying yourself?" and "Isn't this lovely, what a great place." It sounds as if nobody wants to feel bad about either making or hearing a load of complaints. Time is too precious. For Ruth and George, not directly involved, it's like TV, watching who comes to see whom; which of their fellows belongs with which clutch of people. As with residents, women guests outnumber men. There are a few small children but only a couple of teenagers, who don't look happy, but then, as Ruth points out, they probably wouldn't be happy to be anywhere with their families, much less here.

Such long legs young people have, and such large, bright teeth. "Like the wolf in 'Little Red Riding Hood,'" Ruth whispers to George, and not much later she says, "If you don't mind, I think I'm going to escape to my room until dinner. This is such a lot of commotion, it's a little bit wearing. Can I take you to your door, too? I'm afraid on my own I'd get crushed underfoot," and she's not entirely joking.

"Yes," he agrees. "Headache," he adds.

"You have one?"

"A little."

"No wonder. Take an Aspirin and lie down for a while. Whichever of us gets to the dining room first can save the other a seat, all right? We've got a couple of hours."

In his room he buzzes for an aide to help him from wheelchair to bathroom to bed. "Nap," he tells her.

"Good idea. I'll get you up and ready in lots of time for the turkey."

Drifting off, he wonders how Colette is spending the day. At a big table with many friends, Bill at the head? He sees Bill carving, the job of the man of the house. What does Colette's house look like? Or his own house? Why do so many daughters look like their mothers instead of their fathers? Where are the men, all the men? They think they're so strong with their carving knives at the heads of the tables, but it's the women who live. There are Greta's daughters, not Valkyries, whatever those are, but Amazons, as he once thought of Greta herself, with her strong, gripping limbs. His own personal, grave secret; a happy, easy, then painful, tender, private adventure, totally separate, all flung blankets and warmth. Shiny. Peculiar what happens. How everything changes. A busybody spots a car where it shouldn't be. The graceful wobble and stumble, a rememberer begins to forget, George falls to his kitchen floor and rises up, or fails to rise up, a new man. What's true in the first place, if everything can go spinning in a moment in totally unforeseen ways? What's a man really, or a woman, if upendings are so whimsically, randomly possible?

Who's in charge of surprise? Looking down and noticing the back of a woman's neck in a new and irresistible way— there are delicious surprises, not only kitchen-floor ones.

Whoever's in charge, it's hard to forgive. Greta said that; something like that.

"George, Mr. Hammond, wake up, can you smell dinner? The turkeys are out of the ovens, it's suppertime very soon, are you ready to wake up now?" It's Adele something, one of the day-shift aides, saying something about cranberry sauce while he's still betwixt and between where he is and where he was, deeply sleeping, moments ago.

On the toilet, his eyelids droop and he nods.

Next he knows, he's been shifted into his wheelchair and Adele something is pushing him into the corridor outside his room, and he makes out at the far end, as on the first day, Greta, large and brisk, rounding the corner, and by the time they are close, and then side by side, he is in the back room of his store.

He is piling shoeboxes on a low shelf, with Greta hovering above and—his right hand reaches out, slides upwards, cups itself on her big muscled behind, affectionately, inquiringly, twiddles its fingers and—she is making a sharp whuffing noise and jerking away, loudly saying, "Jesus Christ." Not like Greta at all.

Greta, a large, lumpy old woman, appears in her doorway.

Could he really have done such a thing?

How he adored Greta's bottom; and her willingness.

He *revelled*—there's a lost word returned.

The terrible moment was so warm, so soft, so pleasant and true.

He is a disgusting old man. That's what Adele will tell Annabel Walker, even if Greta's daughter does not, and he'll be thrown out. Annabel Walker will also get in touch with Colette—please, don't let Colette hear what he's done.

Who is he asking for help?

Has he ever before been so humiliated, so pleadingly sorry? He doesn't think he has, but he's an old man of assorted experience; only right now he can't remember any single moment so awful.

Greta steps forward. Oh no.

"Emily," she says firmly, "do not fuss. You are a grown woman, you need not take such a mistake so seriously, and I know," her voice turning cold, and even at the end she was never frozen to him, "nothing like this will happen again. Will it, George?" He shakes his head. He cannot meet eyes. To her daughter Greta says, "Wait for me in the dining room." To Adele she says, "I shall take him there, you do not need to wait. Do not to anyone mention this, please."

She's eliminating witnesses to whatever punishment she intends.

When the others have gone, reluctantly and not without glances back, Greta sighs heavily. "George. That was very bad."

"Mistake," he says hopefully, plucking her own word from the air.

"I did not think otherwise. You had a moment of forgetting, did you not?"

He was always lucky with Greta, who any number of times could have done him great harm, and did not. "Very sorry," he says.

"I know. I shall do what I can about Emily, and Adele also, but you must pay attention, you must be more careful. You must *think*, always think." That's another thing about Greta: she often used to say more than she needed to, although maybe only because she wasn't so good with the language and wanted to make sure she was clear. Still, he feels as if he has fallen down and been picked up again.

She's right, he must think. He must pay attention to forgetting what his hand felt sliding upwards; what his affectionately twiddling fingers were able to touch, soft and sweet.

A stranger's softness. That's what he has to remember: a stranger. He must hope Greta can keep him out of trouble, and also will not bar him from the exercise and conversation and company of their little group. Because what would he be here without them? His mind goes white with the thought. How he longs to wheel back into his room, back into his bed, back into a time before this.

"Do not worry," Greta says. "Only remember. In all our lives we make mistakes that are only our own business, yes? And we all keep our secrets."

How good she is; has always been. Mercy. "Thank you." Although it begins to grate, being humble like this. That can't be right, but it's so. She takes the handgrips of his wheelchair and pushes him roughly—is she angry?—to his table in the dining room, and leaves him.

But now here comes Ruth, and she has committed a far bigger, worse crime than his, and nobody has told.

At the table he stares mainly at his plate, turkey, stuffing, sweet potatoes, peas and turnip too much, all the clatter of plates and cutlery, and the unfamiliar volume of high and low voices too much—even Ruth too much, although she too isn't making much effort to talk as she slowly and painstakingly, as she does everything, takes a bite or two of each food on her plate. "It's a lot, isn't it?" she asks finally, and so it is. The whole day.

Across the room they can see Sylvia and Nancy sharing a table with an upstairs resident and two middle-aged strangers. Sylvia and Nancy look to be talking brightly with the others, and everyone is laughing. Well, they're smart-tongued, cutting women, bound to be entertaining as long as they're not turned on each other. "Mothers and daughters,"

Ruth says, following the half of George's gaze that is follow-able. "They're a funny pair, aren't they?"

George does not want to talk about mothers and daugh-ters, does not want even to think about them; but of course they're everywhere in this busy, crowded room, an unfurling of generations like flags. There's Greta, with two of her Amazons and the granddaughter, still a young woman unfleshed. She has Greta's broad shoulders, though. Maybe she's how Greta looked at her age, before she came to this country, and years before him.

They are a whole raft of people he knows nothing about. How do they feel about vengeance?

Greta is in earnest, head-bent, private conversation with one of her daughters, while the other one and the grand-daughter eat and talk with each other. He can't tell the daughters apart at this distance, or perhaps at all, but the one with Greta's hand on her arm must be the one. The daughter's expression goes from angry to, he thinks, resigned finally. He glimpses her nodding, although also frowning. She has a sister, as well as a daughter or niece, right there to tell. Still, they seem to be girls who are generous toward Greta's desires. The daughter Emily might care for her mother more than she cares to hurt him. "George, are you all right, are you ill?" Ruth is asking. Why, what does he look like, is he pale, is he weeping?

What if Greta, because they're used to telling things, tells Ruth and Sylvia? It doesn't take much, or long, for a man to be ruined. "Fine," he says. "Thanks."

"All the noise, it's exhausting in a way, but it's nice too, hearing so many happy voices."

Happy? There's an H-word a fellow doesn't much hear around here. "Yes," he says doubtfully. "Nice."

When the meal finally ends, and as Ruth rises and leans into his wheelchair to push him out of the dining room, people are rising from other tables as well. Greta looks across at him and smiles slightly and nods slightly and lifts her hand slightly; it looks as if she's saying that he's okay. But oh, what a stupid, stupid thing to do. She was right, he has to *think*, he has to try hard and be on his toes. Bad things happen when a fellow caves in. "Thanks," he says to Ruth again, as she leaves him at his door. Because it is Thanksgiving, and he is grateful that the day, for him, is more or less safely over at last.

Even so, wasn't that a sweet blunder? Greta can't mind if he lets himself remember now and then, just a little bit, can she? And nobody can stop a man's dreams. It would be warm and even exciting to have a sweet dream or two. Big, bad things happen in the night, leaving a fellow sprawled on the floor helpless as a sack of grain, so tender and delicious things should be allowed too, and if they can't get him in trouble, or ever even be known—just his own private, dreaming secrets, asleep or awake—where's the harm?

26

ALL THE MORAL BUSYBODIES . . .

*N*ANCY IS INDEED MORE GAUNT than the last time she visited, and for good reason. "You should know I'm having a hysterectomy next month," she told Sylvia at Thanksgiving. "I'm just mentioning it because I figured if I was going to be mad at you for not telling me important things you were doing, I shouldn't turn around and do the same thing myself. If I'd remembered to have kids my insides would probably be fine, but oops, I forgot, and they're not, so it's best to ditch the whole shebang now."

Sylvia recognized the brittle tone. Other mothers might chip at it till it crumbled—might speak the word *cancer*, for one—but, expert herself in the maintenance of useful walls, she recognized one when she saw it. "Thank you. I'm glad you told me." Because whatever Nancy said, she wouldn't have revealed any weakness, including sickness and surgery, if she didn't need comfort. Which left Sylvia to gauge the precise amount of comfort desired against the precise amount that would offend. She put an arm around Nancy and tugged gently, stepping away as soon as she felt Nancy's shoulder tense, which was quite soon.

"Can you tell me what's involved and what you're setting out to get fixed?" *Get fixed* was an unfortunate turn of phrase, in the context. She might have hoped Nancy wouldn't notice, but of course Nancy did. "Myself. I'll be getting myself fixed. Spayed. Whatever. But seriously, it's mainly pre-emptive. One or two things are out of whack, so this'll catch them before they maybe get dangerous." And that's all she would say.

"Who will look after you? Do you have someone?" What a thing not to know—who cares for Nancy?

"A bunch of friends will take turns and I'll have a little home care, but the surgeon says I'm in better shape than most patients my age, so I should bounce back fast."

Nancy has promised to phone after surgery the first moment she can, and so for the first time in her life Sylvia has equipped herself with a cellphone, which she now takes with her everywhere, practising its use, no easy matter with her cramped, lumpy hands. More mysterious by far than any tiny mobile, though, is this new, electrical fear for her child. The one Jackson cradled under his chin, cherished infant. Her happy little pre-sorrow child performing somersaults off the porch, diving into the deep end, doing cartwheels over the lawn. The one, too, with an unknown, unheard-of band of friends prepared to take care of her—oh, for heaven's sake, she's getting as maudlin as George.

When George goes to his GP he comes back with not only the standard blood-thinners for survivors of strokes, but batches of little pink pills, one for morning, one for nightfall, for raising his spirits. Sometimes he takes them, sometimes he doesn't. Maybe they work, maybe they don't. Hard to say how downhearted he'd be if he skipped them entirely. Would he share them if Sylvia asked? Not that she would. She needs to be alert, not open to misunderstanding bad news or to taking mistaken delight either.

Greta says, "It would be a hard thing to have a child become ill. I too would be very frightened." Presumably this is her version of solace. "I have not thought often before of such things coming the wrong way around." By which she means, Sylvia assumes, backwards. That in the right order of things, children are not supposed to suffer, and definitely not die, in advance of their parents. People bury wives and husbands, sisters and brothers. They bury their parents—Sylvia has been known to imagine Nancy erupting at her funeral in great grieving regrets, she has taken a gleeful motherly pleasure, in a *ha-bet-you're-sorry-now* sort of way. But it must be a permanently broken-hearted business to bury a child.

The fault of Nancy's father? Some dubious medical inheritance from his side of the family bringing Nancy to grief? Perhaps someone should warn Annabel Walker, but it's not going to be Sylvia.

Ruth lightly touches Sylvia's hand. "Don't worry. Or, sorry, that's stupid, you're bound to worry. I mean, be strong. She is, and she'll be fine." But having a child does, as Greta contends, make a difference. Any number of differences. Lucky Ruth, in her way.

Nobody needs to advise Sylvia Lodge to be strong, but she finds she does, after all, have a regret or two although, as she expects is the way with regrets, there's not much to be done about them. So what she's stuck with is this uniquely frantic concern for a vulnerable, out-of-reach daughter. What if

Nancy died? Then Sylvia might be tempted to feel she'd lived on for too long herself. This comes as part of the surprise.

They're used, almost, to the falterings of their own bodies, toppling in interesting and dull ways like dominoes, one ailment or pain leading to a medication that threatens to create another kind of ailment or pain and—on and on it goes, in careful kill-or-cure calibrations. Sylvia's specialist measures dicey bones and swollen joints, and while doling out anti-inflammatories and supplements and pain meds, may or may not recommend trying a newly authorized drug, fresh from the lab, that may or may not cascade into happy or unhappy long-term effects. Tough decisions.

Greta's cardiologist listens for fluctuating, wavering heartbeats, and encourages her mild exercising and prescribes this and that and otherwise says, "Just be careful, you know the routine." In Sylvia's view, "If you were younger, he'd have operated, I bet. Done a bypass, or even a transplant. When you're old, they figure it's a waste of resources."

Even Greta acknowledges the possible harsh truth of that. Still, "I would not myself care for such surgery. It would be hard, and for my girls also." Because they would be at her bedside through a long convalescence? Not likely, not on the evidence here, where apparently they're happy to phone Greta often enough, and chip in for her rent, but really don't all that often show up. Sylvia doesn't say that. There doesn't seem much harm, at this stage, to illusions that comfort.

It looks as if Greta, who's already produced enough scarves for an army in winter, is moving up in the world, attempting more ambitious creations. At the moment her *sweater du jour*, as Sylvia calls it, involves the knitting of fifteen red rows followed by the purling of seven green ones—

exceedingly festive, coming up to the seasonal, but who
does she imagine would wear such a thing? She is working
on the broad back section of a simple-patterned, wide-
sleeved number—her girls are not small women, so her task
is not minor. Each is to receive one for Christmas, partly
because Greta is weary of scarves but also in aid of reassuring them, after George's bad act, that she is in a good place
sympathetic to her busy new interests. She expects Emily
has told her sisters about George's error. She imagines that
all their lives, they have told each other things they do not
mention to her. As she has not told them why George could
make such a mistake.

It is most important to be kind to each other, to be not a
burden. Let them go, and they will return. As they will do
soon for Christmas, although not, except for Patricia, on the
very day. Meanwhile it is best to be busy. Darkness matters.
Snow falls and thaws, turning the world white and then
muddy brown, dawn arrives late and dusk early and, as
Annabel Walker has remarked, "I understand how it can
take special effort to be cheerful at this time of year." Yes, it
does. "We're planning a great celebration of our own,
though," she has said, and already there is a big piney-plastic
wreath with a red-ribbon bow and little golden bells hanging
in the front entrance. "Much more to come," promises
Annabel Walker.

The fact remains that the world closes in. This is a season when it is easy to lapse into too much gloomy thinking.
Also too much feeling. It takes particular determination even
to go outside, a cumbersome effort of coats, boots, scarves,
time. Therefore the busyness and the brilliant colours of
wools. Greta is illustrating lively memory with these clashing

colours of Christmas: of excited, high-pitched, laughing, bickering girls; the heat of baking in the small kitchen; the secret handmaking of gifts—bookmarks, pot-holders, drawings of her and each other—such careful, poor days, always worrisome, but recalled cheerily now in the green and red of warm, heavy sweater.

Soon also: Ruth. The bright entranceway wreath a burning hoop yet to be leapt through, or not.

Ruth continues to keep her medical appointments, partly because she enjoys the Idyll Inn van's high, slow vantage point as it traverses the city, streets lined with maples gone stark. This won't be a bountiful time in which to die, but it's a truthful, uncamouflaged, bare-to-the-world one.

Flashing feet bear people, click, click, click like Greta's needles, toward their mysterious, dreaded or ordinary or anticipated destinations, all of this movement familiar, and most of it piercingly lovely for reasons that do not have to do with familiarity. Ruth's attentiveness, she supposes, is a kind of grief for herself; a premature mourning.

A scruffy young blond-bearded, unwashed-looking fellow has recently been catching her eye. She sees him standing at a downtown street corner with a panhandler's sign—*Please give*, it says bluntly in big black-marker print—and with a shiny-eyed golden retriever. There was a time when people here kept their troubles hidden indoors. Or, if need be, in parks, or under bridges. They're more blatant and unashamed about their needs and desires these days, which may or may not be progress. At any rate the dog looks cared for and healthy. An unconditionally warm creature to love, Ruth imagines. Sometimes, rescuing children, she had to call the Humane Society to get animals rescued as well. Matted, thin dogs, cats collapsed in their own waste—people's careless cruelties cross all sorts of boundaries. The young panhandler may be a boy she once triumphantly carried to safety. She rarely had high hopes for those children, but at least some of them might have learned a thing or two about mute affection.

She could add that to a tentative plus column when she's making her totals.

Besides the grand tour through town, Ruth visits her doctor to request sedatives along with her usual pain and osteo meds. "I don't sleep well any more. I'd give anything to get through the night."

Sedatives will help on the night she doesn't intend to get through. She wants to be calm but awake. Maybe she can't expect revelation, come the time, but something— who knows what interesting information may arise? Not that it could be particularly *useful* information by then.

Thoughts of last moments are becoming nearly obsessive, but how could they not be? Of course she tries to place herself in the dimness of night with the slippery sound of plastic descending. Naturally she wonders what her last clear and then last blurring view will be of, how readily the true blackness will descend, and if there will be, after all, a terrible moment of suffering. The removal of Ruth, the process of creating the absence of her particular Ruthness—that's surely a large effort, a major extraction. She's afraid, she supposes; but if she has no anticipation of ecstasy, she does not conjure dread, either. Fear is different from dread. Fear is spiky and quick and these days frequent enough, but dread would be a deep, dark, continuous drumming.

To feel dread, she would probably have to be able to feel its opposite, which would have to be hope.

The pictures are haunting but unavoidable, part of the necessary adding-up preparation. Still, some questions won't be answerable, at least not until the point and moment of no return, precisely when it's too late for answers.

"I'm bound to be anxious," she tells Sylvia, Greta and George. Anxious at best. "Don't be surprised, and please don't mistake nervousness for changing my mind." Speaking as if events are inevitably in train helps set a tone, and not only for them. Time is ticking along. Bare tree limbs and wreaths mark its very slow, very quick passage, and still there are points on all sides that evidently need to be made.

Please give is Ruth's.

She was born at 2:19 on the sixteenth morning of December nearly, very nearly, seventy-five years ago. She was a little creature and caused only about eight hours of labour, a small trouble, her mother said, compared with what other mothers went through with their burlier, more recalcitrant infants. "Right from your first moment you were a sweetheart," said her father.

She expects to experience only an early hour or two of her seventy-sixth year. That seems about right. She shows the others her calendar: a real date, a Friday this year. The date's square on the calendar is blank and jarring.

For their part, there are basic arguments they can make, and do make, while avoiding as best they can the grim visualizing of the doing itself. No one may know exactly what the moments would be like, but the actual tools, the actual struggle—those would give anyone but a psychopath pause, and her friends, of course, are not psychopaths. It would help if they were.

"Here's what I can promise you," she tells them. "An extraordinary experience." Which scarcely needs saying. And an extraordinary experience is by no means necessarily a delightful one. And did any of them suggest they'd acquiesce if only they got a decent return on investment? "Truly, there's a kind of grace to it."

Really? Would it not make a difference, grace-wise, that Ruth loved Bernard? Or that he was dying and she is not, except in the regular, general way of all humans? There are lots of big words like *extraordinary* and *grace* she can pull out of the hat, but their interests are in other words, such as *murder* and *guilt*.

Greta, somewhat astonishingly, has still another one: *nobility*. Noble in the sense, she means, of *superiority of mind, character, ideals or morals*. "You read to us of pain and grief," she tells Ruth, "but there are people who sacrifice and suffer for good purposes—to make others free and safe, and people who go to prison and risk their lives or travel in terrible places to help those in danger because they believe in every life—we know there are many wicked people but I think of those good ones and I feel, perhaps, is it in some way, what is the word I want, an *insult* to them to give up on a life instead?"

Imagine—Greta saying such a thing to Ruth, even if the history they take exquisite care not to speak of has nothing to do with the two of them, at least not right here and right now. "But," Ruth says instead of any of that, "I'm not a hero like them, and it's a little late to become one. Nothing I do now is going to make any difference to the world rolling on willy-nilly, but I've done what I could, and even if I don't measure up, this is just another choice about what to do with a life, not an insult to anyone else's."

Greta frowns; possibly snared in Ruth's circular words? Or possibly not, because she says, "But then there are the people who have not so many choices, that you tell us about. The ones you read us only this morning, for instance."

Ruth's own tactic returning to bite her? This morning's was a long account of tens of thousands of people in a single faraway city spending their lives picking plastic and metal out of a huge garbage dump, living on terrible air and whatever pittance they can trade their scavenging for, always hungry and barely able to breathe—Ruth's point had to do with cruelty and despair. Greta appears to have heard another one. "Those people who struggle to be alive. When we are safe and comfortable here—they feel their lives are precious even when they are so very difficult, but you do not feel your life is?"

"Oh, but I do think my life's been precious, and if I could share what I've had with every blessed one of those people, I would. The best I can do, though, is that maybe one or two of them will benefit from what I'll leave in my will. Other than that, since they don't know I exist, they won't be offended if I choose to depart. It'll just mean a bit of extra air and a morsel of spare space for whoever can use it—removing my footprint entirely from the earth, as some would say."

"So now we're back to the environment, are we?" But in some ways Sylvia is surprisingly easier to deal with than Greta. She at least starts from the principle that Ruth has a right to do as she wants with herself. Sylvia bears a useful grudge against what she calls "all the moral busybodies who think it's up to them if somebody wants a child or an abortion or, for heaven's sake, a tummy tuck or a facelift, as if everything that happens is not only their business, but falls under their rules. And it's not as if what you want doesn't go on all the time anyway, only of course quietly and discreetly, and with people who are already on their way out. And with the help of experts, which I would point out we are not."

The trouble with Sylvia's principle is this: "If you insist on the right to your choice, you have to grant ours, as well."

"Of course. I know it's a fearsome thing I'm asking you for. Big act, though, big reward. Bear that in mind."

"So you say." Because Ruth's the only one of them who would know. As if she needs reminding.

Sylvia can be cruel. Fair enough.

Nor is she finished. "Do you know the time among all the good and bad times I liked best in my marriage? The years Jackson and I had, just the two of us, once he retired. They felt so benign, as if we were just very close comrades. We *knew* each other. And we were free to do nearly anything we felt like, and go almost anywhere we wanted, just us. We did a lot more travelling, mainly Europe, and oh, I miss all that—pointing out a painting, discussing a cathedral, pretending we were perfectly accustomed to sitting at midnight at an out-door café, having a drink, planning the next day. Not to say it couldn't be maddening being together so much, but having at hand the oldest of friends—do you miss that too, Ruth?"

Greta has paused in her knitting to stare at Sylvia. Such easy talk of travel to such places Greta has never returned to, and with a husband, a friend of many years. If Dolph had lived—but it does not do to think of how a whole life might have been.

Also it does not do to look back too directly. If ever she let herself do so, she would feel such harsh blows to the heart, as painful as real heart attacks. She used to speak to the girls, she thought vaguely and without true intention, of someday returning to visit her first home. Pictures she had of the same mother and father and sisters and brothers, only older like her and now with their own children, but in the same place, although in better circumstances after so many years—how they would laugh and confide and admire, how fond they would be of each other, how at home she would finally feel. They would speak of lives since she and Dolph left, not from before. It would be like a painting of a picnic, happy people gathered around a basket of food under a big spreading tree.

So pretty.

The girls must have been listening in a different, real way, however, because some years ago they came to her, all together, and said that since to journey back was her dream, they would send her. They would send a friend, too.

She did not have a good friend to invite; but that was not the trouble with their large gift. The trouble was—no. An entire reluctance, a great sinking fear. Her precious pictures, but what if those pictures were no longer true? What if they never were true?

"That is so very generous, thank you," she told Sally, Emily and Patricia, "but I think the place is too much changed, and so many of my people are gone, and others are strangers to me. Now it is best, I think, to leave that home in my memory." How could she have better explained? They looked almost betrayed: proud to have arranged the fulfilment of her desire—to have that rejected was hard for them. "I am grateful, though. You are such good, thoughtful girls."

They did not intend this, of course, but they caused her a grave loss. Perhaps also a cowardice to be faced. She embraced them each in turn, in order not to see their eyes, but more so they could not see hers.

Now Sylvia speaks of such journeys lightly, fondly, as only eating and drinking and pointing out beautiful things—as a delight, not a dream. How distant their worlds have been—Greta is reminded, again, how fortunate she is to have this place now, at this table.

Ruth is yet another matter. "We couldn't afford anything as splendid as those kinds of vacations, but I know what you mean, Sylvia. The years after we retired were just as you say: companions doing almost everything together. Well, of course we always did. But then, my goodness, we could go to the beach at the drop of a hat, or off to a movie—sometimes the best fun was the planning. Or maybe the best part was waking up in the morning and one of us saying, 'Let's do this today, or that,' and off we'd go. At first we still did a little volunteer work around town, but then Bernard said to hell with it, we should start getting the most out of what was left of our own lives. Which wasn't"—and isn't it suddenly hard not to weep?—"nearly long enough for Bernard."

And whose fault is that? "Nor for Jackson," Sylvia snaps. Ruth needn't think she's got the only dead husband. "It did surprise me, though, that those were the calmest, happiest years of our marriage. In a way, they put a golden light over the whole thing, start to finish."

Bitches. Although George manages not to say that out loud.

By the time he sold the store, Alice was already slipping, though he didn't know it and thought she just wasn't trying, and often enough he was probably cross and maybe even kind of mean—calmest, happiest years? These women, throwing it in his face. Like Alice, in a way: not thinking.

He's the one, not Alice and for sure not Colette, who knows how bad it was. Alice's anguish only lasted as long as she could comprehend anguish; as far as he could tell, anyway. Now there's things it seems he can't make clear to anyone else, and it's enraging, and what if Alice too is humming with words and ideas that only come out in those little gobbledy sounds that don't make any sense? Or for all he knows, she's gone totally silent by now. Poor woman. A fate worse than death? Maybe, but he can't imagine not existing at all, and who can?

Besides Ruth, according to her.

Ruth: who is still considering Sylvia's *golden light*. The bathing of decades in a particular glow.

It doesn't matter, though, does it? Deceptive or true, lights have to go out.

Sometimes Ruth sees Bernard, almost young, almost fairhaired, almost plump, nearly ordinary, in her office doorway, tapping lightly, bearing goodwill and coffee.

Sometimes she feels him under her hands.

In between, their two little lives.

No. Stay on firm, practical ground, keep focused on discussing a plan.

Which is: at the appointed hour Sylvia, Greta and George would rouse and collect themselves one by one from bed or chair, from sleeplessness or by alarm clock—the former more likely, according to Greta's "But who would be able to sleep?" Well, George is apt to doze off anytime, day or night.

On the other hand, in the very precise, useful process of devising the details, he comes in handiest when he blurts, "Duck."

What?

"Duck." Then, irritated, "Tape."

"Oh, *duct* tape. That's excellent, George." And how would they get their hands on it? "You could put it on your shopping list for Diane, and if anyone asks, although why would they, tell them you're packing up something to send to your daughter. Of course then you'd need to do it. How does that sound?"

It sounds like something important to do. He could send Colette something for Christmas. Usually he gives her a cheque and tells her to buy something she wants, but a cheque doesn't need duct tape. Maybe a framed, forlorn photograph of himself: just a reminder.

Then there's the plastic. According to Ruth's research, "Dry-cleaner bags are best, for the very reason they're supposed to be kept away from children and pets. And of course they're easy to get and then to dispose of."

"I've got a couple of winter coats, although they don't actually need to be cleaned. How much?"

Sylvia means how much plastic, but Ruth hears something different and says, "I know coats are expensive. I'll pay."

"How much *plastic*, Ruth. Good lord, I can afford my own dry cleaning."

"Sorry, of course you can. I just don't want anyone to be out of pocket. Including for the duct tape, George, by the way. As to plastic, two long bags? To be on the safe side." Ruth smiles. "Well, you know what I mean."

Yes, they know. How amusing. "And I have these small scissors for wool," Greta says. "They fit in a pocket."

"Perfect." The aftermath is not Ruth's concern, but she would certainly not wish harm—discovery—on her friends. The legal perils are clear, although have not been much discussed—the least of their concerns, all in all, since Ruth is so usefully reassuring on that score.

Would they really do this? "Even if I promised," Sylvia says, "well, frankly, I've never in my life killed anything, not even a mouse. I mean with my own hands. And not counting the occasional insect. But if I couldn't put a bag over a mouse, what're the odds I could possibly manage to do it to you?"

But that's where planning and training come in. Like recruits in an army, they need to be drilled until obedience and action come automatically, although unfortunately that's easier to achieve with young, freshly out of school, freshly signed up, unformed minds than with those that have had decades to build up resistance.

There are mobs too, though: demonstrating that acts that wouldn't be contemplated individually may be swiftly, brutally accomplished by groups.

People get swept up, carried along in the crowd. It's a matter of impetus and momentum.

So there they'd all be, awake and moving in the middle of the night: Sylvia arranging two dry-cleaner bags, as carefully folded as parachutes for quick, efficient unfurling, tight beneath the belt of her robe, and checking to be sure the coast is clear before making her way down the hallway to Greta; Greta putting her small scissors in the pocket of her robe before she and Sylvia steal off to George's room—a stretch to come up with a role for him in all this, but he doesn't like being left out of things, even, apparently, this.

They'd make sure the duct tape is tucked in his bathrobe pocket. The end of the roll would already be pulled free and folded back on itself, probably by Greta, so there'd be no fiddling and fumbling come the moment smooth action is urgent.

Dry-cleaner bags, duct tape, little scissors—primitive tools, but as Ruth says, "Simple is best."

Then the trio would set off down the dimly lit, silent corridor to Ruth. Who, hopefully made serene by a sedative or two, would be waiting. Whatever was said then would have to be said quietly, and when they were ready, and Ruth was ready, George would shift back to the doorway where theoretically he'd keep watch and give warning if anyone came along, blocking the way if need be, as well as he could: flailing his arms and jostling his chair. "You can roll back and forth and turn sideways and basically get in the way," Ruth tells him. "Not that you'd need to. But just in case."

He'd have to stay sharp. It could be a big job, jamming the doorway. But one good thing, he wouldn't have to do anything else, not even look.

There are other potential crises and impediments to consider: what could happen in the event of a restless resident, an unexpectedly strolling staff member, an alert signifying stroke, heart attack, tumble, or an alarm throughout the whole building warning of fire, break-in, breakout—oh, a myriad of entertaining, diverting, worrywart concerns.

They could do a dry run, creeping along the corridor in the middle of the night, approaching Ruth's bedside, but "Speaking of creeping," Sylvia says, "that'd be altogether too

creepy." Also possibly a complete waste of time. "Not that
we don't have time to waste, but I'd just as soon be asleep."

Or sitting at her window with a glass of wine, looking
out into darkness, trying to unravel love and Nancy and lies.
What might still be fixed, and what cannot ever be.

At this late date.

If they've made no promises yet, they do find themselves
watching Ruth with surgical eyes. They try to hear the rustle
of plastic, the ripping of tape. They regard her tissuey throat,
and then touch their own. Ruth, for her part, sees herself
straining to catch George's silhouette outlined by the faint
light from the doorway, tries to hear Sylvia issuing final
commands and to see Greta's fingers, adept at moving needles stitch by stitch, row by row, getting the thing done at
the same steady pace.

How very strange it is, sitting here in the Idyll Inn
lounge wondering, *What if these are the last faces I see? Is it all
right if these are the last faces I see?*

It probably is. What did Bernard think as her face above
him disappeared behind the soft billowy pillow descending—
was he as surprised as she by that impulsive obedience to his
last words?

Help me, please help, he said, and she did. Oh.

27

THE MAGICIAN AT THE FAIR . . .

O N RESIDENTS' BIRTHDAYS, the Idyll Inn provides
the cake for a congratulatory come-and-go tea in the
lounge. The typically organized Linda Swain asks Ruth's
cake preference well in advance. "Banana," Ruth suggests.
"With white creamy icing," to add the verisimilitude of
detail. Later she asks the others, "Is that okay? It won't matter to me, but if you'd rather have chocolate or carrot or
anything else, I can change my order."

"Ruth," Sylvia says, relatively gently. "I very much doubt
that if you weren't here, they'd forge on with a birthday party."

Oh. Of course, how silly to forget. There are these little
slip-ups. Failures of imagination.

She's not alone in that. Sylvia says, "You know, Ruth, I
still have such trouble with the why of the thing. The business about just feeling done, I can't seem to get it. I'm sure
I'd have an easier time if you had an awful illness that was
going to be fatal."

"The reason Bernard and I had. A clear matter of mercy."

"Well, clearer. But yes, that."

Ruth sighs. It takes a great deal of energy, week after week, pressing her one remaining desire. "Try thinking of doneness as an awful illness then, and bound to be terminal. If you can't even imagine feeling finished, you must think it's a pretty terrible state to be in. So it's about accepting what a person—me—regards as the end of the line. My definition of a fatal disease, which isn't necessarily yours."

"Oh, accepting"—Sylvia waves a thick-knuckled hand—"I can do that. I can accept all kinds of human perspectives, but that doesn't remotely mean I feel a need to agree. It's that further step—I do feel we're rather dodging the depths of that, skittering about on its surface."

"No, truly, I think this is as deep as it goes. Maybe what you're missing are words that *sound* under the surface but really are exactly what we've been talking about. Only we've done it in two-syllable words rather than five-syllable ones. You're wanting something that *sounds* more profound."

"Profound, yes—*au fond* you're probably right." Ruth and Sylvia smile at each other, while Greta does not understand why they smile, and George keeps on not listening.

"It's not that complicated, boiled down," Ruth says. "There's just yes or no. Only two options."

She sounds tired; impatient, too. "Then," Sylvia says, "I guess we should be getting around to fish or cut bait. Get down to brass tacks. Shit or get off the pot"—that last what Jackson used to say, waiting for a client to decide whether to sue a brother over a father's will, or for a homeowners' association to appeal a rezoning.

This, like one or two other things on her mind, is rather more vital.

"I do not know *cut bait*," Greta says, "or *brass tacks*." For heaven's sake, how long has she been in this country? Sometimes she looks to be losing language rather than gaining it.

"I don't know the origins either, but they all mean the same thing, and *shit or get off the pot* could hardly be clearer." They're into the earliest days of December now, and there's mistletoe tacked up over the entrances to the dining room—an invitation to certain kinds of interpersonal mischief, a miscalculation on the part of Annabel Walker? In the fake library, the bushy fake Christmas tree is awaiting its tinsel and bulbs, and Linda Swain's craft keeners are busy with the creation of crèches and wreaths.

Naturally, December's main festivity for Ruth has always been her own birthday. "Our little saviour," her father used to joke, back when he joked.

There's not much funny about the month this year. Despite their dithering, there's a new roll of duct tape in the top drawer of George's bedside table, and Sylvia's two freshly dry-cleaned winter coats already hang in her closet. As to Greta's little scissors, they're right here on the table, ready for wool-snipping as needed. Which is rather tactless; much as it would be tasteless if George brought the tape and whatever gift he's sending off to his daughter here to the lounge to be wrapped up for mailing.

At least Sylvia has had the good grace not to go around wearing those coats, which hang still encased and untouched in their plastic.

The opposing way of regarding all this is, if Greta's the only one who can stomach the tools, what hope is there that any of them will come through with the deed?

The answer is coming. Not only because of Sylvia's "shit or get off the pot" but also because her cellphone should ring anytime, bringing a verdict on Nancy. Which in turn will affect the peculiarly superstitious bargain she proposed to Ruth in an *I'll chance anything* moment last week. "I realize that on the face of it this doesn't make sense," she offered, "but if my hope comes true, I'll try to do my best for yours, how about that?" Her hope being that Nancy will sail through her surgery, fit and cancer-and-any-other-disease-free.

Except for sounding unserious, it was an unlikely pledge coming from Sylvia: inexplicably irrational to suggest that Ruth's death could be fair return for Nancy's life. Then again, Sylvia has become strikingly solemn about Nancy, no doubt about that; which means that two of them are waiting for Sylvia's phone to ring, two of them are relying on an unknown surgeon—young or old, thin or fat, deft or clumsy?—in a distant city to do his work well.

Maybe Sylvia just finds it comforting to have a companion in helplessness. She's certainly tense. Now and then she sighs, and she keeps staring at the little blue phone on the table as if it already contains the answer but is refusing to tell. Apparently fierce maternity can kick in anytime; as in fact Ruth already knows, from her dealings over the years with lackadaisical, cruel or inept mothers transformed on the instant into ferocious defenders of family. Alert, suddenly, to the potential for loss.

Ruth wouldn't mind borrowing one of Greta's ghastly scarves. She is freezing.

Greta is learning the use of circular needles for manufacturing red sleeves with green cuffs. How intent she looks, but then, she has her gift deadline coming up fast. It's a bit hard to comprehend that all these lives, with their various catastrophes and celebrations, events and non-events, even their bold sweaters and scarves, will go on whether Ruth's a witness or not. The Idyll Inn will have its wreaths, its lights, its seasonal concerts and foods and morsels of nostalgia, with or without her. Even George, half-frowning in a world of his own, must have a sense of a future.

George is wondering if Colette is coming for Christmas. Probably she has told him, he's not sure, but he's not going to ask, unless he forgets and asks anyway. But if Colette doesn't come, and Greta's girls do, and who knows about Sylvia's, who will he celebrate with? At Thanksgiving there was Ruth at his table, but apparently she doesn't plan on sticking around.

There was also a terrible moment of shame that weekend, wasn't there? And, he hasn't forgotten, one of delicious delight. Words that maybe make it a D day.

Colette should be here. It used to be that nothing got in Christmas's way, not shoes, or Greta for the years that she lasted, or anyone else. It was just Colette, him and Alice, dolls and sweaters and watches, swaths of wrapping paper and scraps of Scotch tape, pancakes in the morning, the smallest of turkeys at night—everything, all of it, to do with Colette.

At Alice's nursing home, last time he checked, Christmas looked a lot the same as it seems it's going to look here. Alice, still rousable by music from her vast bewilderment, was apt to weep along with the carols, which could only bring a guy down. Exactly when did the season turn sad? Cruel, phonying it up like this. And mistletoe! He'll want to watch out for that.

When the blue cellphone on the table finally makes its jolting little trill, Sylvia almost drops it in her hurry to answer. Even George looks up. "Yes?" they hear. And then they wait, and wait, unable to read Sylvia's expression, until they are astonished by a tear; and then another. Trembling-voiced, she says at last, "Oh, thank God. I'm so relieved. Yes, you rest now, but thank you for letting me know. We'll talk again later. Sleep tight, dear. Be well."

Sleep tight, dear? That's Nancy she's talking to?

Sylvia's eyes close briefly, and when she opens them— what radiance! Ruth is dazzled by an unexpected explosion of silver. "Nancy says she's fine, and they got everything that was wrong. Oh, but I wish I was with her. I'd like to see for myself."

When Nancy was little, if she was sick, Sylvia took dry toast and ginger ale to her bedside, and read stories out loud. "Hospitals are tough places these days. She says they're going to make her get up in a couple of hours and take a few steps. I hope she has somebody with her to lean on."

"I'm sure she does. Hospitals may be brisk about getting people moving, but they're careful."

"Still, I'd like to be there."

"Of course you would." Greta reaches across, pats Sylvia's hand.

What Sylvia would like to do is tell Nancy she's sorry, although not exactly for what; and how likely is it that she'd say any such thing in Nancy's actual, forbidding presence?

Some lies, whether of commission or omission, grow too old and deep for undoing. But can there not be such a thing as an apology, a regret—even, if she were so bold, an embrace, stubbornly and it now seems stupidly delayed for decades and decades?

Well, they'll see, the two of them, although not till Nancy next comes to visit—by which time who knows what will be the same and what will be different?

"That is most wonderful news," Greta says. Look at her—her hobby may strike Sylvia as in equal parts garish and dull, but she's dependable and apparently loyal, if not by any means vastly amusing. She is generous toward George, when she must have had, at least years ago, every good reason not to be kind—for sure, even now, if Peter lived among them, Sylvia wouldn't be wheeling him around or urging life-saving exercise—so the fact is, if Sylvia were in hard, genuine need, it's Greta she would want to rely on, not Annabel Walker, or a nurse or an aide, or Nancy, or definitely, obviously, George.

Without Ruth, though, Sylvia really can't see sitting here with just Greta and George. Of course, who Sylvia would choose to have a glass of wine with in the future is scarcely the crux of the matter, but it's one crux. It matters to her.

Did she make a deal with Ruth, or just an airy suggestion? The former, she fears.

Still, if they were to do this thing, everyone involved would be changed in the doing—who knows what could emerge, for better or worse? George might discover good humour and benign gratitude, Greta bitter temper and rancour.

While Sylvia might find herself soft and pliable as a dishrag, which she wouldn't care for at all.

Who was Ruth before she did what she did to—for— Bernard? She's not exactly a gentle soul now, but she's not a brute, either.

Jackson would have been frantic waiting for the news about Nancy. Parents should be together when their children have trouble. They would have talked, and understood silences, and held one another.

How ecstatic together they could have been now.

Help me, he whispered near the end. *Help me*, Ruth's husband cried, and she did. "All right, then," Sylvia hears herself say. "Still no guarantees, but I haven't forgotten my bargain, so okay, I'll give it a try. In a way I'm *honoured* you've asked me to try."

Can she mean that?

Honour, trust, compassion, respect, regret, debt—big words. "You know, one *behaves* in certain ways for the most part, and perhaps one even *is* certain things, but one doesn't often put words to them. Perhaps one should. Then one would know more precisely and be better prepared."

What on earth is she talking about, and who calls herself *one?*

Ruth doesn't care. She heard Sylvia's conclusion well enough.

Greta assumes it must be her own fault that she couldn't follow these words that sounded passionate and important. George, though, George has caught a glimmer of something at the edge of his vision—*honour, trust, compassion, respect, regret, debt?*—and slams his hand flat on the arm of his wheelchair again and again, and calls out loudly in rhythm, "Yes, yes, yes," and if he's not entirely sure what he's saying yes to, he knows it's some big deal of a thing.

"Thank you, Sylvia, thank you, George." That leaves Greta: the one with the sure, strong, quick fingers.

All their public discussions and private deliberations about gods and eternities, punishments and rewards, sins as opposed to virtuous acts, the affections and obligations of friends, natural unfoldings versus Ruth's forcible one, most of all the fundamental human drive, will and duty to keep breathing, keep *being*—and today it comes down to something irrelevant like Sylvia's daughter coming safely through surgery; to George's muddled pounding out of his *yes, yes, yes*. To what, with Greta? Capable thumb up, or efficient thumb down?

So: here Greta is, at this table in the Idyll Inn lounge, under the eyes of her new friends and George, needed and important and even desired. An old woman with other old people; differences that have wounded and mattered smoothed under blankets of common and uncommon experience, and of age—this is a moment, yes.

In his struggle Dolph must have watched, not a long, full past disappearing, but a long, impossible, glorious future. He would have seen her and their girls, and his heart must have burst.

That is nothing like Ruth. Nor did Greta choose to be shot through by heart attack, nor did George choose his stroke. Only Ruth has decided to decide. She wants to whip her own fate out from under herself. She is like the magician at the fair who left a whole set of unrattled china in place when in a single, swift, almost invisible motion he flicked the tablecloth out from beneath. The girls later tried that at home, and broke plates.

"I am like Sylvia," she says finally. "I can also not promise for sure when the time comes, but if it is truly what you want, I shall try. If it is too hard"—because of course it seems impossible—"I hope you will forgive me. Us."

Well. All right then. How abruptly frightened they are; like children who've lit a fire that spreads fast and far beyond anything they know how to put out—here it comes, flames roaring over grassland, leaping through treetops, racing toward them.

28

SO THIS IS HOW IT HAPPENS . . .

*A*ND SO THIS IS HOW IT HAPPENS that at three o'clock of a mid-December morning, at that defenceless hour when anything feels possible and nothing human or inhuman out of the question, three Idyll Inn residents are joined in the main-floor corridor to make a journey under pinkish, translucent, ridged and uptilted wall sconces to the suite where their fourth is waiting.

The building itself is silent at this hour except for the hum and thrum made by its structural versions of breathing and blood. The people, too, are quiet as can be, and wary, even though this is the same plain-sailing corridor they've been navigating for months. How have they come to this? Not easily, not without objection and fuss, but all in all, remarkably swiftly. Now, although wearing robes, slippers, pyjamas and nightgowns, they're as equipped for their mission as any soldiers heading for combat. One way and another, they come bearing weapons. The suspense is a killer, which in other circumstances might be a good joke.

Instead it's a wonder skin isn't scorched, a miracle the whole place doesn't burst into flames.

If not smoke, something murky does hang in the air. Busy hearts leap and bang, legs wobble, hands shake—easy to desire an event that would halt them, right now, in their tracks: a staff member's patrol, an alarm going off.

How fragile flesh is. How warm, soft and vulnerable a body can be.

If it was a long, long way from the thought to the word, it's now much farther still to the deed.

It's also an excruciatingly short distance from a lithe little girl tumbling and vaulting through the air to a woman waiting in an Idyll Inn bed, springing around memory, flying through purpose. Only a moment on earth; only a moment to contain the entire story of Ruth.

She can't—won't—doubt her decision, but there are jolting, eye-opening moments when she disbelieves it. This is a form of being in shock, she expects. It wouldn't be right to call her fearless, but shock, as in a catastrophe like a bombing or car crash, provides its own anaesthetic. Also she took two sedatives at midnight, and has completed her sums. The total appears to be that she is a woman turning seventy-five who is no longer loved and, empty of even the desire to desire, sees nothing to love.

So tonight is only the final hollowing step.

It would be nice to suppose that on the other side of the hour will be Bernard. That sort of belief must be a balm for others about to take final breaths, but instead she'll be, like him, only the silence, the space.

The no-Ruth.

How can she do this? Does she have Bernard's resolve,

his desolation? Is the method she's chosen truly merciful—
how would anyone really know? This is not a new question.
She has seen the plastic, she has regarded the tape. She has
examined the eyes and moreover the hands of her friends.
They must be very good friends. She can hear their slight
stir and rustle out in the corridor. Her senses are terrifically
keen; she can feel, too, the gentle touch on skin of her new
flannel nightgown, light blue and scattered with small yellow flowers. She bought it last week, out shopping with
Sylvia. This is the first time she's worn it. Helping her into it
hours ago, Diane remarked on its prettiness. "I wanted something cosy for winter," Ruth told her. She is glad that Diane's
shift ended at midnight; that she won't be the one coming
through Ruth's door in the morning.

There are no loose ends, as far as she knows. Her will,
updated thanks to one of the lawyers who bought Sylvia's
husband Jackson's practice (Sylvia's lover Peter's practice, as
well) leaves half her remaining assets to the children's
agency she worked for, the other half to an organization that
helps children in even more dire need overseas. She has
placed a copy of this will, and instructions for what's to be
done with her remains, her poor breathless body, in the top
drawer of her dresser. She'd have left it all out in plain view,
except that would look suspicious come morning. She has
told Sylvia, Greta and George about it, though, in case it
needs pointing out. "No service, and just cremation. But I've
left a little budget to cover lots of wine and a few sand-
wiches, if anyone feels like raising a glass somewhere. Or
nowhere. It's hardly important."

No casket, open or closed, no formal funeral, but besides
this nightgown she has also, entirely irrationally, bought a

dress: a silvery grey silky number, along with silvery grey silky stockings to match, a splurge she would, as she remarked to Sylvia, "never have made while I was alive." It's the luxury of the material, the soft swirl of the skirt—"Bernard would have liked me in this."

She intends it to go up in smoke, unseen and irrelevant, right along with her, and where's the sense in that? "Oh, go ahead, treat yourself. At least it's virtually certain," and Sylvia laughed, "to last you the rest of your life."

There. Not many people are able to leave life to sounds of laughter.

To be sure, not many people probably want to.

"So far I haven't imagined a cheery scenario," Sylvia said, "but you never know."

No, you don't.

How much of this has been fanciful and what is going to be fact?

Fact arrives in the doorway on slippered feet. A pink nimbus from dim corridor lights shimmers, a pale radiance surrounding an awkward, three-headed silhouette. Is it that time already? Not too late to say, *No, go away*, but still a little too soon to say, *Now*. Idyll Inn bedrooms aren't large. Suddenly Ruth's is filled by one narrow body and a bulky one, both breathing as if the journey here has been long, hard and uphill, and a third arriving at the foot of Ruth's bed on wheels and canting leftward. Obviously Ruth isn't the only one for whom this is a difficult night, although just as obviously her claim is unique. Then these three will have the morning, as well. This too has been carefully planned, except for the amount of sleep anyone who's not Ruth is likely to get.

When whatever will happen has happened, Sylvia and Greta are to wheel George back to his room and roll him into his bed. He'll be the one practically guaranteed to fall fast asleep, they assume. Sylvia and Greta may or may not have words to say, such as "Oh my," or "Good night," and they may or may not care to touch each other's warm, living skin before they head to their own suites, where they will begin learning to believe whatever they've done and not done.

They will have left Ruth's door open. She likes to keep it ajar anyway so she can overhear passing conversations, random bits of gossip: aides speaking of how best to handle certain residents, their complaints about strict management, meaning Annabel Walker, their romantic evenings or difficult marriages, conflicts and triumphs with parents or children; passing residents, too, confiding feuds, alliances, judgments. "I have no idea what she's doing in a place like this," Ruth has heard, presumably not about herself. "She should be in a nursing home, she's a real ding-a-ling." The words have been life floating in mildly interesting fashion into Ruth's ears; but in the morning her door, with a different purpose this time, should stand open; an invitation to discovery—avoiding delay is the goal.

In their suites, Sylvia and Greta will close their own doors behind them. They do not expect to welcome disturbance.

Will they go directly to bed? Will they sleep? Awake or asleep, will they prefer to leave bedside lights on? Will Sylvia sit with a glass of wine in her chair by the window, staring out into darkness?

What will they see in their minds' eyes? If they sleep, of what will they dream? This is all, as Greta has said, fantastic to contemplate. *Fantastic: so extreme as to challenge belief*, as well as *bizarre* or *grotesque*.

It's too bad, although nothing new, that the innocent are the ones who most often suffer for others' decisions. At some moment as morning lights are flipped on, as pots and pans start clattering in the kitchen and breakfast dishes are laid out on dining-room tables, as residents are rousing themselves or being roused from another silent sleepless or wakeful Idyll Inn night, one unlucky staff member will walk through Ruth's open door. She will call Ruth's name softly, then a little more loudly. Perhaps she will reach down, gently shaking Ruth's shoulder. Once she catches her breath she'll hurry off to alert Annabel Walker, and immediately the usual process of doctor-calling, followed by corpse-whisking-away, will kick in. "Just make sure before you leave me that I'm wearing a peaceful expression, okay? No pop-eyes or dropped-open jaw." Which came out less lightheartedly than Ruth intended; in fact, caused a brief silence during which each mind screened a picture of terrified eyes, and limbs strained from fighting a losing, last-minute battle against the hands of her friends.

"Won't happen, though. Nobody'll notice a thing wrong, including the doctor. If I were eighteen or forty there'd be an autopsy and questions, but I'm not, so there won't be." Ruth has done her best to comfort and assure. She's a kind woman, if a deadly one.

Whereas blunt Sylvia said, "What you mean is, if you're old nobody'd even *imagine* noticing you've died for no obvious reason. Or you can *kill* somebody. We could do *anything*." As if she had something further in mind? Or more likely had just had at least one drink too many.

They'll all be entirely sober come morning. No matter how shocked or unshocked they are, they're bound to fall asleep eventually—"We're old," as Sylvia says. "We nod off"—which means they probably won't make it to breakfast, and will miss all the coming and going. By some means, however, they'll learn that Ruth's gone. How will this happen? "I bet Annabel Walker would come tapping around, since she knows we've been friends. For that matter, she'll wonder why we all slept in, if that's what happens."

Well, it's a challenge, trying to account for every eventuality. "You could put it down to the mystical. That without knowing what's happened to me, you must have fallen into an extra-deep sympathy sleep." Another of Ruth's failures to amuse on the subject. "Or seriously, you could say I wasn't feeling well and you all sat up with me till quite late, which is why you slept in."

"And we didn't call anyone to say you were sick, and you didn't either?" Sylvia frowned. "Irresponsible, surely."

"No, you'd say it just looked like an upset, nothing particularly concerning. Honestly, nobody'll have any real questions."

"Still, we'd be pretty horrified."

"I expect you should look as horrified as you can manage, in any event. If nothing else, that should get you all sorts of special treatment. Look on the bright side, maybe Annabel will order you up a late breakfast in bed. Let you loll around all day in your housecoats without nagging. You can probably milk it for quite a few days." Such merriment. What an extraordinary conversation, making these plans, examining multiple possibilities for the hours after she would no longer exist. Real plans for unreal circumstance.

The only sensible, sane approach.

Whatever works.

What does work? Not George's call for "duck" tape, or his fist-pounding "Yes, yes, yes"—that couldn't be called a proper argument; unpersuasive even to Greta, but then why *has* Greta arrived here at Ruth's middle-of-the-night bedside, with her frailties of the heart but also her necessary strong hands? Still, or awkward, waters evidently run deep. Perhaps now it's just a matter of in for a penny, in for a pound, not that Greta would know the expression, but how to account for the penny to start with?

Gratitude. Loyalty. Desire. One would have to know more about Greta than Ruth does, or Sylvia, or even George. One would have to know about shame, as well as the weight and longings of years as a foreigner and a stranger—loneliness, although that is a word too hard and sad to speak—and a redemption found here. *Redeem: save or rescue or reclaim; fulfil.* One would have to know the force of will, and feel the full, unexpected beneficences of the Idyll Inn.

There is a life-saving debt owed to Ruth. There is, then, this debt to them all, and a payment Greta can make that no one else swiftly and mercifully can.

If she can. If she is called to.

It is Sylvia who is to remove the carefully folded dry-cleaner bag from under the belt of her robe, Sylvia who is to hold it up between her knobby, outstretched hands, ready, but it is Greta who is to help Ruth raise up her head so the plastic can slip smoothly over it, Greta who is to reach for the roll of duct tape with its end already folded back so there's no fumbling, Greta who is to quickly, as smoothly as she can, wind and wrap the tape around and around, pinning plastic to throat.

As George keeps watch in the doorway, ready or unready to warn of intrusion, it's to be Greta and Sylvia hovering right over Ruth, witness to the whuffing in and out of the plastic, the O of last breaths, the brief but bound-to-be-frantic struggle. It's Greta, when the room is still again, who is to finally take the small pair of scissors from the pocket of her robe and snip carefully through the tape. Sylvia will raise the plastic away. Then they will see—what? Ruth's terminal hope, or terror, or peace, or for that matter an entirely unanticipated future coming to view? Or nothing at all.

That's the plan. "Don't be surprised," Ruth has advised, "and remember, don't leave me looking surprised, either."

Then there's the other plan.

"No guarantees," Sylvia said. She has her own brand of chin-up courage, it seems to Ruth, and has learned from tough experience, as people either do or do not, to stick by nearly every one of her words. None of them can save anyone. Sylvia couldn't even save her own daughter, if Nancy were in real trouble. "That's the most helpless I've felt in a long time," Sylvia said, "and I'm more than furious that almost every damn thing that matters in this world is out of our hands. This is one thing that isn't. Whatever anyone says—lawyers, doctors, governments, religions, all those nincompoop moral busybodies that float around like weed seeds—we should be in charge of our own selves. Even if we hardly ever are." And so here she is. Standing beside Ruth's bed in her cream-coloured, ankle-length chenille robe, with two plastic bags, one for real, one for spare, carefully folded and tucked under its belt. Proving that her mind is with Ruth; but hearts do not always—do not often—naturally and automatically follow minds. Ruth's own great struggle has been to align determination of mind with the terror and grief of the otherwise empty heart. What can she expect of these others?

Sylvia lowers herself with some caution and difficulty to sit on the bed. It's easy to forget that she's in fairly severe pain a lot of the time. She's a prideful person, even with herself. Ruth, for one, finds that invigorating, reliable and even contagious, although it's obvious that some people are put off by a stiff upper lip, assuming it marks the absence of an equally strenuous heart.

"What time is it?" Ruth whispers.

"Five after three. Do you mind if I turn on the bedside light?"

Oh, five after three. Minutes dissolve, sugar in water. How many did Ruth calculate she has wasted over her years? Did she think to multiply and divide time into minutes or did she stop at the hours? What if in every single minute she'd seen people surrounded by colours in the shape of electrical arcs, and she'd smelled every scent as if it were her mother's bath powder or Bernard's aftershave? What if so many moments hadn't slipped past, a regiment of grey shadows? "Sure, go ahead."

In this light, which is not pink, translucent or especially dim, features come instantly clear. George is drooping but Greta looks alert, fearful and tense; as for that matter Ruth must as well. Whereas Sylvia—Sylvia's smiling. Not broadly, but how can she smile at all, what's the matter with her? Now she's reaching under her robe. For the dry-cleaner bags—is she that keen to get this over and done with? No, for something else: a slim packet of paper. Now what?

"Here's the deal. We're here and we'll do our best if we must, but we're not going down without one more fight, and neither are you. Okay? Got that?"

So brusque. As if Sylvia and not Ruth is in charge. As is the case at the moment, given Ruth's supplicant position. She has spent months, weeks, days and hours, right down to these last minutes, inching her way up to this high, breath-taking ledge, nearly ready to jump—and now they want to tug at her sleeve, grab her belt, one more time? There can't be anything fresh to be said, any new argument to be made, any remaining qualm to surprise—unless there's a last-minute, queasy qualm when fingers touch plastic and skin; there's always been that possibility. "How can you do this to me now?"

Greta looks stricken. Too bad. "We are sorry." She too sits beside Ruth, across the bed from Sylvia. "But we thought this could be a time when you would hear."

"You mean, when I'd be vulnerable?"

Sylvia frowns. "Well, admit it, that's partly why you picked this hour: because it's a tricky, unreal time for doing tricky, unreal things. You're right, we knew this could make you angry, and as Greta says, we're sorry about that, but occasionally making a friend angry is among friendship's jobs. Now just listen. Listen to this."

Outrageous, bargaining right to the end.

The paper Sylvia's produced from under her belt is newsprint—Ruth's own weapon turned against her once more? Now Sylvia's going on about some kid who, having seen a TV documentary on child slaves used for mining diamonds, harvesting coffee, providing sex to old men—children are useful for many purposes, as Ruth already well

knows—this boy now travels the world speaking to governments and international organizations and schools, visiting
hard-pressed villages and destitute orphanages, giving over
his adolescence, as he will, he says, his adulthood, to sham-
ing and improving, if not humanity, at least a portion of its
malevolence. "See?" Sylvia says.

See what? "He's young. The young are optimistic and fit,
they can do that sort of thing."

"I'm way ahead of you on that. So here's a ninety-four-
year-old named Lily Meisner—obviously a good deal older
than any of us—who's damn near blind but still writing
politicians and religious types and everybody else she can
think of, campaigning for absolutely-no-cost-to-anyone
birth control. In every place on earth, mind you. She says
that's the basic way to make women free, and she's pushed
for it all her life and isn't about to stop just because of a bit
of old age and blindness."

"Well, bully for her and her letters, and much good may
they do her or anyone else. But I expect if she's such a fan of
freedom, she'd be bound to agree to mine, too."

"Maybe, but I bet she'd have some alternative sugges-
tions as well. And you'll notice that even though it's an
utterly hopeless cause, she's never given up hope. She
keeps trying."

"Very inspiring." Ruth too can be dry when she needs to
be. "And no doubt you're making a point?"

"It's George's, really." At his name George raises his
head, his eyes flying open. No, nothing happening yet. "It's
what he keeps reminding you: that there's always good news.
I admit I had to scrounge and scrape to find it, but look at
that boy, and old Lily Meisner—we're a funny bunch,

humans, is all I mean. A more mixed bunch than it's always easy to bear in mind. And whatever we're doing, whoever we are, most of us don't care to quit."

Not fair to pull out an apple-cheeked do-gooding boy and an ancient sight-losing zealot when Ruth is waiting in her nice new nightgown to be dead—dead! What will that be? What will it not be?—within the hour. A waste, too. There's nothing new about what Sylvia's saying except in the particulars, and of course in her uncharacteristically chipper view of the nature of humans. Nevertheless a show of temper wouldn't be smart. It'd be easy for them to turn on their heels, and then what would Ruth do?

"We're *interesting,*" Sylvia is saying, with, Ruth admits, an interesting passion. "We're good and bad and everything in between and we're always finding fresh ways to show it. Whatever else that is, don't you find it absorbing? Just look at us—how fascinating is this, even if we can only be here right now because to anyone but ourselves we're about as transparent as four very old crystal balls." Albeit, Sylvia adds, "four crystal balls somewhat fogged up in our own minds when it comes to the future."

Not really. That's not been Ruth's impression, but then her view of the future has been limited to this very hour.

"I mean, never mind longing for this and that, aren't you still at least curious? Don't you want to know what happens next? I realize we're all bound to be cut off in the midst of something suspenseful, but don't you want to know who wins and loses different elections, and how wars are going, including the war on the planet you're so worried about? Don't you want to know whose house gets built or burned down, or which local rapscallion is selling drugs or making fake money? How about whether that Diane you're so fond of makes a go of it with her boyfriend, or another crazy geezer starts waving knives in the kitchen? And look, what about tomorrow, aren't you even mildly interested in whether it's snowing tonight, and what the sunrise will look like when the light hits the river?" Sylvia must be desperate; it's not like her to go soft about sunrise.

"There's us, too, don't you care about us? Because if we go through with this, nothing could be as enormous for any of us ever again, and the end of enormity would be an awful thing to get used to. You should want to save us from that. And we're your friends, you know—wake up, George—so we'd also like you to take into account that we'd miss you, very much."

They've said that before, too; but "Miss, miss," cries George, jolting upright.

"Shhh," Greta whispers. "We must be quiet."

There's a great deal for George to be quiet about. Greta herself is his secret, he believes, one that's such a long-standing habit it's lodged in his brain like a nut in the throat. Quiet, she says. What's going on? Still nothing, it looks like.

Oh. Ruth. "Miss," he repeats softly. It's hard to let go of people a person's got used to. "Fond," he says.

"Thank you, George. I'm fond of you, too." So why's that not good enough? It's a sad thing, not being enough in the eyes of a woman. Maybe he's not the man he once was, but then again, look, not every fellow his age has three women caring about him, and even caring for him just about every day. "Miss," he sighs one more time; now meaning something complicated about four that would be different if they were three. The whole bunch of them could fall apart, and then what would happen to him?

Does Alice get lonesome, does she feel adrift with no daughter or husband holding her hand? He can see, right now, how she might. She was a good woman, by and large. Like Ruth, as a matter of fact, at least in the way of being small and mostly meaning well. Not so demanding, though. That's why they're here, because of Ruth being demanding.

Still, he's trusted to be here. Alice is in a locked wing at the nursing home, since some people—not her any more— are likely to wander away. There are numbers to push on a lock to get in. He has no idea now what those numbers could be, but somebody'd probably help.

It's not nice hearing a door lock behind you. There'd be the problem of getting out, too.

"If I had not met you first here, Ruth," his old, once-upon-a-time Greta is saying, "I would have been frightened, and I might still be alone. I, too, wish you will see that it is possible to make new things to be interested in. It is not possible always to be having new friends, however."

Surely that's Greta's problem, not Ruth's. Ruth will have no need for anyone, old or new, so what does she care about gratitude, or whatever struggles and disruptions she leaves in her wake? She'll be dead and untouchable.

How cold. It's one thing to be empty of desire, but it would be . . . unworthy . . . to leave cold-hearted. That would be a failure of character. Ruth reaches for Greta's hand and finds hers painfully clasped. Greta's hand is large, which is good, and hot, which is distressing. "I'm sorry," Ruth says.

What would happen if she said, "Enough"? If she said, "Do it," and pulled her hand free and closed her eyes and set her mouth in a firm, go-ahead line—would they obey? Ah, but there's this spikiness in the atmosphere that needs flattening before she goes forward into—well, into nothing. Really, in its way that's even funny. Would they laugh, or would it lose effect, as so much does, in the explaining?

Sylvia is fiddling with papers again. "You'll never guess what else I've been looking up. Well, of course you won't, so I'll tell you: astrological signs. Which you won't be surprised to hear I've never done before, but there you go, as we've just been pointing out, there's always something new to be learned. And I find you're a Sagittarius, so you're, let's see, full of enterprise, energy, versatility and adventurousness. Which I guess in the circumstances is fairly true."

She has to be kidding. "Don't make fun." Ruth is angry. "This is my *life*."

"I know it is, but it's ours too, and it's actually a compliment, how far we're willing to go to keep you among us. Horoscopes, for heaven's sake, that's how far." Sylvia does not point out that Ruth just referred to her life, not her death. It's not a bad thing if Ruth's angry, either. Even in this light they can see that her skin's flushed, her eyes have narrowed, her jaw is tightened—she doesn't look on the verge of saying, *Go ahead, kill me now.*

"This also says your mind is open to new thoughts, and you're ambitious and optimistic even in unhappy times. You're also honourable, trustworthy, truthful and sincere, and you fight for the underdog. You have foresight and you can be witty. You're strong-willed and good at organizing—and we can certainly see that that's true, too. You're outspoken but forgiving, and good at coming up with principles to explain the universe. It seems you also have a strong gambling instinct—that's interesting, isn't it? In which regard we might note that you can be impatient and overly hasty when you take on a project."

If events had moved as intended, without this foolishness, the others could be headed back to their beds by now. Ruth would be lying here already dead. How . . . odd . . . to be not dead. To be present when she ought to be absent. This seems to make the margins between life and death somehow flimsy. Or perhaps she means flexible.

"You're vulnerable to arthritis and rheumatism—well, there you go—and you like freedom and getting to the nub of things, but you may tend to feel disillusioned. Apparently you should try harder to think positive thoughts. I imagine we'd all agree about that.

"Then, since this is your birthday, I looked up the specifics, too. For the next year you're to expect big positive changes. I realize that's somewhat ambiguous, but I think we can assume it means you should be alive to appreciate them. It also says that in the next twelve months you'll benefit from alliances with senior people, and you're supposed to be sociable and take good care of friendships. On your birthday itself—today—you're supposed to go slowly and guard against knee-jerk reactions, and cheer up because your troubles are minor and your life is about to be highly positive. Although again I realize there's some ambiguity there. Still, you get the drift: good times ahead."

The room's getting warmer. There's even a scorched scent, as if a hot iron's been left flat on cotton. Maybe it's anger, maybe it's fear. Maybe it's coming from one of them, maybe from all, maybe it's just a smell that regularly arises from the Idyll Inn during these sleeping hours. Sylvia lets her papers fall onto her lap. "All right, Ruth. We know you think you've had enough. All we want to do is tell you one more time that there can't be enough—not time, affection, breath, anything. Not even horoscopes. Of course it's hard knowing that once we're born we'll have to die, and at some stage—ours, obviously—we should be teaching ourselves how to do that, preferably with some grace. But in the meantime we hope. We always want more."

George stirs again. "More," he says.

"I don't. I've told you, I have no *longing*."

"Have you thought," Greta suggests, "that this is perhaps only ordinary?" Only ordinary, to have no desire except a certain yearning for absence—how dare she?

"That this is not a time for longing," Greta continues, "but for other matters. You talked once of a curve in the shape of a life. As when you and Sylvia have spoken of when you and your husbands were retired and free together, that time would be to you a nice part in a large curving. But for me, I see life in separate sections, and each portion with its own customs and purpose. So mine would be a section before Dolph and I came to this country, which was a part we had to leave behind, and forget. And then the first years here, and having the girls. There comes a new section after Dolph died, and another after my girls left home, and then after other things, too. Now I think this can be only another portion of life, to be old. Our bodies change, and sometimes our minds, but we can learn also now different affections. So that maybe our days are in some ways painful and difficult, but they can be as well new. There is grief when one part of life ends, but then there comes finally a courage, and we set ourselves to find what is next—what I have learned here already from you, Ruth, I cannot say it all. Do you not still learn? I think you do."

How flushed—dangerously flushed?—Greta looks in this light. Ruth hasn't heard so many words from her before, at least not like this, in a rush. "And if we search in the world like Sylvia, and George too, for what is good as well as what is wicked, then look at us. Because if we are not your good friends, we would not be here now, do you see?"

What Ruth sees is that Greta's muddled, fierce words have their own sincere kind of entrancement.

Which is, as Greta would say, something new to be learned.

Entrancement must be a kind of longing; a puzzle of sorts. "What time is it?"

"Almost four."

Seventy-five years ago this very moment Ruth was entirely new to the world: pink, wrinkly, full-heartedly adored by two people, and completely unknowing.

Now she's pink, wrinkly, unadored, and knows far too much.

As well as, according to Greta and Sylvia, not yet enough.

Oh, and unexpectedly, she's still alive, too. There's always that kind of suspense, of plans delayed, or denied, which Sylvia didn't mention when she was rhyming off curiosities. No one suggested that tempers and sharp tones might arise. Or hot, leftover, uneloquent, heartfelt debate.

Sylvia's right that whenever death comes, it's in the midst of something at least vaguely interesting: an election, a war, a toppling or a rising-up. But all these events, they fold over on themselves. They build, one by one, layers of history like rock. They bury themselves, much like humans, and much of the time this must be proper.

Say it *now*. Go ahead.

What does Ruth leave in her wake? Only lives saved and not saved. Love made and love put out of its misery.

Also whatever remains of her in the hearts of the people right here at her bedside.

Also perhaps other, more elusive, vapour trails of her Ruthness—words she has said and forgotten that have made a difference to some person or other. To Diane, possibly, or the many children, with and without their haphazard parents.

In these respects she must be splendidly unique, as well as merely one star in the multitudes of the sky, one minuscule grain of sand in the desert, a comfortingly insignificant one among billions, no gain and no loss.

"I think," she begins.

A strange, surprised, quiet "Oh" interrupts. It is an *Oh* that causes everyone, even George, to look sharply at Greta; an *Oh* accompanied by a frown, and a look in the eyes that says Greta has suddenly gone to a remote place of her own, far away, or inside.

The hand holding Ruth's painfully tightens. Greta's other hand goes to rest on her cheek, as if something important and puzzling has cropped up that she needs to consider right now. In this light, to Ruth's eyes, Greta has been instantly washed in very dark blue, like a storm sky, but touched at the edges by flares of brilliant yellow and red. "Oh," Greta says.

Sylvia stands, papers falling from her lap to the floor. "Greta?" she asks, too loudly for the hour and place. "What is it, what's wrong?"

"A pain. My medicine." Greta's voice is faint and echoey, as if she speaks from a cave.

"Where is it?"

The crisp question seems to draw Greta closer to the mouth of the cave. "Bedside," she says as her hot hand leaves Ruth's and moves to her chest.

"Your bedside table? Hold on then, I'll go get it." How swiftly Sylvia takes in new information, and acts. "Ruth, you get up. Greta, you lie down. George, get out of the way."

That takes a moment of backing and forthing. He has set himself so firmly in the doorway, ready for action; but not this action. Between them, he and Sylvia finally wrestle his chair into the room, and she says, "Ruth, get a cool, damp cloth for Greta's forehead," and then she is gone. Where, what's going on?

George sees the little one, Ruth, standing now beside her bed. She's covered up in a soft-looking blue nightgown with little yellow flowers all over, and is clasping her hands. His big thick-skinned Greta is lying back on the bed. "Oh," she says several times, in that same strange, surprised, quiet voice.

Her arms fold against herself, her hands at her ribs, pressing. Lying down, she is breathing shallowly but more evenly. Ruth, obeying Sylvia, makes her way to her bathroom by the reflected light from the bedroom and finds her facecloth, runs it under the cold-water tap, wrings it out, returns to Greta's side as quickly as she can manage. It's interesting, she thinks, noting also the irrelevance, that her own body seems to be liberated from pain by this urgency.

Greta looks grey, although Ruth can't be sure any colour she sees is a true one. Greta winces as the cold cloth touches her forehead. "Does it hurt very badly?" Ruth asks. "We should get you sent straight to hospital, don't you think?"

"There is the angina, yes, tight in my chest." Greta takes a deeper, steadier breath. Cool drops of water run from the cloth, down her temples, into Ruth's pillow. "But it should not get worse, I think, with the medicine. Sylvia has gone for it?"

"Sylvia's back," comes the voice from the doorway. "I've got it. You want one pill, two, what?"

"One. It goes under my tongue. Thank you. Now there is only to wait for a few minutes."

In the silence, as Ruth and Sylvia watch Greta's face ease, her hands relax, her eyes return from wherever they've been, Ruth finds herself wondering, could this be a trick? A planned-in-advance delaying tactic to keep her alive?

If they'd go as far as a horoscope, why not angina, even a heart attack?

But no, that's mad, Greta couldn't fake this, even if she would, and Ruth believes Greta would not. They have seen her once or twice before, discreetly taking the plastic container out of her knitting bag and putting a tablet into her mouth and resuming her listening and talking and knitting, but people's medications are ordinary and personal, and she hasn't said why, and they haven't asked. They haven't seen her on a journey quite like this one, though, travelling away from them so fast and so far. No, no chance of a ruse.

Sylvia, now—she's a different story. There's no telling what lengths she'll go to in order to get something she wants. Or not get something she doesn't want.

Maybe it's odd, when people all over the world are dying cruelly, or sometimes gently, every second of each day and every night, when death is so often random although on occasion deliberate—maybe it's odd how relieved Ruth is that Greta is, right this moment, alive.

She can't tell how she feels about herself still being alive.

Except it's bewildering.

Greta is making a move to get up from Ruth's bed. "I am better now. I am so sorry."

"What," and Sylvia laughs in that sharp way she has, "for interrupting the evening? It wasn't one of our better nights anyway. Now just lie still, don't stir yourself. Ruth, you might as well sit down while we wait another couple of minutes. We still might decide to call on somebody for help."

Sylvia, the natural chair of their four-person board.

While Ruth was staring at Greta, slow on the uptake, noting Greta's warning new colours but failing to realize what a drastic disruption they'd mean, Sylvia sprang into action. She may have saved Greta's life. Give the woman a badge. Briefly, Ruth feels an acidic churn of bitterness; but who is there to blame? Hardly Greta or Sylvia. Certainly not George. Possibly only herself.

"I do not think more help is needed," Greta says finally. "I already feel not so much tightness or pain. It is why there is the medicine, to act before there can be again a true heart attack. But I am sorry. There was much to think about, but it should be all the time with me, and I should not have forgotten."

That's so. Ruth's very bad luck to have her moment pre-empted by so small an omission: a little plastic container of pills.

"Lucky you did, though," Sylvia says. "In a way. As it turns out."

Is it too late, then?

Sylvia turns to Ruth. "You were starting to say something just when Greta took her spell, what was it?"

Yes, she must have been on the very verge of making a move, time running out, time up. She remembers that. But now she isn't sure how the sentence was going to unfold. Whatever it was going to be, she should have spoken it sooner, she shouldn't have let them go on and on, shouldn't have assumed there was time to be as gracious, as well as graceful, as the occasion suggested.

She should have known, as she does know, as they all must, that something unexpected can leap anytime out of the night, or for that matter the day, blindsiding, bushwhacking. She gestures slightly in Sylvia's direction, not answering, but asking instead, "What time is it now?"

"Just about five."

The first kitchen staff start arriving at five, the Idyll Inn begins stirring, and then there's only a couple of hours till dawn. Sylvia thought Ruth should wonder what the sun's first pink light would land on, but if Ruth wasn't alive she wouldn't wonder and wouldn't care. That was the point.

George is dozing again. Sylvia reaches out, shakes his knee. "George, wake up. Greta should rest, but we need to get moving. We still don't especially want to get caught."

Why, what has happened, and why won't this bloody woman let him alone? Why is Ruth standing while his Greta is over there on the bed, and why is he not in the doorway—has he somehow failed in his purpose?

No, because it's still just the four of them in the room. No outsiders.

"Do you feel up to helping me get George back to his

suite, Ruth?" Sylvia asks. "Then maybe he'd let us borrow his wheelchair to come back here and get Greta."

She's very good at logistics; would do well on a battle-field. "I guess so," Ruth says. She's having some trouble col-lecting her wits. Abrupt reversal is disorienting, as well as deflating: like being all geared up to go over the top with guns blazing, and being ordered instead into retreat.

While George nods at Sylvia. Whatever they want, he supposes.

"I can walk, I am better," Greta offers, but her voice is half-hearted. She sounds exhausted. Well, at this hour and stage of the night they're all likely exhausted, Greta just in a different, pale and palpitating way.

"Not a chance. You wait here and gather your strength," Sylvia tells her, "and we'll be back in a few minutes. I could probably manage George myself, Ruth, but two are always better than one, and we need to be as quick and efficient as we can be."

Suddenly that is the urgent and very practical problem to be overcome. Matters of life and death evidently get left in its dust.

Ruth pushes George's wheelchair, leaning into it for sup-port, keeping up with a striding Sylvia as best she can. "Up and over, George," Sylvia instructs once they're at his bed-side, and he manages to rise from the chair and more or less tumble onto his bed. Sylvia lifts his legs, tips him back, and Ruth covers him with his blankets. Now he looks wide awake, not sleepy at all. "There," Sylvia says. "As if you'd never been up. We'll have the chair back here as soon as we get Greta tucked up in her room too, so don't worry about that, just go to sleep. Come on, Ruth, let's go."

Again too much hurry, too much change of purpose and plans all at once. Ruth can't catch her breath, or catch up. Sylvia, framed in bright yellow like a lantern ahead, is again moving too fast. Everything is too fast. "Sorry," Sylvia says at Ruth's doorway. "We've made a mess of your night, but I don't see we had any choice."

In Ruth's room Greta is still taking up much of the space in Ruth's bed, and seems barely awake. "Oh dear," Ruth whispers.

"No, no, do not worry, I am better, I am well." Greta turns in the bed, propels herself to a sitting position. If better, she is clearly not yet well. Even in the glowing light of Ruth's bedside lamp, she remains grey-tinged, although Ruth notes that the deep blue around her has paled, and the red flashes are gone.

"If you shift into George's chair," Sylvia says, "Ruth can get back to bed, and I'll take you down to your suite. Then we can decide what to do next."

"I will be fine. This has happened before, but not at a time this . . . difficult. I am sorry, Ruth, I did not understand how I would be so upset. And I should not have forgotten the medicine. Now I have caused us to fail you."

"That's all right." Well, what else can Ruth say? There's no undoing the night, its rhythms so disrupted and its tones so jangled, its time so lost—it cannot be salvaged. "Now Sylvia's right, you should get to bed, but only if you're really sure about not getting checked out at the hospital."

That would be a much earlier than expected and quite different whisking away from the Idyll Inn. Such careful plans they had, such particular pictures. All eventualities they could think of contemplated, deliberated—at their age utterly foolish, imagining any such thing.

"Good night, Ruth," Sylvia says, wheeling Greta in George's chair toward the corridor along which, just a couple of hours ago, they made their way in this direction all unknowing; unknowingness now having shown itself, once again, to be what it is. "We'll see you later, I guess."

"Yes, I guess you will. Take care out there." Don't get caught, Ruth means. "And you take care too, Greta. If there's even the smallest sign of things going wrong, you buzz for help right away, do you promise? Don't take chances."

"I promise. And Ruth? After all, I am very pleased we are both alive."

"Yes." Yes, no doubt they are both alive. Pleased, despairing—those remain up in the air, but apparently Ruth has time now to ponder opportunities taken and missed. To regret or not to regret.

She will have to take this into consideration, too: whether, if life hasn't seemed so important, the absence of death, a somewhat different matter, might equally be not so important.

Oh, she is tired. The little death of sleep is alluring. Seductive.

In Greta's bedroom, Sylvia sits for a few moments in George's wheelchair, watching Greta curl herself into bed, and catching her own breath. How she aches! How every muscle and joint makes itself felt. And still she has a task or two before she too can rest.

Here's Greta, though, doing well enough and safely back, thanks to Sylvia's quick action. There's Ruth, having put them all through this, nevertheless safe and sound in her room. And George in his. Really, these are all things to be proud of: that Sylvia is still good at figuring out fast what's to be done, and then getting it done. And all undetected. Not a bad night, in that regard.

But such a long night. It used to be, years ago, that she could dance, drink and laugh till the cows came home. Certainly until this pre-dawn kind of hour. Those days are long gone. This night is going to take a while to recover from. It won't be like waiting for a small hangover to pass.

Greta is already snoring. A good sign of recovery, if an unpleasant sound.

Up and at 'em.

Surprisingly, George is still awake when Sylvia returns his chair to his room. "Were you afraid I wouldn't bring it back?" she asks, although there's never much sense joking with George.

Predictably, he frowns in his uncomprehending way. But then he surprises her by asking, "Greta. Is she all right?"

Isn't that sweet? Or something. "Seems to be. Last I saw her, a couple of minutes ago, she was sound asleep and snoring. Did you know that she snores?"

There's a pause before he says, "Good thing," and Sylvia doesn't feel like bothering to decipher what, exactly, he thinks is a good thing. Presumably that Greta is well, not that she snores; but possibly that the whole night has been a good thing.

"Get some sleep, George," she tells him; and now finally, finally, she can check the corridor one more time before scuttling home to her own suite. Where, thank God, she can close the door on these harsh, busy hours.

If she previously pictured herself ending the night sitting

with her comforting, calming glass of wine, staring out into the darkness and considering whatever had happened and not happened—whatever she'd done or not done—the time for that has come and gone in an entirely different kind of upset and flurry. She hurts more than she can recall hurting for a very long time, but even so, she thinks she could fall asleep in a blink.

As she pulls off her robe, two carefully folded plastic dry-cleaner bags fall to the floor. They'll look strange to whoever comes to rouse her first thing in the morning, but her body has gone beyond bending to retrieve them.

It doesn't matter. They're just dry-cleaner bags: a minor mystery.

There is, she thinks, as she very cautiously lowers herself into bed, much to be said for the merely minor mystery.

These have been interesting months, and perhaps they won't have such interesting ones again at the Idyll Inn. Or maybe they will. At the moment, although exhausted in every possible way, Sylvia finds that as her eyes close, she is smiling.

For one thing, it's been an absolutely ridiculous night. *Ridiculous*, as Greta would probably note: *unreasonable, absurd*.

More, though, she is smiling because even in the midst of this bone-deep weariness and pride and, frankly, distinct anticlimax, there is, it turns out, a surprising, lilting, unfamiliar upsurging of what appears to be, almost certainly is, at very least definitely passes for, the pleasant and gratifying sensation of—what's it called?—*joy*.

29

AND THEN . . .

A MONSTER BANANA CAKE WITH WHITE ICING it is, then—not a bad effort, really, from the Idyll Inn kitchen, and a treat for everyone but the diabetics, who get their own smaller, sadly sugar-deprived version. The quavering round of "Happy Birthday" is less sweet than the cake, but well-meant, and endurable.

Endurance being, as Sylvia has already noted, "rather the theme *du jour*, one way and another."

The single candle usual for these occasions is within the abilities of most residents to blow out. "Make a wish," Annabel Walker tells Ruth, and poof, out goes the flame. Nobody asks; everyone knows speaking a wish aloud is bad luck.

Annabel leads the "Happy Birthday" chorus. A birthday that falls plunk in the midst of holiday preparations is inconvenient, but anything that makes residents celebratory or even just placid is worth the effort. Old people can be extremely difficult; so can the distant doctor and dentist investors in the numbered company to which, ultimately, she reports. There's no keeping everyone happy, but she goes the limit, she does her best.

Ruth Friedman's little coterie has already caused some alarm and disruption today, but at the moment, in the dulled winter-afternoon lighting of the lounge, all looks reasonably calm and benign. Ruth herself is rather glamorous in a tiny-old-woman way, in a swishy silvery grey silky dress that flares out at the knees.

Something more worrisome was afoot this morning, when not one of Ruth, Sylvia Lodge, Greta Bauer or George Hammond would get up for breakfast. They weren't exactly pleased about getting to lunch, either. Annabel heard from Adele, one of the morning-shift aides, that Ruth told her, "No, please just let me sleep," Greta said, "I will stay in bed longer, thank you," Sylvia said, "Bloody hell, go away," and George said something like "Dutdutdut." "I don't know if you want to check on them yourself," Adele told Annabel. "But it's weird, all four of them still in bed."

"Are they sick?" Perhaps something only they ate or drank. That would teach them a good lesson about self-indulgence; although not if they had actual food poisoning, which can kill weakened old people low in bounce-back abilities.

"Not throwing-up sick."

Annabel sighed. Yes, just in case, she would have to look for herself; but when she arrived at Ruth's bedside, Ruth insisted, "It's my birthday and I'm sleeping in," and closed her eyes again. Next up Greta, who, when Annabel shook her shoulder, stirred only long enough to say, "I was awake late to say to Ruth happy birthday." Of course, like it or not,

George had to be roused, because he had to be helped to the bathroom and stepped by an aide through his toiletries before it was too late. "Dutdutdut," he told Annabel, too, but often enough people who've had strokes need time each day to pull together whatever they're capable of pulling together.

That left Sylvia Lodge, although Annabel would just as soon have as little to do with her as she can. It's difficult to have authority over someone who was friends with Annabel's parents, whose husband worked with Annabel's father, who knew Annabel as infant and girl and who, Annabel's mother used to say, "is a real pill. Poor Nancy, Sylvia must be the most unaffectionate woman on earth." Later there was some mishmash of adult tensions, maybe the strains of a law practice, who knows, and Annabel's parents and the Lodges didn't hang out together so much, and the women, as Annabel recalls, rarely spoke. At this end of time, anyway, it's tricky dealing with Mrs. Lodge, complicated in a former-little-kid way. Still, if somebody can afford the rent and isn't too sick with one thing or another, it's hard to say they're not allowed to move in.

This morning's encounter could have been worse—Mrs. Lodge just said, "I'm perfectly fine. Don't bother me. I'll get there when I get there." As she did, barely, in time for lunch. And now they're all here in the lounge for Ruth Friedman's seventy-fifth birthday party, so whatever kept them late in bed must have been a false alarm. Irritating in itself.

Sleeping late has left them relatively clear-eyed, except maybe for George Hammond. Hard to tell if he's getting better or worse, but he's one of those Annabel keeps a particular eye on in case his situation takes a dive and she has to shuffle him off to, say, his wife's nursing home. He's remarkably uncaring in that regard; hasn't in all his time here even taken the small trouble to visit his wife. Then again, he's a man, and in Annabel Walker's experience men are careless creatures. Spoiled and selfish and vastly unreliable.

This afternoon Annabel's job is to preside over the aides cutting and distributing cake, and to lead the "Happy Birthday" singalong so she can get back to holiday planning at the first possible moment. The trouble is families, mainly. They have all sorts of requests and even demands, and then, come the time, will get in the way. Plus residents, with or without families coming, will have any number of ways of kicking up fusses—all in all, far too much emotion zigzagging through the Idyll Inn over far too many days. However, juggling and managing is her job. The satisfaction, not inconsiderable, is in doing it well, and so when she smiles and says, "I hope you're enjoying this," and Ruth smiles back and replies, "Oh yes, I am indeed," well, that is fairly gratifying.

Who says happy birthday to Annabel Walker these days? Nobody, really. Or if they do, it's not often with a genuine heart. Or maybe that's only her. It gets harder and harder to have a genuine heart. Come the time, she herself will be a less than cheery resident of some Idyll Inn equivalent; although it's true that this job offers quite a few examples of what a person should make an effort not to become— cantankerous, self-centred, ungracious—along with a few models of kindness and courage.

Ruth is surprised by the number of people, however lame, deaf, frail or slightly confused, who come by the table to offer their greetings. Maybe they're mostly grateful for cake, but it's nice of them anyway. In her months here she hasn't particularly cultivated anyone besides Sylvia and

Greta and in a way George—not much point, with no intention of sticking around, and with her carefully laid trail of gloom doing its persuasive work on them. But now here she is when she ought to be not here—this casts a new light on some of the powdery people wishing her well.

This new light has to do also with the ludicrous, grandiose scheme Sylvia proposed here in the lounge an hour ago. "I've been thinking some more," she said, "about how to keep us stimulated after last night—for one thing, how to reward you for staying alive, Ruth, and how to sufficiently entertain you to keep you that way. It's a hard one to top, but it seems to me, just think about it, that we have the tools and we've done the thinking-through part, so we'd only need the circumstance and the request. And of course the guts. Which admittedly we still haven't put to the test."

What?

"I mean, you made your case for, oh, relatively *easeful* death, I suppose we could call it. Granted any of us could go any minute, just *naturally*, as they say. I'm sure we're all aware that we don't have any idea what bullets are lurking inside, waiting for the moment to shoot us down. But if it doesn't happen that fast, that's where your idea would come in handy. So my theory is, we'd agree that if any of us gets in a longer-term kind of trouble and wants out, the others will help her. Or him. If Greta had another real heart attack and couldn't bounce back, or if my mind wandered off into the wilderness. That kind of thing. We'd have a choice. Same as you might have had."

If Ruth had said, *Now*, and if Greta hadn't taken that turn, and if they'd been able to bring themselves to act, in the end.

"And then," Sylvia was continuing, "since we'd be into the law of diminishing returns if we started knocking each other off, and nobody'd want to be left last person standing—or sitting, whatever—anyway, we could keep our eyes peeled for recruits. Carefully, of course. Very subtly."

Ruth wondered if Sylvia's cherished mind might already have gone wandering into a wilderness thicket. Surely she could not be serious.

Typical of Sylvia, though, to turn death into a project. And to elect herself chair. And then to sit back and smile as if at a clever bit of insanely ambitious mischief; although it wasn't an especially benign smile. Nor a particularly insane one, either.

A woman who will not give up ought to have been the first to protest what Sylvia was talking about, but Greta said instead, "I was frightened in the night, and I remembered how my heart has been before, too, and being so frightened. When Sylvia first spoke this before you came to the table today, Ruth, I thought of course, no, but then I think of how I do not want to be helpless, or to be a burden to my girls, and I see that perhaps this could be a strong thing, although I did not dream of it before." She smiled, although not with Sylvia's edge. "This is something more I have learned from you, Ruth. You see again how we keep learning?"

At least one of Sylvia's goals is already achieved: serious or not, mad or otherwise, her suggestion, her project, her plan, means Ruth is now intrigued by a new, interesting arithmetic among these happy-birthday faces collecting their slices of cake: who are these people, and how far might they go—in what state are their minds, and where may their hearts lie? And how about George? It's hard to imagine that he signed on. More likely that when Sylvia asked, he agreeably cried, *Yes*.

Today, at any rate, it's nothing that requires action or even much contemplation. Today is Ruth's birthday: an unanticipated addendum to what was to have been the whole of her life.

The existence of time—that itself, hours into the day, remains disorienting. Fall-down dizzying, almost. If she'd thought of this day coming about, Ruth would have expected it to carry only the sad weight of flat, even foolish anticlimax. Entering the lounge this afternoon, seeing Sylvia, Greta and George at their usual table, was almost embarrassing. "Oh dear," Ruth said. "All that effort and struggle we went through, and here I still am."

"Well," said Sylvia, glancing at Greta, "not entirely through your own choice. And I don't know about you, but I can hardly believe in daylight what seemed sensible enough in the night. That we just gave you your medication and left you, Greta—given that you weren't actually someone who wanted to die, that's pretty unforgivable."

Which was when she described her bright new idea, and the awkward moment—at least that awkward moment—was hurdled right over.

Ruth might have expected Greta to express some regret for the night, if not an apology. She has not done so; but now, with their slices of banana birthday cake on the table before them, she asks, "Are you glad, Ruth?" To be alive, she must mean. It has been snowing lightly for some hours now, so that under a gunmetal sky the Idyll Inn grounds are the flat white of dull paint: clean, but not optimistic. What is optimistic in a temporary, seasonal way are the red, green, blue and white little bulbs strung around windows, the wreaths of fake pine boughs and silver bells and wide red ribbons in bows hung carefully high on the walls here and there, and even the plastic mistletoe sprigs. Glad is not quite the right word—perhaps Greta could consult her dictionary and find a more lavish one.

Ruth's first surprise of the day when she finally woke up, just before lunchtime, and after failed efforts by both Adele and Annabel Walker to rouse her—her first surprise, having forgotten in sleep, was remembering.

And she looked around and thought, just, Oh.

The beauty of her chest rising and falling, breath in and out. The amazement of light.

Funny how, in all her calculations, she had somehow left out the amazement and beauty.

Bewildering, too, the business of light when there was not supposed to be light, sounds when there should have been silence.

An interesting sort of elation nestling in the chasm between her intentions and the ordinariness of that light and those sounds.

She thought, Bernard. The final impression—it's been hard to see past her small hands and a pillow descending, to the grand sweep of her history, and so many faces. Today, with the opening of her eyes it was still hard, of course, but no longer so blinding.

What did she do to Bernard?

She performed a good act as lovingly—as mercifully—as she could. She mustn't forget that.

How her bones ache, especially with the first movements each day. Finally rising slowly and cautiously from her bed,

too late in the day to have help from busy Adele—once on
her feet she felt also, besides the familiar pain top to bottom,
a ballooning in her throat, new and not painful, of something round and brilliantly red. A constricting, monstrous
uplift of . . . gratitude, maybe. Some of that for Bernard.

The grace of shapes: the pewtery late-morning light
touching the yellow shade of the ancient floor lamp that used
to stand at his end of the sofa, and glancing off the walnut
cabinet that holds her and Bernard's old TV set, and swoop-
ing down to the buttery-maple coffee table with its magazines
and their worn remote. The light disappearing, absorbed into
the dull nut-brown softness of their high-backed, wide-armed
sofa and matching wing chair. Bernard's round, freckled face,
all of his faces through the decades, in every possession.

All those possessions that she tenderly and firmly said
goodbye to yesterday, she has had to tenderly and firmly say
hello to today. New eyes from old.

Up on the far hills, through the light snowfall, the bare
trees reached upwards, distinct and bony, with their tap-
tapping limbs. Out on the riverbank, a well-bundled young
couple walking a snow-dappled dog looked up to see Ruth in
her window, and waved: Hellooo, hellooo.

Even so, even so. Was she seduced by words and the
night, until suddenly it was too late to say, *Go ahead, now?* If
she'd remembered in time how very often in life, and apparently also in death, expectations and plans are thrown entirely
off course by unanticipated event, if she'd been quicker, and
they'd obeyed, she wouldn't know any of this today; there'd be
no red balloonings in the throat, no graceful shapes, no merry
hellooos, and nothing would matter because nothing would *be.*

There's no knowing, without knowing the future, what

exactly a person may come to regret—down the road, maybe last night. But that doubt alone must put her, for now, on the side of being alive, she supposes.

So given that she's here, which isn't nothing, she can reasonably say to Greta in this birthday-cake moment that yes, for want of a more suitable word, she is *glad*. She likes this new dress, likes that Bernard would have liked it, likes the airy, fly-away feel of the fabric. She supposes it's nice that it isn't set to go up in flames before she's had some use out of it. The banana cake with its white icing tastes extraordinarily sweet, and is a pleasant gesture by Annabel Walker and the Idyll Inn. And while respect and regard aren't so hard to come by, it's like gold—like redemption, like consolation—that she has friends who would travel to her room at three o'clock in the morning, armed to attempt her wishes, and determined not to.

It must matter, then, that if, for instance, things still were to go wrong for Sylvia's Nancy, Sylvia would need at least a hand on her shoulder, and not that proudly successful mother Greta's hand, either. Sylvia is not necessarily the insouciant person she makes herself out to be. *Insouciant*, as Ruth explained once to Greta: *carefree, unconcerned*. Or if George took another tumble, whose walker would they use to help him upright? Who would help Greta feel safe here, and who would insist on bringing word, bad and good, from the outside, so they don't forget there's a world, for better or worse, beyond Idyll Inn windows?

"I've been so lonely," Ruth hears herself say, and no words could sound sadder.

Although she can see, now she's said them, that they mean much the same as what she has been insisting: that she is empty of longing.

Are they the same? One seems to contain a hint of hope; the other not.

Another thought for another day. They pile up.

"Oh, Ruth." Greta frowns across the table. "Oh, Ruth, I have been often lonely too. It is I think one more state of being we are to learn." Perhaps she means *learn from*; although maybe not. "We do many things for loneliness, I think, but we do not die for it. We do other things that are brave or not brave, but not that."

That sounds . . . tragically companionable.

Outdoors the light may be grey, but around Sylvia, Greta and George there's such a golden-ambery shimmer right now.

Light, colour and shape—those too remain gifts.

"You know," Sylvia says, "some mornings I wake up and think, *Ah, not dead yet*, and just realizing that makes the world look sharper. Do you know what I mean?"

Ruth does. Of course, she had a sharp view yesterday, too. Just a different one. "Life getting in the way of death, apparently."

"Which," Sylvia says, "makes a pleasant change, don't you think?"

Still, "As you've pointed out any number of times, Ruth, it's a choice." Meaning, she repeats—can she be serious, then?—that if they wonder how any occupation can be as compelling as plotting Ruth's death, now they can while away hours plotting more widely an even more deliciously, morbidly sinister trick.

How monstrously interesting.

Or mad.

Or a hoax. *Ha ha ha*, as George would say.

The real test isn't today. Ruth's today is vivid, all refreshed, brilliant vision. It'll be tomorrow and the days after when the grind will begin of learning what's sustainable and what is not.

Speaking of sustainability, though, she's going to have to adjust her budget to account for being alive. Bad news for the children, here and elsewhere—now she herself needs what she has, but here she still is, so what else can she do?

There the children still are too, of course.

"Shall I get us more cake?" Greta asks.

"Not for me, but it's my party. Help yourself."

"Sylvia? And George, would you care for some also?"

"Dutdutdut," he says. This doesn't sound good.

And it is not good. After he was returned to his bed hours ago, George had one tiny stroke, then another. These were little ripples that didn't even wake him, not an avalanching like before, but today he weighed more heavily on the girl who made him get up, not that she noticed, and his tongue feels thick and will not work right. Something uneasy went on, to do with darkness, to do with the women, he thinks. It's good to be here with them now in the day-light. Not alone.

"No more cake for me either, thanks, Greta," Sylvia says, "I'm twitchy enough without adding more sugar. But let me get it for you. You should be taking it easy." She doesn't mention that unless Greta's inclined to live dangerously, after last night she shouldn't be loading herself down with cake.

They are all looking at George, who hasn't answered. "Don't worry," Sylvia says, "the day's all upside down, and we're bound to be discombobulated. He'll come around."

He'd better, hadn't he? Didn't he agree to something big? What use is he to a promise, though, or a promise to him? "Miss," he blurts, or attempts to.

And suddenly, ravenous Greta could weep.

Perhaps she has never had heart attacks, does not live at the Idyll Inn, never knew George before, has never met anyone named Sylvia or Ruth, and is still young, with her little girls and with Dolph, who will not die, and neither will she.

No. But some other things are sharp and true: that life comes and goes in a minute of time. That George is and is not who he once was, which was someone beautiful who in a certain fashion, briefly, she loved, and in that way he means her life as well as his own. Change and so much time—when they fold tight together like this, they make another gripping in the chest, they make again a little of what happened inside her last night. *Twitchy*, Sylvia says: *experiencing a physical or mental pang.* This is harsher than that.

A weakness, one that can come at any moment, can frighten at any moment. Cake soothes, but Greta wants more of much else, as well. Love. Comfort too, although there is already much in being right here, right now, with these people, at this table, under this roof. And always mercy—*mercy: the quality of compassion; an action committed out of compassion, or performed out of pity for a suffering person.* One of her girls—which?—had a schoolfriend named Mercy, a name with a strange sound to Greta's ears, but she did not think then of what the girl's parents might have hoped and intended. Not like *Sally*, or *Emily*, or *Patricia*, with no meanings beyond hope for belonging; a grand enough desire to Greta and Dolph.

What will her girls see when next they see her? She has come very near, with Ruth, to a place they could not dream of, or believe. Does she look different for the long weeks of deciding?

She should want, perhaps, the quiet cultivation of a taste for less, rather than more.

Sylvia raises her glass. "To you, Ruth. You're a tough little cookie, and a useful one, too." *Little cookie* Greta does not quite understand, but *tough*, yes. Who would have imagined all this on that first day, when Greta rounded a corner too fast and nearly ran over a small woman on her way to becoming a friend? "And to you too, Greta."

Sylvia hands George his glass, holding it until his grip forms around it. "Come on, George, drink up. We're toasting ourselves. For God's sake."

For God's sake what? That time keeps running, and running out; that an embracing affection might yet occur, even forty years or so late—interesting what may equally alter and shift when something does not happen as when it does; and that every word Ruth has said and read to them in these months has been true. The encompassing word *doom* comes to Sylvia's mind, along with its less succinct, more nuanced companion *decline*. Really, life in a nutshell, human or planet.

And yet how clear-headed and even clear-hearted Sylvia feels, how very buoyant, if no longer quite joyous, after some sleep and a hit of sugary cake. Of course a good part of today's bounce and uplift must be relief. There are some occasions a person can be just as glad not to have risen to.

At least to have bought time before needing to rise to it. Or to two, three or four such occasions. It depends. Her new notion is still tilted more toward engagement than execution. As it were.

How very enlivening it is, though. Also as it were.

It's a good sign that George understands the day well enough to lift his glass, carefully, between his useful hand and his useless one. He sips first slightly sideways, more or less missing his mouth; misses again; but when he guides his hand a bit to the left, it ends up in roughly the right place. Still hard to see the attractive, tall shoestore man bent over feet, complimenting ankles and calves, but he appears to be in there. Safe for the moment.

Last night they were Ruth's witnesses, they were the people she had. It would be impossibly lonely to be the only witness remaining. Therefore, schemes, bound to be more entertaining than reading newspapers aloud and massaging George's limbs, although there's no reason to stop doing that, and definitely more riveting than playing bridge, watching TV or turning needles and wool, click, click, click. "It's funny," Sylvia says, although it's not, really. "I had in mind when I moved in that in ten years or so I would probably run out of enough money to live as comfortably as I do now, and that would be it. So reassuringly far-off, barring catastrophe in the interim. So much more suspenseful now."

She smiles her wicked Sylvia smile. "Poor Annabel. She has no idea."

Already the late-afternoon lineups of the eager and bored are forming outside the dining room—another Idyll Inn suppertime. "I'm hungry," says Ruth, unwilling to give Sylvia's whimsies more time. Not today. "I need something to tamp down that cake. Shall we?"

Greta stows a partly finished crimson sleeve in her knitting bag and takes the handgrips of George's wheelchair. As
she turns him, his right hand smacks hard on the armrest,
and *Yes, yes, yes,* he calls out, just as if nothing has changed.

What gumption he must have, for all his shortcomings.
The women, Ruth included, find themselves stepping
smartly to the rhythm of his contentious, stubborn right
hand banging out his persistent *Yes, yes, yeses.* And *good*—
he always wants to hear from Ruth at least one story that's
good. Where does it come from, this insistence of his?

In the huge dining-room windows that in daylight look
out over river and snow, they see themselves reflected across
the room, a ghostly, shadowy portrait of four. They can be
proud of the number: not three, and not two either—a triumph. This is not a happy, easy ending. The other way—
that's the one that might have been easy.

George thinks the faint figures in the glass could be
daughters; or maybe only women he's cared for.

Ruth is pleased with the faraway outline of her silky silvery dress, the swirl of its skirt, and thinks that from this distance, for all their lines, stoopings and other incapacities,
the four of them look rather graceful together.

Sylvia repeats to them what she remembers remarking to
herself when the Idyll Inn opened nearly four seasons ago:
that the camouflagings of age provide some happy invisibilities, not only unhappy ones; that this is how secrets are kept,
as well as some kinds of freedom. "Old harpies disguised as
old boots," she says. Greta wonders exactly what harpies are,
although she can guess they're not anything pleasant; while
George is diverted by pictures of well-crafted, strong, go-
anywhere, do-anything boots. They had a good heft, those

kinds of boots. That was back in the days when craftsmen, and he too, took pride in what they could do with their hands, which doesn't happen so much any more.

For the time being enters his head. *For the time being,* he tries to say, but the words come out as something like *Yes,* which is pitiful, but judging from the jaunty—there's a word coming back—way the women are moving again, it seems to make them as happy as anything else. How surrounded he is, and how bright and jolly—another J word—the dining room is. How lucky, all in all. Tilted and bent, maybe, but beautiful as angels, brave as soldiers. For the time being, *yes*.

"Look at us go," Sylvia says, and they're off.

JOAN BARFOOT is the author of ten previous novels, including *Critical Injuries*, which was nominated for the Man Booker Prize, and *Luck*, which was nominated for the Scotiabank Giller Prize. Joan Barfoot lives in London, Ontario.

A NOTE ABOUT THE TYPE

The text of *Exit Lines* has been set in Goudy (often referred to as Goudy Oldstyle), a face designed in 1915 for the American Type Founders by the prolific typographer Frederic W. Goudy. Used with equal success in both text and display sizes, Goudy remains one of the most popular typefaces ever produced. It is best recognized by the diamond-shaped dots on punctuation; the upturned "ear" of the g; and the elegant base curve of the caps E and L.